KISS ME DEADLY

"All right." Detective Chief Inspector Kenneth Harris stood up and moved towards the door. "I'm sure you'll let us know if you think of anything else that might help."

"Yes, of course. Would you care for something before you go? Coffee, or a drink?"

"No thanks, I've already stayed longer than I intended." At the front door he said, "Be careful, Melissa. Don't take any risks."

"What's that supposed to mean? You don't suppose *I'm* a potential victim?" She tried to sound flippant but he did not smile.

"I think you know what I mean but if you insist I'll spell it out."

"If you're warning me against Barney Willard . . ."

"He had motive and opportunity and he hasn't been entirely straight with us."

"But I told you . . ."

His eyes met hers. "Once a man has killed, for whatever reason, he'll do it again if he has to."

MORE MYSTERIES FROM THE
BERKLEY PUBLISHING GROUP...

THE HERON CARVIC MISS SEETON MYSTERIES: Retired art teacher
Miss Seeton steps in where Scotland Yard stumbles. "A most beguiling
protagonist!" —*New York Times*

by Heron Carvic
MISS SEETON SINGS
MISS SEETON DRAWS THE LINE
WITCH MISS SEETON
PICTURE MISS SEETON
ODDS ON MISS SEETON

by Hamilton Crane
HANDS UP, MISS SEETON
MISS SEETON CRACKS THE CASE
MISS SEETON PAINTS THE TOWN
MISS SEETON BY MOONLIGHT
MISS SEETON ROCKS THE CRADLE

by Hampton Charles
ADVANTAGE MISS SEETON
MISS SEETON AT THE HELM
MISS SEETON, BY APPOINTMENT

SISTERS IN CRIME: Criminally entertaining short stories from the top
women of mystery and suspense. "Excellent!" —*Newsweek*

edited by Marilyn Wallace
SISTERS IN CRIME
SISTERS IN CRIME 2
SISTERS IN CRIME 3

SISTERS IN CRIME 4
SISTERS IN CRIME 5

KATE SHUGAK MYSTERIES: A former D.A. solves crime in the far
Alaska north...

by Dana Stabenow
A COLD DAY FOR MURDER

DOG LOVER'S MYSTERIES STARRING HOLLY WINTER: With her
Alaskan malamute, Rowdy, Holly dogs the trails of dangerous criminals.
"A gifted and original writer." —Carolyn G. Hart

by Susan Conant
A NEW LEASH ON DEATH
DEAD AND DOGGONE

A BITE OF DEATH
PAWS BEFORE DYING

MELISSA CRAIG MYSTERIES: She writes mystery novels—and inves-
tigates crimes when life mirrors art.
"Splendidly lively." —*Publishing News*

by Betty Rowlands
A LITTLE GENTLE SLEUTHING

FINISHING TOUCH

A MELISSA CRAIG MYSTERY

Finishing Touch

BETTY ROWLANDS

JOVE BOOKS, NEW YORK

This Jove Book contains the complete
text of the original hardcover edition.
It has been completely reset in a typeface
designed for easy reading and was printed
from new film.

FINISHING TOUCH

A Jove Book / published by arrangement with
Walker and Company

PRINTING HISTORY
Walker and Company edition published 1991
Jove edition / March 1993

ISBN: 0-515-11059-0

Jove Books are published by The Berkley Publishing Group,
200 Madison Avenue, New York, New York 10016.
The name "JOVE" and the "J" logo
are trademarks belonging to Jove Publications, Inc.

PRINTED IN THE UNITED STATES OF AMERICA

10 9 8 7 6 5 4 3 2 1

To my husband
With love and gratitude

ONE

IF A CERTAIN EMINENT ART HISTORIAN HAD not been so absentminded as to double book a certain date in July, thus throwing the Principal of the Ravenswood College of Art and Design into a state of near panic, Melissa Craig would never have witnessed the prelude to a drama that would shortly unfold on her doorstep, inexorably drawing her into its tragic and violent embrace.

The action began quietly enough with a somewhat fulsome letter from the aforesaid Principal, addressed to Melissa's friend and neighbour Iris Ash. Beginning with a personal tribute to 'one of the college's most outstanding and successful graduates', it continued with an elaborately-worded invitation to present the prizes at the annual exhibition of students' work. 'I should be greatly honoured, dear Miss Ash,' it concluded, 'to have the favour of your kind acceptance of my request at your earliest convenience.'

'That's nice,' commented Melissa as she handed the letter back to Iris. 'He's left it a bit late to ask you, though.'

'His first choice must have let him down.' There was a cynical gleam in Iris's grey eyes. ' "Find a sucker to do it at short notice!" says Doctor Mortimer. "That old bird in the Cotswolds who designs curtains and wallpaper . . . let's con her into coming." '

'You underestimate your reputation,' said Melissa. 'Since you won that competition, the glossy magazines are full of your designs and your garden water-colours are all the rage. "Another Helen Allingham", someone wrote the other day.'

Iris scowled. 'Don't like being "another" anyone,' she grumbled.

Melissa nodded in sympathy. 'I know how you feel. People used to refer to me as "the new Agatha Christie". All very flattering, of course . . . '

'Hate flattery!' Iris slammed mugs of coffee on to a tray and added a plate of home-made biscuits. 'Want this outside?' She marched into the garden with Melissa following her, smiling at the show of irritation.

They settled on a rustic seat among the climbing roses that grew in a scented, multicoloured jumble on the wall of Iris's cottage. On this mid-June morning, the garden vibrated with activity. Blackbirds rummaged in the carefully mulched flower-beds and flung showers of grass clippings on to the path. From an elder tree, a chaffinch poured out his exuberant song while bumble-bees hummed a contented counterpoint as they blundered past, laden with pollen. Binkie, Iris's cherished half-Persian cat, lay sprawled on the warm flagstones, too indolent to play at stalking the birds.

Melissa finished her coffee, put down her empty mug, leaned back and closed her eyes. 'Are you going to do it?' she asked languidly.

Iris grunted. 'Haven't decided. Don't like London. Hate making speeches.'

'It doesn't have to be a long speech. Just a few words, telling 'em all how lucky they are to be at this wonderful college where you spent some of your happiest days . . . '

'Huh!' snorted Iris. 'Never learned a thing worth knowing.'

Melissa ignored the interruption. 'And then,' she continued, 'you say "Well done!" or "Congratulations!" to the talented winners and hand over their medals or diplomas or whatever. Piece of cake, and good publicity too.'

Iris fidgeted and sent darting glances in all directions. 'Got nothing to wear,' she muttered. 'Have to buy something.'

'So that's what's bothering you!' Melissa turned to smile at the lanky figure in the faded cotton dress—one of three that, with her gardening trousers, the linen suit that she wore to church and a huge woollen wrap for cool days, constituted her entire summer wardrobe. Iris pulled a face and ran thin brown fingers through her springy mouse-brown hair.

'Hate dressing up. Help me choose something?'

'Of course.'

'Come to Ravenswood with me?'

'If you like.'

'Love your company if you aren't too busy.'

That settled, they agreed on a date for Iris to buy a dress and have her hair done—a suggestion by Melissa to which she agreed with considerable reluctance. They then spent a few enjoyable minutes discussing the relative qualities of farm manure and garden compost before going indoors, Iris to her studio and Melissa to her study to add another twist to the case that was currently baffling her celebrated detective, Nathan Latimer of Scotland Yard.

'I am sure, Miss Ash,' said Doctor Mortimer, looking anything but sure, 'that you would like to see some of our students' work before the formal proceedings.'

His eyelids flickered, his pallid features twitched and his thin hands moved on their bony wrists like pale fluttering birds about to take flight. Observing him, Melissa wondered how on earth such an indecisive character came to be made Principal of the Ravenswood College of Art and Design. Probably because he was everyone's second choice, she thought cynically as Iris rose from her seat.

'Might as well. Coming, Melissa?' The lift of an eyebrow and a twitch of the lips betrayed impressions of the man very similar to Melissa's own. It would be fun to compare notes later.

They left the Principal's office and set off on their tour of inspection. Doctor Mortimer pointed out the winning exhibits in the various classes and expressed what seemed to Melissa a certain over-optimism as to the future prospects of his students. Iris said very little in response but her eyes missed nothing. Melissa, standing apart and observing both, noted with satisfaction how well her friend looked in the blue and white dress and jacket and wondered how long the new hairstyle would stay in place.

'And finally,' the Principal announced, pausing before a painting of a young woman, 'we have the winner of the Lionel Prendergast Memorial Prize for Portraiture. A most promising young fellow—I do hope you agree with our adjudication, Miss Ash! It would not do,' he gave a cough, followed by a nervous giggle, 'to ask you to present awards to creators of works you considered unworthy!' His restless hands implored a favourable response.

Iris, her head tilted back and her eyes half closed, was taking her time in assessing the portrait. Melissa had no doubt that she knew full well that her interlocutor was on tenterhooks, and was deliberately teasing him.

'Hmm,' she murmured and the hands paused in mid-flight. She took a step back and cocked her head on one side. 'Interesting,' she said at last. 'Idealised, no doubt. I suppose he's in love with her?'

The Principal appeared mildly surprised at the notion. 'I've really no idea but it would be only natural, wouldn't it? A lovely girl like that . . . '

A faint hiss sounded a yard from Melissa's ear. Half-turning, she saw a denim-clad girl with cropped black hair and enormous steel spirals dangling from her ears. Her scowl suggested that she did not share the Principal's opinion of the sitter.

'Yes, not at all bad. Better than most of the other stuff here,' Iris said at last and the Principal's smile came and went like a guttering candle. 'Not a good year,' she continued and Melissa could tell that in her mischievous, perverse way, she was enjoying herself. 'Not much originality. A few promising works, the rest of it run-of-the-mill. You've sorted out the pick of the bunch.'

There was a respectful silence while Iris continued her scrutiny of the portrait and studied the signature. 'Ricardo

Lorenzo—Italian, I suppose. So's she by the looks of her.' She gave the portrait a final nod of approval. 'Quite good, he'll go a long way,' she pronounced. The Principal's smile glowed more steadily.

'Yes, we have great hopes for him,' he said and for the first time his hands became still and hung limply at his sides. 'Well, Miss Ash, perhaps you'd care for a cup of tea before we begin the proceedings?' His eyes included Melissa in the invitation.

'Love one,' said Iris.

Melissa shook her head. 'Not for me thanks. I'm sure you want to talk shop. I'll have another look round and meet you afterwards.'

Iris and the Principal moved away and Melissa turned to take a closer look at the portrait. The subject was undoubtedly beautiful. A swathe of rich Titian hair fell on either side of a perfectly proportioned and delicately chiselled oval face. The complexion was pale olive except for a faint flush on the cheeks; the crimson mouth had a curve that was at once gentle and sensual; the parted lips gave a glimpse of white, even teeth. The eyes held a hint of a smile, as if the sitter had been looking in a mirror and was well pleased at what she saw.

The denim-clad girl had stayed behind as well and was hovering at Melissa's elbow. Recognising a need for human contact, Melissa tilted her head sideways and commented: 'She looks like a contented pussy-cat! Do you know who she is?'

The girl's face, chalk-white with black-rimmed eyes and a scarlet mouth, hardened into a malevolent glare. ' "Pussy-cat" is right!' she muttered. 'Cats take what they want and then walk away, don't they?'

'So you do know her?'

'Angelica Caroli. Just finished her final year.'

'What about Ricardo Lorenzo?'

The girl gave a little snort of contempt. 'Plain Rick Lawrence was good enough for him until he met her. His great-grandfather came from Naples so they had so much in common, didn't they?'

'I gather you don't like her very much?'

'I'd like to wring her neck!' The girl's thin hands tugged at the strap of her shoulder bag as if she were tightening it round Angelica's beautiful throat. 'I knew Rick'd get hurt when he took up with her but he wouldn't listen to me.' The small, sharp features crumpled under their veneer of make-up and the voice faltered and died away. Melissa thought how frail and underweight the girl seemed. Poor kid, she was at such a vulnerable age.

A few people standing nearby turned their heads. 'Keep your voice down, people are looking at you,' whispered Melissa but the girl seemed not to care.

'She never even . . . ' she burst out, but before she could reveal what it was that Angelica had failed to do, a voice over the public address system announced that the presentation of awards would commence in five minutes.

The girl looked at Melissa with a beseeching expression. 'Are you going? May I sit with you?' she asked.

'Yes, of course. You lead the way.'

Most of the visitors had already detached themselves from the various exhibits staged around the college and were converging on the main hall. Melissa's companion found two seats at the end of a row near the front and they sat down. The girl seemed restless and uneasy, craning her head from side to side.

'Are you looking for someone?' asked Melissa.

'Rick. I'm so afraid he won't turn up. I told him he's got to come and collect his award. He shouldn't let her do him out of that!'

'Quite right,' said Melissa, somewhat at sea but anxious to boost morale. 'He'll be here, don't you worry. Professional pride and all that!'

'You reckon?' The girl appeared reassured and even managed a weak smile. 'My name's Lou Stacey, by the way. What's yours?'

'Melissa Craig.'

'Are you an artist?'

'No, a writer. I came here with Iris Ash. She's presenting the prizes, you know.'

It was obvious that Melissa's name meant nothing to Lou but at the mention of Iris she became almost animated. 'Her fabric designs are brilliant!' she said. 'So are her garden paintings. They say she's another Helen Allingham.'

'Don't let her hear you say that,' said Melissa with a grin, but Lou paid no attention. Her eyes had lit up like stars. 'He's here, I can see him!'

'There, what did I tell you?' said Melissa, greatly relieved.

All but one of the winning exhibits had already been arranged on the platform and while the members of the audience were settling into their seats, the final item, the portrait of Angelica, was carried in and put on an easel in the place of honour. The Bursar waited beside the table bearing the trophies, ready to hand them to Iris for presentation to the winners.

The Principal plodded through a prolix and platitudinous summary of the college year and followed it with a flowery eulogy to Iris and her achievements which she acknowledged with a glassy smile, her normally healthy colour deepening to a dull brick red.

'She's hating this,' Melissa whispered to Lou. 'She can't stand people going on about her work.'

'Lots of celebrated artists shun the limelight,' Lou whispered back with an air of great wisdom.

Iris stumbled through the short speech that Melissa had helped her to compose and at last the distribution of the cups, medals and certificates began. It gave Melissa considerable pleasure to see Lou receive the Ravenswood Shield for Fashion Design from Iris's hands. How touching, she thought, that the girl had never mentioned her own success, being totally preoccupied with her concern for Rick Lawrence. It was to be hoped that he was worthy of so much loyalty and devotion.

As Lou left the platform, only the Lionel Prendergast Memorial Prize for Portraiture remained on the table. In response to the Principal's final announcement, a young man strode forward, brushing past Lou without appearing to see her, and mounted the stage. He received the silver cup from Iris, kissed her hand with a flourish that brought another blush to her cheeks and sent a frisson round the hall, and turned to face the audience.

That Lou should be so much in love with him was not, Melissa thought, to be wondered at. With his curly black hair, flashing dark eyes, patrician features and proud bearing, he stood like a figure from a Renaissance canvas, his trophy cradled in the crook of his arm.

'Doctor Mortimer,' he began, bowing towards the Principal, 'Ladies and Gentlemen. I am proud to accept this prize and in return I should like to donate to the college the portrait for which it was awarded.' He paused, like an orator waiting for his lines to take effect. The Principal bobbed his head in gratified acknowledgement and there was a ripple of applause from the audience. 'You may not have realised, however,' Rick continued, 'that it is not quite complete.'

The final words were uttered slowly, with a measured interval between them and an underlying note of menace in the tone. The Principal's smile wavered and the clapping died away. Melissa was aware that Lou, who had slipped back into the seat beside her, had grown tense. There was a hush as the artist reached out towards the face on the canvas and ran caressing fingers over the smooth brow, the sculptured cheekbones and the curved lips, lingering for a moment on the rounded perfection of the neck.

'Beautiful, isn't she?' he murmured. His voice had dropped to a stage whisper; there was something theatrical in his stance and a brooding expression in his dark eyes.

'Oh my God,' breathed Lou. 'What's he up to?'

'Just one small finishing touch, that's all my portrait needs,' said Rick, and this time his voice was harsh and loud. By now thoroughly alarmed, the Principal leapt from his seat but he was too late to restrain the hand that plunged a knife into Angelica's throat and dragged it viciously downwards. There was a chorus of gasps and several people screamed as if expecting blood to spurt from the wound in the painted flesh. Bearing the cup aloft like an Olympic torch, Rick descended from the platform, marched to the nearest door and vanished.

Two

THE STUNNED SILENCE THAT FOLLOWED WAS shattered by an anguished shriek of 'Rick, wait!' as Lou raced in pursuit, the Ravenswood Shield clasped to her chest and her grotesque earrings swinging out from either side of her face. In a brave attempt to restore normality, Doctor Mortimer got up to make his closing address but nobody paid the slightest heed. The proceedings were palpably at an end and everyone was too exercised over the drama they had just witnessed to waste time listening to more platitudes.

Melissa made her way through the crossfire of indignation, astonishment and speculation towards the platform, where Iris was offering practical advice to their distraught host.

'Quite a clean slash, easy to repair,' she assured him after inspecting the damage. 'Don't lose any sleep. Never be an old master anyway,' she added with an impish grin.

Doctor Mortimer gave a pale smile and murmured something about refreshments.

'Not for us, thank you,' said Melissa firmly. 'We've got a train to catch.' She took Iris by the arm and steered her towards the exit, cutting short his speech of thanks.

'What's the rush?' Iris wanted to know. 'Train's not till six thirty.'

'I want to look for Lou Stacey. The poor girl's very upset.'

'The child with the clown's face who won the Shield? Saw her go tearing off. What's up with her?'

'I'll explain later.' They had reached the main entrance, washed along by the departing crowds. 'The car park's probably the best bet.'

'Not that way. Students park round the back.' Iris piloted Melissa along a corridor, out through a side entrance and along a path leading to a service road behind the building. They had just reached the gate when a sleek sports car with its hood down tore past, slowing briefly at the junction with the main road before racing away with a screech of rubber and a swirl of exhaust. Rick Lawrence was making his exit from Ravenswood.

'Didn't have the girl with him,' said Iris.

'Oh dear!' lamented Melissa. 'Where can she have got to?'

'Over there.' Iris nodded towards the footpath leading from the students' car park. Lou came trudging towards them, still clasping the shield in her arms and dragging her feet as if ready to drop from exhaustion. When she saw Melissa she ran forward and fell on her shoulder, weeping noisily.

'He wouldn't even speak to me!' she sobbed. 'He'll do something silly, I know he will!'

'Nonsense!' said Iris briskly. 'Made his gesture . . . got it off his chest. Where's your hanky?' Lou fumbled uselessly in her pocket and Iris pushed a tissue into her hand. 'Take this and mop up, you look a sight.'

Lou blotted her eyes and blew her nose. An awed realisation of who she was speaking to chased some of the misery from her face.

'Oh, Miss Ash, thank you, you're so kind!' she stammered.

'Where can we get some tea?' demanded Iris.

'The refectory's open till five.'

Iris glanced at her wristwatch. 'That'll do if we get a move on.' She marched back towards the college building with Lou and Melissa trailing behind in single file like goslings after a goose.

It was a quarter to five; the refectory was almost empty and the frenetic energy of the blue-overalled staff as they wiped tables and upended chairs made it clear that further customers were neither expected nor welcome. Ignoring the hostile glances, Iris installed her charges at a table and strode across to the counter, returning with three cups of tea on a tray.

'Looks ghastly but it'll have to do.' She took a mouthful from her own cup, grimaced and set it down. 'Just as foul as it was in my day!' she observed. 'Now Lou, what's all the tragedy about?'

Lou leaned on her elbows, tugging with nervous fingers at her spiky hair, and gave a huge, melodramatic sigh. 'Oh, it's such a mess,' she groaned. 'I don't know where to begin.'

'Then let me guess. You're in love with Rick, he fell for . . . what's her name?'

'Angelica.'

Iris grinned. 'Sounds like cake decoration!' Lou's red lips wavered into a smile that earned her a nod of encouragement. 'So Angelica spurns Rick and he salves his wounded pride by publicly knifing her portrait. Is that it?' Lou opened her mouth but Iris hadn't finished. 'Not very bright, was it?' she said dismissively. 'Shouldn't waste time feeling sorry for him if I were you.'

'You don't understand!' Lou declared with passion. 'What she did was diabolical! It would have sent anyone over the top.' A tear fell off the end of her nose and plopped into her cup.

'Stop grizzling and tell us then!' commanded Iris. 'We'll have to go in a minute; the staff are giving us dirty looks.'

'It's all such a mess!' Lou repeated, scrubbing her face with the mascara-blackened tissue. 'There was this party for Angy's birthday. Rick's parents organised it with her Uncle Vittorio and her Aunt Rosina—her parents are dead you see—and Rick brings out this ring and puts it on Angy's engagement finger.'

'So Rick and Angelica are engaged?' asked Melissa.

'Not any more, and they never were, really. I mean, he'd never actually proposed to her, he just assumed because they'd been going together, she'd . . . well, I suppose he thought it would be a romantic thing to do. He's like that.' Lou gave a wistful sigh, as if recalling happier times.

'So Angelica said "no thank you" and handed back the ring?' suggested Melissa. Lou's lip curled.

'That would have spoiled the party, wouldn't it? Angy hates to see people unhappy and she hates scenes. She always looks for the easy way out. And there was this jolly crowd of Italians and their guests, happily guzzling their pizzas and their spaghetti alla Bolognese, and dotty old Aunt Rosina crying "Mama mia!" and shedding tears of joy into her Chianti.' Lou emptied a packet of sugar into her lukewarm tea and flailed it with her spoon. 'She couldn't upset all those lovely people, could she? Oh no!'

'But she didn't want to marry Rick?' Melissa pursued.

'No, but she didn't want to part with all the goodies either.' Lou's eyes sparked with malice. 'She had a fancy ring that'd belonged to one of Rick's great-great-aunts, and then when we got home that night Aunt Rosina dived into an old tobacco tin and handed over five hundred pounds she'd been saving up for her wedding dress.'

'You were there?' asked Iris.

'I live with the Carolis, and Angy and I are supposed to be friends, would you believe? I'd been going out with Rick and he called round for me one evening and saw her.' Lou's voice trembled and tears welled again but she fought them bravely. 'They were on different courses and they might never have met if it hadn't been for that.'

'So what happened next?' asked Melissa.

'She took off.'

'Left home, you mean? Don't tell me she took the ring and the money too?'

Lou nodded. 'They were hers, weren't they? Nobody asked if she wanted them; they just handed them over and she took them. That's what she's like. Life is one big cherry tree and if the best cherries fall into her mouth, why shouldn't she eat them? Someone else can clean up the stones after she's spat them out.' Lou finished her tea and slammed down her cup, making the spoon dance in the saucer. 'Poor Ricky,' she whimpered.

'Conceited young fool!' snorted Iris. 'No right to take the girl for granted. Should have asked first and saved a lot of grief all round!'

Lou looked indignant. 'He only meant to make her happy and she's broken his heart!' she protested.

'Rubbish! Fractured his ego, that's all. Shouldn't have hopped off with Auntie's money though. That was naughty. Any idea where she's gone?'

'Not yet, but she's sure to be in touch with her aunt. Old Vittorio's furious with her at the moment but he'll come round. Everyone forgives the lovely Angelica . . . except me, that is. I can't forgive what she's done to Rick.'

'He'll survive,' said Iris drily.

'Do you think he might come back to me?' said Lou pathetically, mopping up a fresh trickle of tears.

Iris's eyes held a mischievous twinkle. 'Quite possibly,' she said, 'but not if he sees you looking like that. Go home and clean that muck off your face!' She stood up. 'Must be off now. You all right to get home?'

'Oh, yes thanks, I've got my bike.' Lou turned from one to the other. 'You've been so kind.'

'Forget it,' said Iris. 'Done my friend here a favour. She'll write a scorcher about an Italian family vendetta, only the villain will knife the real girl, not her portrait!'

Lou gaped at Melissa. 'Are you a crime writer?'

Melissa nodded, smiling.

'Surely you've heard of Mel Craig!' said Iris.

'Of course!' said Lou, once more overawed. 'I should have recognised you, only . . . ' Her cheeks turned pink and she fidgeted with the strap of her bag.

'Only you had other things on your mind.' Melissa patted her shoulder. 'Don't worry about it.'

'But I should . . . I saw you in *Bookworm* on the box last month! I remember thinking, I couldn't believe it when you said you had a grown-up son. You look ever so young!'

'Well, thank you,' said Melissa.

'What do you know, I've met two famous people today!' Almost cheerfully, Lou shouldered her bag, said goodbye and left them.

When they reached Paddington their train was already in the station.

'Thank goodness that's over!' Iris threw her coat on the rack, settled into a window seat and combed her hair with her fingers.

Melissa, sitting opposite, winced as the stylist's careful handiwork disintegrated.

'That Mortimer's an idiot,' Iris continued. 'Must have been everyone's second choice!'

'That's just what I thought,' Melissa agreed. 'I could see you suffering while he was telling everyone how wonderful you are. I was the one who talked you into doing it—I hope it wasn't too much of a bore.'

'Shan't hold it against you,' said Iris. 'Worth it to see that fool's face when young Rick knifed the picture!'

'Angelica can thank her stars it was only the picture he knifed! Some girls have the cheek of the devil.'

'Partly his own fault. Knew a case like that once.' Iris grew reflective. 'Student in my year thought this girl was pining away for love of him and all the time she was having it off with someone else.'

'Don't tell me this guy vandalised the girl's portrait as well?'

Iris cackled. 'Not he! Blacked her eye and then beat the hell out of the other chap. Sensation of the summer term!' She yawned and closed her eyes as the train began to move. 'Let's get home for some peace and quiet.'

THREE

A FEW DAYS LATER, MELISSA LOOKED UP FROM tending her garden to see Major Dudley Ford approaching along the track that connected her own and Iris's cottages with the lane leading to the village of Upper Benbury. She always thought of him as an eccentric, slightly comic individual and his appearance today reinforced the impression. The open collar of his baggy shirt was frayed and his amply cut khaki shorts, a relic of his service in the tropics, flapped round his thighs. He had evidently been sitting in the sun, for his bare knees were salmon pink above long woollen socks. Sinbad, his fat King Charles spaniel, rolled along behind him; at the sight of Binkie sprawled on the path outside Iris's front door the dog plunged forward, yapping excitedly, then skidded to a halt as the cat formed a croquet hoop, spitting defiance.

'Heel sir!' ordered the major, flourishing his stick above Sinbad's nose.

'What's going on?' Iris appeared, snatched Binkie into her arms and cuddled him protectively. 'Oh, it's you, Dudley. Do wish you'd keep that beast under control. Did the nasty doggie frighten him then?' she crooned into the cat's ear.

Seeing the opposition immobilised, Sinbad began yapping again.

'Quiet!' Ford's normally florid face turned a deeper purple under its crown of thick white hair. Then, remembering

15

his manners, he gave an affected bow. 'Good afternoon Iris, good afternoon Melissa. My good lady asked me to deliver these.' He handed each an envelope. 'We're giving a little drinks party on Friday evening. Just an informal affair to welcome our new neighbours to the village. I do hope you can come.'

'What a kind thought,' said Melissa. 'Thank you very much.'

'You've decided to forgive them, then?' said Iris with a smile that held a hint of malice.

'Eh? What's that?'

'The newcomers!' Iris raised her voice a decibel or two. 'You've forgiven them for having the cheek to come and live here?'

Ford coughed. 'Yes, well, the real culprit was old Freda Gallard for selling the land.'

'Can't blame her. Henry Gallard left her with hardly a bean to her name.' Iris and the irascible old warrior had fought in opposing camps over the elderly widow's battle to secure planning consent for four houses in part of her garden.

'Hrmmph!' Ford glowered, then remembered that his mission was one of friendship. 'Well, now it's done we have to let bygones be bygones. I must say,' he went on condescendingly, 'the two families who've moved in so far seem quite a decent class of people. Perhaps you've seen them around?' Iris and Melissa shook their heads and he beamed at having information to impart. 'Chap called Shergold, some sort of academic at Stowbridge Tech with a mousey little wife, and a civil engineer. Kent, I think the name is, or Essex . . . some county or other, *haahaahaa!*' When he laughed he sounded like a sheep with something stuck in its throat. 'Young Mrs County's a smart little filly,' he added with a leer. 'Make some of the wives round here sit up, and the husbands too, *haahaahaa!* Well, I must be getting along.'

With a jaunty wave of his stick he retreated, oblivious to the lukewarm response of the two ladies to his jocular remarks.

'What an old gossip he is!' remarked Melissa when he was out of earshot. 'However does Madeleine put up with him?'

Iris grunted. 'She's as bad as he is. Proper old busy-bodies, the pair of them. Only invite people to sus them out. Do it for all the newcomers; got the treatment yourself, remember?'

Melissa did remember being entertained by the Fords one evening soon after her arrival. She had appreciated the opportunity of meeting some of the local residents but had no recollection of gratifying anyone's interest in her own affairs. Rather the reverse.

'I seem to remember asking quite a few questions myself,' she recalled with a smile. 'Writer's natural curiosity, you know.'

'That's probably why you've been invited. They'll pump you later to see if you've found out anything they haven't.'

'What a cynic you are!'

'You'll see.'

'We're going then?'

'Might as well.'

On their way home from the drinks party at Tanners Cottage, the Fords' draughtily genuine Queen Anne residence, Melissa and Iris, in mellow mood, exchanged impressions of the new arrivals in the village.

'Eleanor Shergold's a bit of a mouse,' observed Iris. 'Nice little thing, though. Didn't take to what's-his-name—the husband.'

'Rodney? Neither did I,' agreed Melissa.

'Self-opinionated ass!'

'Yes, isn't he. He informed me,' here Melissa began chanting in exaggeratedly sonorous tones, 'that he has a Pee Aitch Dee in history, is Head of the School of Extra-Mural and Non-Vocational Studies at Stowbridge and is writing a book on neolithic burial mounds. Declaimed it like an actor reciting a Shakespearean prologue. When I asked his wife what her interests were and she said she did a little painting, he practically squashed her flat.'

'Never mentioned her painting to me,' said Iris, sounding a trifle piqued. In recent months she had developed an interest in nurturing amateur talent.

'Probably scared off by your reputation. Incidentally, *Doctor* Shergold,' Melissa gave the title an ironic emphasis, 'has offered me a job.'

Iris's jaw dropped. 'Doing what, for goodness' sake?'

'Running a writers' workshop. I said I'd think about it. He said I could have a free hand, and it'd only be one afternoon a week,' Melissa continued, in response to Iris's dubious frown.

'Up to you. Couldn't work for that pompous twit myself.'

'I think it could be fun.'

Iris shrugged, then gave a grin that fleetingly reduced her age from fifty-something to twenty-something. 'Talking of fun, did you notice our Dudley making up to Harriet Yorke?'

'I did.' Melissa chuckled at the recollection. 'She is rather dishy, isn't she? Madeleine was fairly baring her teeth. You could almost see the vitriol dripping into the avocado dip!'

'I've had an idea!' Iris came to an abrupt halt by the roadside and made a sweeping, melodramatic gesture with her arms. 'How's this for a plot for one of your novels? Ford and Shergold are both after Harriet, who is found in a cowshed with a hayfork through her gizzard. Whodunnit, Madeleine Ford, Eleanor Shergold or the postmistress?'

'Iris, you are a goose!' cried Melissa, and the two women laughed like schoolgirls and devised variations on the absurd theme for the rest of the way home.

Four

THE MID-COTSWOLD COLLEGE OF ARTS AND Technology, known to its administration and lecturers as MIDCCAT but to most of the residents of Stowbridge as 'the Tech', had long outgrown its nineteen-sixties campus and at various times had acquired further properties in other parts of the town. The School of Extra-Mural and Non-Vocational Studies was quartered in a draughty Edwardian house, supplemented by a group of prefabricated buildings in the extensive gardens and presided over by Doctor Rodney Shergold. In his office on the ground floor, the learned doctor planned his courses, wrote his reports and made pronouncements to his staff to the accompaniment of feet tramping up wooden staircases and the scrape of chairs on the uncarpeted floors of the rooms overhead. It was here that Melissa found him when she arrived to conduct her first writers' workshop.

It was a large, well-proportioned room with a high ceiling and tall sash windows which had a dwarfing effect on both the furniture and its occupant. There were bookshelves along two of the walls, a wooden cupboard, a filing cabinet, some chairs and a table and two desks. On the smaller of these a covered typewriter proclaimed the territory of the part-time secretary, who was not at the moment in attendance. Rodney Shergold, sharp-featured, bespectacled and balding, sat at the other making notes in the margin of a closely-written sheet of foolscap, his head propped on his free hand, the epitome of a dedicated scholar.

'You're in very good time,' he commented, raising his head after what appeared to be a deliberately measured interval.

'I thought it would be a good idea to arrive extra early on my first day,' said Melissa, ignoring the unsmiling manner that robbed his words of any hint of welcome or approval. 'I don't even know where my classroom is and I wanted to ask you about registers and so on. I haven't done this sort of thing before, remember.'

'Oh yes, of course.' He put down his pen and glanced across at the empty desk in the corner. 'My secretary hasn't arrived yet. I suppose I'd better take you to the staff room myself. There'll be someone there to show you the ropes.'

He rose, rather grudgingly it seemed to Melissa. He was only a fraction taller than she was but by holding himself rigidly erect with his neck stretched and his chin tucked in, he managed to give the impression that he was looking down at her. He was no shabbily-dressed, out-at-elbows academic; his jacket was well-cut, his white shirt immaculate and the crease in his trousers razor sharp. Melissa had a swift vision of a flushed and anxious Eleanor bent over a steamy ironing board.

'This way.' Shergold led her up two flights of stairs and opened a door marked 'Staff Room' to reveal an untidy arrangement of battered desks littered with books and papers, rows of shelves and cupboards and a photocopier in a corner. A man sat at one of the desks, reading the *Guardian* and eating sandwiches from a yellow plastic container.

'Mr Willard, this is Mrs Craig,' Shergold announced in his abrupt monotone. 'She's running my new writers' workshop. Just tell her where everything is, will you. My secretary has made out a register for her but perhaps you'd explain how to fill it in. Your room is C3,' he added to Melissa and went out.

'Certainly, Doctor Shergold.' Willard put down his paper, returned a half-eaten sandwich to his lunchbox and stood up, brushing crumbs from his paint-smeared jeans. 'Pompous ass!' he muttered as the door closed. ' "*Mrs* Craig", "*Mister* Willard", "*my* secretary"—thinks he's living in the nineteenth century.' He was about fifty, tall and spare with a high forehead, a trim grey beard, receding grey hair and round eyes the colour of milk chocolate. His cheeks were hollow and his fingers long and tapering. An artistic type, Melissa guessed as they shook hands. 'I'm Barney,' he added with a smile. 'Do I have to call you "Mrs Craig"?'

'No of course not, I'm Melissa. Glad to meet you Barney.'

'Melissa Craig . . . would you be Mel Craig, the crime writer?'

'That's right. What's your subject?'

'Senior Tutor in the Faculty of Fine Arts—that's the second hut on the left behind the bike sheds!' His smile had a gentle, aesthetic quality. He began wandering round the room. 'The registers are kept in these pigeonholes. Yours should be under Thursday afternoon—yes, here we are.' He flipped open a folder. 'You've got twenty students and they've all paid. Room C3 is upstairs, immediately overhead. Staff toilet next door but one. Leave your register on Angy's desk at the end of the afternoon. Angy is *his* secretary, by the way,' he added with a grin and a jerk of his head towards the door. 'You'll find her very helpful. Anything else you need to know?'

'I think that's all, thanks. Do go on with your lunch.'

'I will, if you don't mind.' He bent down to switch on an electric kettle half-hidden among heaps of books on the dusty floor before polishing off his sandwich and sinking his teeth into an apple. 'Care for a coffee?'

'No thanks.'

Barney spooned instant coffee into a mug. Melissa was about to go in search of her classroom when the door burst open to admit a heavily-built young man with an untidy mop of fair hair. He was clutching an armful of books which he let fall in a slithering heap on a chair.

'Hi,' he said to Barney and cocked an eyebrow at Melissa.

'Meet Doug Wilson, the Campus Casanova,' said Barney. 'This is Melissa, alias Mel Craig, crime writer extraordinaire.'

Doug beamed. He had large, spaced-out teeth and an air of pugnacious sensuality. Far from showing any sign of resentment at Barney's introduction, he appeared quite proud of it.

'Welcome to the sex maniacs' department!' he said, enthusiastically pumping Melissa's hand. His grin broadened at her look of perplexity. 'Rumour has it that the County Education Officer and his staff are still trying to think up an innocuous acronym for a School of Extra-Mural and Non-Vocational Studies,' he explained. 'Meanwhile we use our own but it doesn't seem to have caught on at Shire Hall.'

'Nor with the Head of Department, I imagine,' said Melissa, remembering with amusement the humourless response that gentleman had made to some harmlessly flippant remark at the Fords' party.

'Rodney has engaged Melissa to instruct the citizens of Stowbridge in the art of writing blood-and-thunder fiction,' Barney explained.

'Not just blood and thunder,' she corrected him. 'They can write what they like. My brief from Rodney is, and I quote, "to assist them in the improvement of their basic writing skills and the development of their latent creativity"!'

'Always supposing they have any,' said Doug cheerfully.

'How did you come to know him, by the way?' asked Barney. 'I thought he only moved in learned antiquarian circles.'

'He and his wife moved into my village a short while ago. I met them at a party.'

Doug's eyebrows vanished under the overhanging thatch. 'Randy Rodders at a party? The mind boggles!'

Melissa stared at him with raised eyebrows.

'If his name was Sidney we'd call him the Sizzler,' explained Doug obscurely. 'We like to spice our good-humoured raillery with alliteration,' he continued as Melissa still looked blank, 'so we call him Randy Rodders because he's humourless, sexless and most probably bloodless. If he cut himself he'd ooze mineral water. I'm surprised to hear he's married. What's his wife like?'

'Pleasant but very quiet,' said Melissa, recollecting the dumpy woman of about her own age, neatly turned out in a style of some twenty years ago, with remarkable sea-green eyes that continually strayed in admiration to her husband. 'She seems to dote on him,' she added.

'How any woman could dote on Rodders is beyond me,' said Doug. 'I wonder how she'd react if she knew what a dish his secretary is!' His eyes glowed with undisguised lust. 'Have you met our delicious Angy yet?'

'I spoke on the telephone to a girl with a very alluring voice.'

'That's Angy!' Doug made whinnying noises and his hands described an imaginary female form. Out of the corner of her eye, Melissa noticed Barney's jaw set in disapproval but Doug went rattling on as if unaware of the fall in temperature.

'Every red-blooded male on the campus would like to bed her but I'll bet old Rodders hasn't so much as cast a prurient eye over her cleavage. It must be sad to be so cold-blooded,' he reflected, busy spilling papers from a briefcase on to an already over-loaded table. 'Someone should try and arouse his interest in the joys of the flesh. I think I'll suggest it to Angy. It'd be quite a challenge for her!'

Barney rammed the lid on his lunch-box and began jerking drawers open and slamming them shut. He grabbed a portfolio, picked up his mug of coffee and strode to the door. 'You'll do nothing of the kind!' he snapped. 'And I'll thank you to show a little more respect!'

'Okay, okay, only kidding!' Doug turned and winked at Melissa as the door banged. 'He gets like this from time to time,' he explained. 'Clings to the old Victorian values and all that. He was once heard to refer to "the sanctity of womanhood"!' One corner of his mouth lifted in a kind of indulgent contempt.

'It's quite a refreshing change to meet someone like that,' said Melissa pointedly.

'Ah, yes, well, I suppose . . . ' He had no need to finish the remark—his condescending smirk said it for him: I suppose at your age you appreciate that sort of crap! Aloud, he said flippantly, 'Do I detect disapproval in your bright eyes?'

'No comment,' she replied, trying not to sound curt.

He shrugged, took some papers from a folder, went over to the photocopier and switched it on. He stood with his back to her, watching the machine ejecting copies into a tray.

'What do you teach?' she asked.

'English to foreigners,' he replied over his shoulder.

'That must be very rewarding,' she said politely.

He shrugged. 'More often than not it's bloody frustrating.'

Melissa moved towards the door. 'I think I'll go and find my classroom.'

Doug fed more paper into the machine. 'Best of luck!' he said.

She reached room C3 ten minutes before her class was due to begin but already nearly all the students had arrived. When she entered, heads were raised and eyes swivelled silently in her direction. She read appraisal in their gaze, and an almost tangible hope that she had the power to unlock for them the door to the fulfilment of their literary dreams. It was a daunting moment.

She took a deep breath, introduced herself, outlined her plans for the course and marked her register. 'Now,' she said with what she hoped was a sympathetic, encouraging smile, 'has anyone brought something they'd like to read to us today?' A few tentative hands were raised, one was chosen at random and the writers' workshop was under way.

At the end of the session, as instructed by Barney, Melissa went back to the office with her register. Rodney Shergold was not there but the secretary's desk was occupied by a young woman wearing a cream silk shirt that fell open just far enough to invite adverse comment from the prudish, while a gold pendant lay at exactly the right point to focus the attention of a lascivious eye. Titian-red hair framed a perfect, oval face. As the girl looked up, Melissa found herself looking at the original of Rick Lawrence's portrait.

'Can I help you?' The half-smile that the young artist had caught with such accuracy lifted the corners of the mouth and gave a slight tilt to the amber eyes.

'Is your name Angelica Caroli, by any chance?' asked Melissa.

'That's right. Most people call me Angy—except Doctor Shergold, of course.' A hint of mischief crept into the smile.

'Didn't you do an art course at Ravenswood College?' Angy's eyes grew larger.

'That's right, I did. How did you know?'

'I was at last year's prize-giving and I saw your portrait. I can see now just how good it is.'

'Thank you.' The voice was low and a trifle husky, like a young cat purring with pleasure. 'I suppose you saw Ricardo's knife-throwing act, then?' She spoke the name with a perfect Italian pronunciation.

'You heard about that? It must have been a shock!'

'It was rather, but so typical of him. He loves a bit of drama.' She held out a hand for Melissa's register. 'You must be Mrs Craig. Was it a good class? Did all the students turn up?'

'Yes, they all turned up and they seemed to enjoy it.' Melissa handed over the folder and Angy dropped it on to a stack of similar ones on her desk. She drew a sheet of paper from a drawer and fed it into her typewriter. A garnet ring accentuated the ivory whiteness of her hands, the fingers tipped with pearl like a kitten's velvet paws.

'Forgive me if I sound inquisitive,' said Melissa, 'but how did you know about the portrait being slashed? I was told you'd gone away.'

'My aunt wrote to me. Who told you I'd left?'

'Lou Stacey.'

'You know Lou? How is she? She never writes to me.' The concern in Angy's voice and expression seemed genuine.

'I've only met her once, at the prize-giving. She was very upset by what happened.'

Angy sighed. 'I suppose she's still angry with me for speaking with Ricardo.' Again the musical, Italian lilt, accompanied by a sad shake of the head. 'And we used to be such friends. I thought she'd be glad to have him to herself again but . . . ' The quick lift of the hands and the movement of the shoulders were not quite English either. 'What else did she tell you about me?'

'That you broke off your engagement and left home without saying anything to anyone, that's all.'

Angy spent several seconds fiddling with the sheet of paper. Melissa had the impression that she was trying to make up her mind to what extent, if any, she should confide in her.

'Did she tell you about Ricardo's grandiose gesture?' she said at length. Melissa nodded and Angy leaned forward, planting her elbows on her machine. 'It was so embarrassing!' she declared. 'And so . . . so medieval! Worse than medieval. At least, in a proper arranged marriage, the bride knows what's going on. His parents and my family knew what he was planning and they never said a word to me. I ask you, in this day and age! I simply didn't know what to do.'

'So you decided to disappear?'

Angy's gestures became wider and more dramatic. 'I had to. Everyone was over the moon about the engagement— everyone but me, that is—and I knew how upset they'd be when I broke it off. I do so hate seeing people unhappy.' A sorrowful shake of the head proclaimed infinite compassion for the suffering of the world. 'But it wasn't my fault. Ricardo had no business to take it for granted that I'd marry him, just because I . . . we . . . well, you know how it is!' Her hands, her shoulders, her smouldering eyes, all registered despair at the unreasonableness of men. 'Even that was a disaster—for me at any rate,' she added, half to herself. Then she looked straight at Melissa. 'What else could I do but go away?' she pleaded.

'I suppose you could have told Rick . . . Ricardo, privately after the party, that you didn't want to marry him,' said Melissa.

'I couldn't possibly!' Angy looked appalled at the prospect. 'He'd have made a terrible scene and he'd never have
let me break it off. He's got this furious Italian temper and
he can be quite terrifying at times. I thought, if I just disappear for a while, they'll all get over it. I knew I could get
a job; I did a business course before going to Ravenswood.
I had some money Aunt Rosina gave me . . . '

'For your wedding dress!' Melissa could not resist pointing out.

Angy showed no sign of contrition. 'I never asked for it,
did I? Any more than I asked to be engaged. I was going to
write to Ricardo and send his ring back but I was so afraid
he'd come looking for me.'

'What made you choose Stowbridge as a bolt-hole?'

Angy gave a faint, slightly contemptuous smile. 'Ricardo
and I once agreed that the Cotswolds were a refuge for
folksy artists to come and paint their birthday card pictures.
I figured I was unlikely to run into him down here.' She
wrinkled her forehead and pursed her lips. 'I suppose,' she
reflected, 'I could send Aunt Rosina's money back now.
Eddie doesn't charge me much rent for my flat.'

At that point the door opened and Rodney Shergold
entered, leaving Melissa to speculate on the motive behind
Eddie's generosity. He strode over to his desk without
glancing at either of the women and stood there reading
a paper he had brought in with him.

'Have you finished that report yet, Miss Caroli?' he
asked, his eyes still on the paper.

'Just one more page, Doctor Shergold,' said Angy. She
winked at Melissa and began to type.

'See you next Thursday,' said Melissa, eager now to get
home and tell Iris about this extraordinary coincidence. She
decided, however, to say nothing about the reference to
'folksy artists'.

Angy smiled and nodded. There was no response from
their Head of Department.

FIVE

IN MID-DECEMBER, MELISSA DROVE DOWN TO
Sussex to spend Christmas and the New Year with the
couple whom she always thought and spoke of as her in-
laws. They were a lively, generous-hearted pair who doted
on their grandson and had no difficulty in overlooking the
fact that his mother had never been married to the son they
had lost.

The festivities passed pleasantly enough and Melissa
returned home refreshed and ready to start work again.
She had plenty to occupy her days but the evenings often
seemed long and there were moments when she reflected
wistfully on Iris's invitation to join her in the South of
France, whither she had departed according to custom early
in November and whence she would not return until the
end of March. The high spot of her week was Thursday
afternoon when she could look forward to a stimulating
chat with Barney followed by a rewarding hour and a half
with the members of her writers' workshop.

The telephone was a lifeline. Her son Simon called once
a week from Texas, where he worked for an oil company;
Joe Martin, her agent, rang from time to time, ostensibly
to enquire about the new book. At first she was able to
report encouraging progress but now she had run into a
snag and, after a few attempts at prevarication, felt bound
to admit it.

'The plot simply won't jell,' she complained during one
of his calls. 'I'm going to leave it for a while and do some

short stories.' Joe was sympathetic.

'Would it help if I came down for the day and we had a brain-storming session?'

'It's a lovely idea but there's more snow forecast. You might not be able to get back.'

'I can imagine worse fates,' he said with unmistakable meaning.

'*You* might be able to!' she retorted with equally unmistakable levity.

A plaintive sigh echoed in her receiver. Since his divorce from Georgina, Joe had sent out strong signals that he would like his relationship with Melissa to be more than that of author and agent.

'Cruelty, thy name is Melissa!' he lamented. 'So tell me, how are things at college? What news of the lovely Angelica?' Joe had heard all about the slashed portrait and how the subject had taken refuge from the avenging artist in a small Gloucestershire town.

'She's a sweet little pussy-cat who purrs for everyone,' said Melissa, 'and there's going to be mayhem in the staff room before long.'

'How so?'

'It's all quite ridiculous. I think I've told you, Barney Willard sees her as the embodiment of all that's chaste and pure.'

'And is she?'

'She has this air of childlike innocence. I'm sure that if men fought and died over her, she'd sit there shaking her head and wondering quite sincerely why they couldn't all have been friends.'

'And you think there might be a fight to the death?'

'Nothing quite so drastic as that but Barney does get very tetchy when Doug Wilson throws out hints about how Angy distributes her favours. I'm sure it's only aggro but Barney's sense of humour doesn't extend to jokes about her virtue.'

'Well, maybe there's a plot in there . . . but make sure you keep out of range when the fists start to fly!' advised Joe. 'I'll be in touch again soon.'

*   *   *

The year advanced and the days began to lengthen. On the bank behind the cottages, clumps of primroses glowed like pale miniature suns and the winds that came roistering along the valley carried with them the high-pitched, staccato protests of new-born lambs. Melissa's daily walk became once more a pleasure instead of a self-imposed discipline and she tramped the lanes and footpaths with a light heart, feeling the fresh sweet air wash over her face and rejoicing at the prospect of another Cotswold spring.

From time to time on these outings she met Eleanor Shergold exercising Snappy, her aptly named Border terrier, and the two took their walk together. Eleanor, invariably band-box neat in clothes that were years out of date, trotted beside Melissa, picking her way round puddles and patches of mud, tugged along by the straining dog and punctuating her remarks with little puffing breaths.

Towards the end of March, she invited Melissa to tea.

'I've been wanting to ask you for a long time,' she said in her soft, rather precise voice, 'only Rodney wouldn't let me invite anyone until everything in the house was the way he . . . the way we wanted it. We've had so much trouble with the builders, you know, and the decorations weren't right, and then we had to wait ages for the lounge curtains . . . '

'I'd love to have tea with you,' Melissa interposed gently, having heard it all before. 'But really, you needn't have worried about the curtains!'

'Well, I wanted to ask you long ago. I said to Rodney, I'm sure Mrs . . . Melissa I mean, must be lonely with her friend away, but he said I had to . . . ' She stopped for a moment to allow Snappy to place his territorial mark on a gatepost. 'How about tomorrow afternoon at three o'clock?'

'I'll look forward to it,' said Melissa.

The Shergolds had called their house Cotswold View and the name was carved on a varnished slice of wood with the bark retained to give a rustic appearance. Already the new houses, although built to the same design, had begun to take on a measure of individuality: a carriage lantern in a porch, a tub of daffodils about to break into flower beside a front door, a flagged path and a planting of trees and shrubs alongside a lawn painstakingly laid the previous autumn. Two of the owners had hung slatted blinds in their downstairs windows, another had crowded the sills with potted plants and antique glassware. Only the Shergolds had chosen to veil themselves in looping folds of lace.

'It's so nice to be able to have visitors!' said Eleanor, as she and Melissa sat drinking tea from china cups patterned with violets. 'Everyone has been so kind and hospitable, and I've felt really guilty . . . '

'These scones are delicious. Do you think I could have another?' said Melissa, anxious to forestall a further outburst of apologetics.

'But of course! Would you like the recipe? I'll write it out for you!' Delight illuminated the homely features. 'What about some more tea?'

'Yes, please.'

'I'm sure you must miss . . . Iris, isn't it?' Eleanor was still not entirely at ease with first names but, like a child reciting a difficult lesson, she showed a determination to persevere.

'Oh, I do,' Melissa admitted. 'I'll be glad when she comes home at the end of the month. I have Binkie, of course, her cat. The minute she goes away he moves in with me and really he's quite companionable.'

'Animals are company, aren't they?' Eleanor agreed. 'I wouldn't be without Snappy. Rodney didn't want me to have a dog; he says they make the place smell if you're not careful and they spoil the carpets so he's not allowed in here . . . Snappy I mean of course, not Rodney, *khikhikhi!*' She gave one of her throaty giggles. 'I don't often argue with Rodney but I told him, if we're going to live in the country I must have a dog, so in the end he agreed.'

'Good for you!' said Melissa heartily, greatly encouraged by the note of determination that underlay this speech.

'Rodney tells me that your writers' workshop is a great success,' Eleanor went on.

The remark took Melissa by surprise. Not once had he made any enquiry or shown the slightest interest in her classes, but since she could hardly say as much to his wife she merely replied, 'I'm glad he's pleased with it.'

'Oh yes, he says the numbers have kept up very well. He has to keep an eye on numbers, you know, because of the cuts. As soon as the numbers fall below a certain level, the class has to go.'

'Ah yes, the cuts,' agreed Melissa.

'I do so envy people who can write,' said Eleanor with a sigh. 'Rodney writes books you know. I sometimes wonder . . . *khikhikhi* . . . why someone as clever as him married someone as ordinary as me! I should have been clever,' she continued in response to Melissa's encouraging noises. 'My father was brilliant . . . he was the Principal of Brigston University you know . . . but you don't want to hear about me. Do have some more cake!'

'Thank you,' said Melissa, thinking how awful it was to be so inhibited. If ever anyone needed a boost for their ego, it was Eleanor Shergold. Well, she'd see what she could do. 'If you're interested in writing,' she said casually, 'why don't you come to my workshop?'

'Oh, I couldn't possibly do that! Rodney wouldn't like it at all!'

'Whyever not?'

'I wouldn't be very good and he'd hate other people to know how stupid I am . . . *khikhikhi!*'

The giggle was becoming wearisome and Melissa felt herself growing impatient. 'That's ridiculous!' she said firmly. 'I'm sure you're not stupid. Do think about it.'

'He might see me at the college.' The prospect appeared to cause Eleanor great alarm. 'And my name would be on the register.'

'Give a false name!' said Melissa cheekily. 'Put on a wig . . . go in disguise!'

The attempt at humour was greeted with an uncomprehending stare. 'Oh no, I couldn't possibly!' Eleanor repeated obstinately.

Exasperated, Melissa knew a brick wall when she saw one and tried another topic. 'What about your painting?' she asked. 'Have you done anything lately?'

'How kind of you to ask!' Eleanor's cheeks grew pink and she seemed to come alive, like a drooping flower refreshed by the rain. 'As it happens, I've been working on a little picture. I'll show you if you don't mind coming into the kitchen. I work there because the light's good . . . '

She got to her feet as she spoke and led the way. Snappy, curled up in his basket in a corner, lifted his head and growled softly at the sight of Melissa.

'Silly boy, Snappy!' chided his mistress. 'Mrs Craig's a friend!'

'But this is good!' said Melissa, as Eleanor shyly pointed to an unfinished water-colour of the church. 'Have you shown any of your work to Iris?'

'Oh no, I wouldn't like to bother her.'

'I'm sure it wouldn't be a bother,' said Melissa. She was still examining the little painting. 'Iris would like this, I know she would. Have you had lessons?'

'Not since I left school but I study a bit from books and go to art exhibitions when there's one locally. Do you really think it's any good?' A mixture of pleasure and disbelief transformed Eleanor's features. With those extraordinary eyes, she could be quite attractive, Melissa thought, if she'd only get a new hairstyle, buy some fashionable clothes and polish up her abysmally low self-image.

'I like it very much. They do painting classes at MIDCCAT, you know. Why don't you enrol for a course?'

Eleanor's face slumped like an unset blancmange. 'Oh no, I couldn't possibly.'

Because your flaming husband wouldn't like it, I suppose, thought Melissa, mentally grinding her teeth. 'I must be going,' she said. 'I'm sure you want to start getting Rodney's supper.'

'Oh yes, I expect he'll be hungry after his day out. Did you know he's been asked to organise a summer course in local history for a party of Americans? He and Miss Caroli

—his secretary, you know—were planning to drive to some of the places he wants them to visit, just to see how long the journey will take and where they can have lunch, and so on.' Eleanor's tone grew wistful, as if she would have enjoyed being included in such an expedition. 'Do you know Miss Caroli?' she asked. 'Rodney says she's very efficient.'

'Oh, she is—very efficient,' said Melissa guardedly. 'Haven't you met her?'

'Oh no, I never visit Rodney in his office . . . he wouldn't like it at all.' Eleanor seemed to find the notion almost shocking. 'I'm so relieved that he has a good secretary. It's made so much difference to his work, you know, to have someone reliable, and his new book's coming on very well, he says.'

'I'm glad about that,' murmured Melissa. 'Thank you so much for the tea. You must come to me soon.'

What a pity, she thought as she made her way home, that Iris was still away. There was no one else to whom she could express her indignation. What gave a pip-squeak, third-rate academic like Rodney Shergold the right to make his wife feel so inadequate, and how could Eleanor be so spineless as to submit to his petty tyranny? She had real talent that should be encouraged.

On second thoughts, she must have some backbone. Snappy's presence proved that.

Six

IRIS RETURNED AT THE END OF MARCH FROM Provence where a few years previously she had bought a renovated cottage in a small town a few kilometres from Avignon. She looked happy and healthy; her fine skin was tanned and her eyes bright. The climate down there suited her, she said, and she had evidently made a number of friends. In her usual laconic style she told of mild winter days spent out of doors sketching and evenings at local restaurants with parties of neighbours. There were also intriguing references to a certain Monsieur Bonard, who ran a small private *'centre culturel'* and who might possibly, Melissa guessed, have something to do with the general air of well-being that Iris had brought home with her. In due time, perhaps, she would reveal more.

Meanwhile, she demanded to be brought up to date with the village news.

'There isn't a great deal that I haven't told you in my letters,' said Melissa.

'No disasters or scandals?'

'Nothing to rock the headlines.'

They were settled in front of Iris's log fire after supper on her first full day at home, Melissa in an armchair and Iris in her favourite place on the hearthrug with Binkie on her lap.

'Tell me about your class. Any budding Shakespeares yet?'

'Hardly. One or two have had odd bits published and several others show quite a lot of promise. There's one called Sybil Bliss who writes poems about flowers. She had one accepted last month by *Madame* magazine and she was positively euphoric!'

'And who's this Barney character your letters are so full of?'

Melissa, feeling she was being interrogated, made her reply deliberately casual.

'Oh, he's the chap in charge of the art department.'

'You haven't got a thing about him, by any chance?'

'Certainly not!' Melissa avoided Iris's penetrating eye. 'He's got a thing about Angy though. He seems to regard himself as her minder.' She could hear a hint of asperity in her own voice, and was annoyed by it.

'From what I've heard, that girl can look after herself,' commented Iris with a sly look which Melissa ignored.

'I think so too, but Barney is almost fanatically protective towards her. I went into Rodney Shergold's office once to find him lecturing her on the innate wickedness of men, like a Victorian papa.'

'Surprised she puts up with it.'

'Oh, she just smiles and agrees with everything he says.'

'And then goes her own sweet way!'

'Probably.'

'Barney sounds an oddball.'

'No more than any other artist!' countered Melissa. 'He can be aggressive, though,' she added reflectively. 'I thought he was going to clobber Doug the other day after one of his lewd wisecracks. Oh, and he suspects Rodney Shergold of dishonourable intentions.'

Iris cackled in disbelief. 'That pretentious twit? Only interested in himself and ancient history, in that order.'

'Mmm . . . maybe.' Melissa became thoughtful, remembering the day the office door had been left ajar and she had entered without knocking. Rodney Shergold had been standing behind Angy, who was seated at her desk and seemed to be drawing his attention to something on the sheet of paper in her typewriter. Nothing remarkable about that, except that he was leaning forward with a hand resting on her shoulder, his thumb caressing her neck, looking at her rather than at the paper and wearing the same fatuous expression that came over Iris's face when she was talking to Binkie. When he saw Melissa he had snatched his hand away and jerked upright like a clumsily handled marionette, the hint of a blush spreading over his thin cheeks.

Iris's eyes were gleaming in the firelight, her interest aroused by Melissa's non-committal response. 'You've noticed something? Do tell!'

Melissa recounted the episode. 'I don't suppose it means anything,' she said, thinking of Eleanor and hoping it was true. 'But he did look guilty when he saw me. It was quite comic really. Angy of course didn't bat an eyelid.'

'That doesn't surprise me. I wonder if she's discovered what it is Eleanor sees in him!' speculated Iris wickedly.

'Or he's heard about his nickname and is trying to live up to it,' said Melissa. 'There's something about that girl . . . everyone eats out of her hand. It's not surprising really. She just oozes charm, and she's so incredibly beautiful. By the way, talking of the Shergolds, I've been trying to persuade Eleanor to enrol for a painting class, but no luck. Maybe you could make her change her mind? I've seen some of her work, and I think it's quite good.'

'I'll have a go next time I see her. Hate to think of talent wasted.'

'It might give her morale a boost. That dreadful little man has brainwashed her into believing she's no good at anything.' Melissa stood up and yawned. 'Let me help you with the dishes and then I'm going home.'

'Never mind the dishes. Gloria comes in the morning.'

Easter came and went. During the short break Melissa, alternately bullied and blandished by Iris, spent the greater part of each day in the garden, cultivating her vegetable plot. She dug and hoed, weeded and sowed for hours on end. Her back ached but the hours in the fresh air seemed to revive her creativity and the plot of her book began at last to knit together. Almost before she realised it, the holidays were over and the college reopened.

It was gratifying to find all last term's names, and several new ones, on the writers' workshop register. Everyone seemed to have returned refreshed and stimulated. Sybil Bliss, who had spent Easter in the Scilly Isles, brought a new collection of floral poems and at the end of the class she lingered after the others had left and hesitantly laid a folder on Melissa's table.

'I wonder if you'd care to see these,' she said, and spread out half a dozen or so water-colour paintings of flowers. Melissa had learned enough from Iris to know that they were competent, if not outstanding, and she praised them warmly.

Sybil's response was rapturous. She was a slender creature of about forty, with bright blue eyes and straight grey hair falling like soft wings on either side of an expressive little face. Her voice was carefully modulated, her manner a shade theatrical and, despite her wedding ring, there was something gauche and spinsterish about her.

'Oh, I'm *so* glad you like them!' she breathed. 'I was thinking of putting together a little book of my poems and illustrating them myself. Do you suppose there's *any* chance of getting it published?'

Melissa felt a little out of her depth. 'I'm not sure,' she murmured. 'This sort of thing's outside my field. Why not ask your art teacher?'

Sybil looked dubious. 'I thought you'd be more likely to know about publishing, but I could ask Miss Caroli, I suppose.'

'Miss Caroli? You mean Angy—Doctor Shergold's secretary?'

'That's right. Our regular teacher was taken ill during the holidays and won't be back until next term. Miss Caroli is only part-time with Doctor Shergold and was free on Tuesday afternoon so she's standing in for her.'

'Really? I knew she'd had an art training, but . . . '

'She's going to be an absolutely *splendid* teacher!' Sybil, like everyone else, had evidently fallen under Angy's spell. Her voice rose and fell as if every other word was in italics. 'So *talented!* And so *beautiful* too!' She clasped her hands together and widened her eyes, like a drama student asked to mime delight and astonishment.

'Well, that sounds a very handy arrangement,' said Melissa. 'Would you let me take these home?' she added, indicating the paintings. 'I live next door to Iris Ash. I'll ask her if she's got any ideas.'

The prospect of her work being examined by the celebrated Miss Ash sent Sybil into fresh transports. 'Oh, how *wonderful!* I'd be *thrilled* to let her see them!' She placed the folder in Melissa's hands and departed, stammering thanks.

In the office, Angy was looking stunning in tangerine silk. Rodney Shergold was nowhere to be seen.

'I gather your first painting class was a great success,' Melissa remarked as she handed over her register. 'Sybil Bliss is singing your praises!'

'Oh, I'm so glad to hear that. I was a bit nervous, it being my first day, but I'm sure I'm going to enjoy it.' Angy turned on one of her breathtaking smiles. 'Wasn't it a bit of luck, Mrs Levy being taken ill like that!'

'I'm not sure Mrs Levy would see it in quite that light,' said Melissa drily, at which Angy gave a little purring laugh.

Well, it wasn't a bad start to the term, thought Melissa as she drove homewards. Everyone seems happy, the book's going well and all's right with the world!

And so it seemed at the time.

Iris readily promised to try to think of a possible market for Sybil's work. Accordingly, one Wednesday afternoon about three weeks later, she invited her to tea.

Accompanied by Melissa, who had undertaken to introduce her, Sybil approached the door of Elder Cottage as if she were treading on hallowed ground, her face pink with excitement.

'I can't tell you what a *thrill* this is,' she began breathlessly when the door opened. Iris, who hated being treated like a celebrity, made a dismissive gesture.

'Come on in,' she said. 'You going to join us?' she added, with a glance at Melissa.

'Later, if I may. I'm just off to the post office.'

There was a small white car parked outside the little general stores. Snappy, sitting in the back behind a metal grille, recognised Melissa and set up a furious whining and yapping, leaping up and down and scrabbling at the window as she passed. Inside the shop, Eleanor was at the counter, rummaging in her purse with the agitated movements of someone afraid of missing a train, while Mrs Foster, the proprietress, stood by with one plump, pink hand extended.

'Hullo, Eleanor,' said Melissa breezily. 'I was just thinking about you.'

'Oh, really?' said Eleanor, counting coins into Mrs Foster's palm.

'One of my writers' workshop ladies is having tea with Iris this afternoon and I was wondering if you'd like to meet her? She goes to Angy Caroli's art class as well,' she added, as Eleanor gave her a blank stare. 'She says she's really a very good teacher and I thought . . . '

'Oh no, no!' Eleanor shook her head distractedly. 'It's kind of you but I'd rather not. In any case, I have to hurry back. Rodney isn't at all well.'

'Oh dear, I'm so sorry.'

'He came home early, saying he'd been sick. He must have caught something . . . he said Mr Willard was off-colour yesterday and Miss Caroli didn't come in at all this morning.'

'Sounds nasty,' Melissa murmured. 'Could it be something they ate in the college refectory, do you think?'

'I'm not sure. Rodney hasn't been himself for several weeks. I've been putting it down to overwork but he's never been like this. I'm really worried.' She looked it; her movements as she gathered up her shopping were uncoordinated, she had an unhealthy colour and her cheeks sagged.

'Shouldn't he see a doctor?' Melissa suggested.

'I want him to but he won't. He can be very obst—' she checked herself and substituted 'determined', as if afraid of sounding disloyal. 'Please excuse me, I must get back.'

'Of course. I do hope he'll be better by tomorrow.'

'She doesn't look too well herself,' commented Melissa as Mrs Foster entered the cage that served as a post office.

'That's what I told her this morning, when she came in for her paper,' said Mrs Foster, eager as always for a gossip. With her round, babyish face and snub nose, she reminded Melissa of a small pink piglet. 'She wouldn't have it though. "There's nothing the matter with me," she says. "I'm perfectly well so don't you go telling anyone I'm not." Quite shirty, she was.' Mrs Foster gave a little toss of the head as she handed over stamps and counted out change, clearly offended by the rebuff.

Back in Elder Cottage, Melissa joined Iris and Sybil for tea and wholemeal scones.

'Well, how did you get on?' she asked.

Immediately, Sybil began a paean to Iris's brilliance when compared with her own mediocre talent and went on to extol her kindness, her encouragement and her helpful advice.

'She suggests that I paint my flowers on greeting cards with one of my verses inside. She knows someone who would print them for me, isn't that a good idea? So much more practical than trying to get a book published. I must tell Angelica, she'll be so interested. She's such a sweet girl and so encouraging to everyone in the class. Really I feel quite inspired!' She rattled on, every sentence peppered with italics, her tea-cup in one hand and a half-eaten scone in the other, the wings of hair flipping across her face as she turned from Iris to Melissa and back again.

'Angy seems to be a great success,' commented Iris, pouring second cups of tea.

'Oh, rather!' The schoolgirlish expression made Sybil seem extraordinarily young. 'Mrs Levy was good, of course . . . I mustn't criticise. She taught us a great deal, but Angelica has such enthusiasm!'

'Barney Willard must be delighted,' Melissa observed when Sybil paused to recharge her energies with tea and another scone. 'He thinks of Angy as his protégée.'

'Is Mr Willard the tall man with the beard? He's rather strange, isn't he?'

'Strange?' Melissa frowned. 'I've always found him very pleasant.' She spoke with a warmth that caused Iris to cock an eyebrow and Sybil to colour in confusion, as if she had taken the words as a reproof.

'Oh, I'm sure he's a very nice person really,' she said hastily, 'only he does seem a little possessive towards Angelica . . . or perhaps "protective" would be a better word. He came into her class on her first day . . . but then, it was only natural I suppose, when she's so new . . . only he came again last week when she was showing young Godfrey, the disabled lad, he's in a wheelchair, such a shame, he's so gifted and a really nice boy although why he should want to shave his hair off and wear earrings I can't imagine . . . anyway, Angelica was leaning across him, helping him with the highlights on his vase and her hair . . . such a lovely colour, isn't it . . . her hair was brushing his face and I think he was rather enjoying it but when Mr Willard saw he told her quite sharply to come and help me . . . and I didn't need any help at all, not just then . . . anyway, she did what he said and didn't seem at all cross . . . she's got such a sweet nature, hasn't she? No sign of artistic temperament . . . oh, I do beg your pardon, Miss Ash!' Sybil's face was a comical study of dismay and embarrassment.

'No offence.' Iris's eyes sparkled with fun.

Sybil put down her empty cup and looked at her watch. 'Oh dear, is that the time? I must be going.' She stood up and made for the door, expressing voluble thanks which Iris received with a set smile and a minimum of words.

After Sybil had left, Melissa told Iris about her encounter with Eleanor Shergold and the story of her husband's indisposition. 'It's probably a bug,' she said. 'I hope it doesn't go round the department.'

As it turned out, it was no bug . . . but by the next day the entire department was afflicted.

SEVEN

THE FOLLOWING DAY, WHEN MELISSA ARRIVED at the college to take her writers' workshop, there were two police cars outside.

'Oh no, not another bomb scare!' she muttered as she manoeuvred the Golf into a parking space. Shops and offices in Stowbridge had suffered a spate of them lately; only last week, classes had been disrupted for over an hour because of a false alarm.

On second thoughts, she reflected that a bomb scare would have brought out all the emergency services. During last week's incident the campus had been alive with fire engines and ambulances as well as police cars, all arriving at high speed with sirens howling and blue lights going like party poppers. There had been clusters of gaping sightseers as well, and the staff and students had been herded across the road to the tennis courts, where they stood being counted, shivering and grumbling in the cool breeze. Today everything was quiet. There must be some other reason for the police presence. Some property stolen perhaps, or another outbreak of vandalism.

A young uniformed constable intercepted her in the hall.

'Are you a member of staff, madam?'

'That's right. I tutor the writers' workshop. What's going on?'

'May I have your name?'

'Mrs Craig, but what—?'

'Do you spell that C R A I G?' he asked, writing in his notebook.

'Yes. Do you mind telling me—?'

'And which room do you use for your writers' workshop, Mrs Craig?' His eyes were smoky brown, like trouser-buttons and about as expressive.

'Room C3,' said Melissa impatiently.

'What floor would that be?'

'Second.'

'What time does your class begin?'

'Two o'clock.' Melissa glanced at her watch. It was just after half-past one and she had arrived in comfortable time to do some photocopying before her students arrived.

'Perhaps you'd be kind enough to go into the office,' said the policeman with smooth, impassive courtesy. 'Detective Sergeant Waters would like a word with you.'

'Would you mind telling me what all this is about?' Melissa demanded.

There was not so much as a flicker in the trouser-button eyes. 'We'll try not to make you late for your class, Mrs Craig. The office is that door in the corner.'

'I know very well where the office is, thank you,' said Melissa through her teeth. She stalked across the hall, knocked and entered.

Rodney Shergold sat at his desk, staring down at his blotter. He glanced up as Melissa came in but he did not speak. He looked ghastly; his drawn features had a greenish tinge as if he had still not recovered from his upset stomach. Doug Wilson was peering out of the window through the slats in the venetian blind, his broad shoulders hunched and his hands in his pockets. When he heard the door open he swung round, nodded to Melissa and swung back again without a word.

Angy was not present; one of the other Thursday afternoon lecturers was standing beside her desk and a second was sitting in her chair. Melissa recognised the latter from casual chats over cups of tea in the staff common room: Miss Knott, a thin, stringy-haired woman of uncertain age who taught dressmaking.

The other woman was a stranger to Melissa but from the green plastic bucket of flowers and foliage on the floor beside her, she deduced that this was Mrs Pearce who taught floral art.

When Melissa entered, both women turned their heads towards the door and then hastily looked away. Miss Knott took out a packet of cigarettes and mimed a request for permission to smoke but wilted under Shergold's look of distaste. Mrs Pearce, her face partly concealed by a shawl of silky brown hair, stooped and fiddled aimlessly with her flowers, lifting them a few inches and then letting them fall. The movement released a sweet, cloying fragrance that hung in the edgy silence like vapour. The place had the atmosphere of a funeral parlour, thought Melissa uneasily. And still nobody spoke.

'Could someone please tell me what's going on?' she pleaded. 'That policeman in the hall is suffering from selective deafness.'

Mrs Pearce and Miss Knott glanced across at Rodney Shergold, evidently considering that as head of department it was up to him to respond, but he did not appear to have heard the question. They then held a consultation, wordlessly, with pursed lips, raised eyebrows and shakes of the head. It was Doug who finally turned from the window and said:

'It's Angy. She's dead.' A faint sigh went round the room, like air escaping from a balloon.

Melissa stared at Doug with her mouth open. 'Dead?' she repeated. 'How? What happened?' It couldn't be true, she must have misheard . . . but from the glazed look on Doug's face she knew there was no mistake. She glanced round the room, searching for someone else who should have been there. 'Where's Barney?'

'We're not sure but we think he's still at the police station,' said Doug. His voice was an unsteady monotone. 'He found her body, you see.' He swallowed and inhaled, jerkily. 'She was murdered.'

'Murdered? Angy murdered?' It was unthinkable, impossible. Bemused with shock, Melissa switched her gaze away from Doug and her eye fell on Miss Knott, who was fiddling with her packet of cigarettes and her lighter and looking peevish at not being allowed to smoke. Melissa felt a sharp spurt of anger. That was Angy's desk. Angy the beautiful, with her Titian hair and amber eyes, her soft, lilting voice and her kittenish smile. Friendly, charming, complaisant Angy, the 'sweet little pussy-cat who purred for everyone'. Someone had killed her and there was this stupid, nondescript creature with nicotine-stained fingers sitting in her place.

As if she read hostility in Melissa's stare, Miss Knott got up and edged towards the door. 'Just going outside for a fag,' she muttered. At that moment there was a tread of feet in the hall. The constable popped his head into the room and asked if Miss Knott could spare Detective Sergeant Waters a few minutes. She followed him, her eyes glazed in terror.

'I suppose they want to know when we last saw Angy and what we were doing at the time of death,' speculated Doug, breaking the heavy silence.

'They can't possibly suspect one of us!' declared Mrs Pearce. She spoke with the confidence of one who has nothing to hide.

'At this stage of an investigation they don't rule out anyone,' said Melissa.

Mrs Pearce looked at her with curiosity in her large eyes. She was a graceful young woman whose slender white hands might have been created to arrange flowers. 'Have you some . . . er . . . knowledge of how they work?' she enquired.

'Some,' Melissa replied.

'She writes about crime,' said Doug Wilson. Now that a conversation had started, he seemed more relaxed and some of his natural flippancy began to show. 'She's the MIDCCAT celebrity, didn't you know? Mel Craig, creator of that infallible sleuth, Nathan Latimer!'

'Oh, of course! I've seen the films on the telly!' exclaimed Mrs Pearce.

'Ah, but have you read the books?' pursued Doug. 'Have you made your contribution to the author's royalties?'

Mrs Pearce pushed back the shawl of hair that had fallen across her cheek and shook her head, smiling an apology. 'Not yet, I'm afraid,' she admitted. 'I keep promising myself . . .' She took a notebook from her handbag. 'Do give me the titles!'

For a few moments, the three of them kept up a pretence of having forgotten that they were in the office of their head of department, waiting to be questioned about the murder of a colleague.

A strangled sound from the other end of the room made everyone jump. Rodney Shergold was on his feet, a handkerchief held to his mouth. He lurched to the door and wrenched it open; they could hear him gagging as he hurried across the hall.

'Anyone would think he'd found the body,' said Doug with a sneer.

The policeman returned and requested a few minutes of Mrs Pearce's time. Miss Knott scuttled in after him and scooped up her possessions. She laid a hand on her colleague's arm. 'Don't worry dear, they don't bully you,' she murmured comfortingly, 'but they do take your fingerprints!' She sounded quite excited, as if she had just had a memorable experience, and for a second Melissa saw the ghost of a smile on the constable's lips.

'I must get along to my classroom,' said Miss Knott and followed him out, leaving Doug and Melissa alone in the room.

'Do you know what happened?' she asked. 'How did she . . . ?'

'Stabbed,' said Doug laconically. 'Couldn't get any details out of him.' He jerked his head towards Shergold's empty desk. 'He's been rushing out to puke ever since I got in.' His pursed lips suggested that this could be significant.

'He's not been well lately,' said Melissa. 'A tummy bug or something.' She had no particular affection for their head of department but one had to be fair. 'I met his wife in the village yesterday and she seemed quite worried about him.'

'Tummy bug—huh! Uneasy conscience, more like!' said Doug.

'Whatever do you mean? You aren't suggesting . . . ?'

'That Randy Rodders killed Angy? I doubt if he'd have the guts. No, what he's worried about is that his little bit on the side will be made public.'

'Do you really believe there was anything between them? He may have fancied her but I don't suppose he was the only one.' Melissa shot Doug a meaning glance, at which he gave an impudent grin. 'Anyway,' she went on, 'whatever could a girl like her see in him?'

'Services rendered, maybe. What was it worth to her to get some teaching experience? Or maybe,' Doug added with a leer in response to Melissa's frown of disapproval, 'she saw him as a challenge!'

She was silent, remembering the scene in the staff room on her first day. She went over to Angy's desk, straightened the chair and adjusted the cover on the typewriter. Anything to avoid doing nothing.

Her thoughts turned to Barney. He was the one who had found Angy's body. The shock must have been appalling. Was he still at the police station? Was he a suspect? His protective attitude towards Angy amounted almost to an obsession. Supposing there had been something between Rodney Shergold and Angy, and Barney had found out, and in a fit of rage . . . but no. Barney was far too kindly, too gentlemanly. And yet, such things had been known. It was a relief when Mrs Pearce returned and the constable called her name.

He directed her to an empty classroom opposite the office. Detective Sergeant Waters was seated at the teacher's table and a second uniformed constable sat at a desk at the back. When Melissa entered, Waters stood up and waved her to a chair facing him. She saw a middle-aged, grey-haired man with keen eyes. A soft Gloucestershire burr accentuated his disarmingly pleasant manner as he ran through his list of prepared questions.

'When was the last time you saw Miss Caroli?'

'Last Thursday afternoon, when I'd finished my class.'

'What time would that be?'

'A few minutes after three-thirty. I took my register into the office and gave it to her.'

'Was that usual?'

'Yes. It was part of her job to keep a record of the students' attendance.'

'Did you simply hand over the register and leave, or did you stop for a chat?'

'You mean on this occasion, or generally?'

Detective Sergeant Waters sat back in his chair. 'Let's say both. Were you on good terms with Miss Caroli?'

'Of course, everyone was. She was a very friendly girl.' Perhaps a little too friendly for her own good, Melissa thought. 'Complaisant' was a word that had occurred to her when she first learned of the murder. Hating to upset anyone. Always willing to do whatever was asked of her. Perhaps there had been times when she had been over-willing? Was this why Barney had watched over her so jealously? Aware of the detective's scrutiny, Melissa dismissed this line of thought as pure speculation.

'So you would sometimes stop for a chat with her when returning your register?' Waters pursued.

'Sometimes. When Doctor Shergold wasn't there.'

'What did you talk about?'

'Oh, things in general. Her students, my students. I presume you already know she'd been taking one of the art classes as well as her secretarial work?'

'We do.' Of course they knew and very soon they'd be interviewing all Angy's students. Almost certainly, someone would mention the incident between Barney and young Godfrey Mellish. She pictured Barney at the police station, shocked and dazed by his awful discovery, longing to be left alone with his misery yet being asked endless, probing questions. In no time at all his feelings towards Angy would come out.

Meanwhile, Waters pressed on with his own line of questioning. 'Did she ever tell you about her background or her family?'

'As it happened, I knew a little already.' Briefly, Melissa told what she knew of Angy's affair with Rick Lawrence, alias Ricardo Lorenzo, and its melodramatic conclusion. The policeman's face remained impassive but she sensed his mounting interest as he put more questions and made notes.

'Now, Mrs Craig, back to last Thursday. Was Doctor Shergold present then?'

Melissa thought for a moment. He had been there, she remembered, and when she entered he had been looking across at Angy and she had been looking at him. They had obviously been discussing something that continued to hold their attention for a brief moment after Melissa's appearance and from the strained, almost pleading look on Shergold's face, that something might have been personal. He had dragged his eyes away and begun fiddling with the drawers in his desk while Angy—cool, relaxed, smiling her pussy-cat smile—held out her hand for the register as if she had not a care in the world.

'Last Thursday, Mrs Craig?' Detective Sergeant Waters broke into Melissa's recollection.

'I'm sorry, I was thinking. Yes, I remember now, he was there.'

'So presumably you didn't stop for a chat with Miss Caroli?'

'No.'

'You just handed over your register and left?'

'That's right.'

'Without saying anything at all?'

'I expect we exchanged a few words. She might have said, "Was it a good class?" and I'd have said "Yes, fine, see you next week." Something like that.'

'What about Doctor Shergold? Did he speak to you?'

'No.'

'You're sure?'

'Quite sure. He isn't given to small talk.'

'Did he speak to Miss Caroli while you were in the room?'

'No.'

'But this wasn't unusual?'

'Not in the least.' For a moment, she thought that Waters was about to ask point-blank if she knew of any relationship between her head of department and his secretary, and was relieved when he did not. She wanted more time to think before deciding whether to voice her suspicions.

'You say she was a very friendly girl,' Waters continued, with a subtle emphasis of the adjective. 'Did she have any particular friends at the college?'

'Not that I know of but I'm only here once a week for a couple of hours. I don't know a great deal about relationships among the staff.'

'But presumably you chat to people over coffee, or in the staff room?'

'Yes, sometimes.'

'So did you ever hear anything to suggest that there was anyone in particular . . . ?'

Melissa side-stepped the question that Waters had pointedly left unfinished. 'She was an extremely attractive girl with a delightful personality and a charming manner. I'm sure plenty of people enjoyed her company.'

'What about Mr Willard?' Melissa almost jumped at the sudden switch in the line of questioning. She sensed that Waters knew she had been evasive. 'Mr Willard,' he repeated. 'I understand he was particularly attached to Miss Caroli?'

'He was very protective towards her.'

'Protective.' Waters repeated the word reflectively, as if he were considering a clue in a crossword puzzle. 'Protective against anything—or anyone—in particular, would you say?'

Melissa shifted her grip on the folder of papers she had brought for her class while Waters' eyes delved into hers.

'Mr. Willard has rather old-fashioned—you could say chivalrous—ideas about men's attitudes towards women,' she replied. 'Some of the male members of the staff are apt to make comments that he considers disrespectful. He gets very annoyed at times.'

'Especially when such comments refer to Miss Caroli?'

'She is . . . was . . . quite young, living alone and a long way from her family. I think he saw her as particularly vulnerable.'

'How about you?'

Melissa smiled faintly. 'Me? I don't think he's particularly concerned about *my* welfare.'

'I mean,' explained Waters patiently, 'did you consider Miss Caroli in need of Mr Willard's . . . protection?'

Melissa thought for a moment before saying, 'Some people might have thought her naïve but she didn't strike me that way. I'd say she had a cool head on her shoulders but I can understand how a man, especially an older man, might feel concern for her.'

'Well, thank you Mrs Craig, you've been very helpful. Perhaps you'd be kind enough to allow the officer over there'—he nodded towards the constable, who peeled the backing from a sheet of black-inked paper and laid it on his desk with a sheet of white paper beside it—'to take your fingerprints? Purely for elimination purposes, you understand?'

'Of course.' She knew the drill, had referred to it in more than one novel, but this was her first experience of it. While the constable guided her fingers she asked casually, 'Detective Sergeant Waters, would you mind telling me who is in charge of this case?'

Waters looked faintly surprised, but answered without hesitation. 'Detective Chief Inspector Harris is leading the enquiry.'

'Thank you.'

In the hall, the constable was still waiting patiently by the front door. In response to a sign from the detective, he popped his head into the office and spoke to someone inside.

Doug Wilson emerged. He walked without his usual jaunty swagger and looked distinctly uneasy. When he saw Melissa he hurried across and murmured: 'Take my students into your class until I'm through, will you? They might bugger off if I don't show up and that'll upset Rodders.

Give 'em something to write. They're an easy bunch, their English is quite good . . . '

'I'll see what I can do.' Already it was almost half-past two. Melissa hurried upstairs.

EIGHT

THE MEMBERS OF THE WRITERS' WORKSHOP were horrified by the news of the murder. Sybil Bliss, the only one besides Melissa who had actually known Angy, was in tears. The members of Doug's English class, all young and excitable, discussed the affair among themselves in a babble of different languages. Unable to interest them in any other topic, Melissa finally managed to impose some sort of structure on the group by leading a discussion on capital punishment until Doug came to take charge of his students and enable things to return to something like normal for the remainder of the session.

When the classes dispersed there was still no sign of Barney. Apart from Doug and Melissa, the staff room was deserted. The same thought was in both their minds.

'You don't suppose they've arrested him, do you?' she asked.

Doug stared at her. 'Don't tell me you think he's the killer! Not our saintly old Uncle Barnaby?'

'Of course not,' she said, smothering the uneasy doubt stirring at the back of her mind. 'He adored Angy. He wouldn't hurt a hair of her head. Where can he have got to?'

'He's probably gone straight home,' said Doug, ramming books into an already over-full briefcase. His jaw was set, his movements hurried and nervous.

'He'll be in a fearful state,' said Melissa. 'He lives alone, doesn't he? Someone should be with him.'

'He'd probably rather be on his own.'

'He must feel dreadful after finding her like that. Do you know any more details?'

'Not many. It seems he went round to her flat this morning and found her there. He rang the police and then he rang Rodney, who's been gibbering ever since.'

'What was he doing at Angy's flat?'

'Trying to find out why she hadn't been in college since Tuesday, I suppose. By the way, wouldn't you love to have been a fly on the wall when the fuzz were questioning our beloved head of department?' Doug assumed a passable imitation of Detective Sergeant Waters' voice. ' "And what was your relationship with the deceased, Doctor Shergold? Purely professional, you say? Are you sure there wasn't more to it than that? What would you say if I told you that at least one witness . . ." '

'Witness? What witness?' Melissa cut in. 'Just what have you been telling the police?'

'Only what I've seen for myself—burning looks, lustful glances. Don't tell me you haven't noticed them!'

'I've seen you give a few lustful glances in Angy's direction but that doesn't mean you got anywhere,' retorted Melissa, still reluctant to agree with Doug but unable to contradict him outright.

'Ah, but who's to say Rodders didn't?' countered Doug. A sly, lascivious grin spread over his fleshy features and she felt a wave of disgust. There was something about the man's preoccupation with sex that suggested graffiti on lavatory walls; in the present circumstances it seemed especially repugnant. The gleam in his eye was an open invitation to share and savour his prurient thoughts.

Abruptly, she changed the subject. 'Do you know if Angy rang to say why she wouldn't be in yesterday morning?' she asked.

'That's hardly possible.' Doug put his hands in his pockets and shuffled his feet. His face became grim, his brow knotted under the tangled thatch of hair. 'It seems she was killed some time on Tuesday afternoon or evening.'

'You mean she's been lying there dead since . . . oh, how awful!' A queasy spasm in her stomach sent Melissa's hand flying to her mouth. Doug hastily pushed open the window.

'Let's have some fresh air. We can't have you keeling over.'

'Don't worry, I'll be all right in a moment.' She began drawing deep breaths and expelling them noisily through her mouth, thankful for the instruction in yoga that Iris insisted on giving her from time to time.

'Okay now?' said Doug when she had pulled herself together.

'Yes thanks. How come the police told you all this?'

'They didn't, not in so many words, but that chap Waters kept banging on about my movements after leaving here on Tuesday so I put two and two together.' He began prowling round the room, fiddling with filing trays and adjusting books on the shelves. 'I've got an alibi of sorts. I went for a jog and then to the sports centre for a shower and into the bar for a drink. Lots of people saw me but of course there were gaps and it seems I'd have had plenty of time to sneak into Angy's place, do the deed and reappear.'

'Where is Angy's place?'

'She's got a studio flat in Tranmere Gardens.'

'Have you ever been there?'

'No, I bloody well haven't!' Doug snapped. 'You're as bad as Waters . . . that was his angle. "Where do you go jogging, Mr Wilson? In the park? How do you reach the park? Along Millers Road? That intersects with Tranmere Gardens, doesn't it? Are you sure you didn't turn down there to number twenty-two now and again? On Tuesday afternoons, perhaps?" ' His breathing had grown heavy and his face red; he stabbed the air with his fists in an explosion of rage and resentment.

'Barney's the one I feel sorry for at the moment. He doted on that girl,' said Melissa, hoping a change of subject would calm him down. The effect, as it happened, was disastrous.

'Yes, his little virgin lily!' sneered Doug. 'Well, my guess is that he'll soon learn how far out his judgment was . . . if he hadn't rumbled her already.'

A hand grabbed him by the shoulder, spun him round and sent him reeling under a blow to the face. Barney had entered unnoticed and had evidently overheard the end of the conversation. Melissa was appalled at his appearance. Untidy tufts of hair straggled round a face that seemed to have caved in around the skull and his eyes were glaring.

'You grubby-minded young oaf!' he panted, his voice unsteady and barely recognisable. 'How dare you speak of her like that!'

'Sorry,' muttered Doug, massaging his jaw. All the bluster had left him and he silently gathered up the rest of his books and shuffled out, avoiding eye-contact.

Barney lurched across the room, slumped into his chair with his arms sprawled on the table and bowed his head. For a moment there was silence; then, softly at first but swelling like an incoming tide whipped to a frenzy by the wind, grief and shock poured out of him in wave after wave of dry, juddering sobs.

Melissa stood helplessly by, waiting for the worst of the storm to pass. Presently he grew quieter; like an exhausted swimmer seeking a handhold he made helpless, groping movements among the papers on his desk. Melissa reached out and took one of his hands in hers. Ice-cold fingers closed like a trap and she gasped with the unexpected pain. Immediately, he relaxed his grip and raised his head, mumbling an apology.

Melissa put her free hand on his shoulder, unable to think of anything to say but: 'Poor Barney! Oh, poor Barney!'

'Dear God!' he whispered, staring at the wall as if the dreadful sight was there in front of him. 'The blood . . . there was so much blood! And her eyes . . . they were open!' His fingers, still grasping Melissa's, gave an involuntary jerk as he relived the sheer horror of the memory. 'They looked bewildered, as if she was saying "Why? Why are you doing this? What have I done to you?" ' Tears spilled down his cheeks. 'She was so lovely . . . Angy, my little girl!'

Melissa, standing motionless at his side, felt the hairs rise on the back of her neck. One question hammered at her mind but to voice it was unthinkable. To break the tension, she glanced at her watch and said: 'Have you been at the police station all this time?'

He shook his head. 'They let me go some while ago. I didn't notice the time. I went and sat in the park for a bit and then I wandered around and came back here.'

'Have you had anything to eat?'

'They gave me cups of tea . . . they offered me a sandwich but I couldn't face food.' His face was the colour of parchment, the flesh taut, the lips bloodless. He rose suddenly to his feet and gripped Melissa by the shoulders. Despair contorted his face and his eyes were wild. 'What am I going to do?' he pleaded in a thin, high-pitched wail. 'Oh God, tell me what I should do!'

'You're in shock. You should really see a doctor,' said Melissa uneasily. It was nearly five o'clock; all the students had long since left and the building had become silent.

'Doctor?' Barney threw back his head and gave a harsh laugh. 'What can a doctor do? He couldn't help her, could he? He couldn't pour back the blood and sew up the gash in her throat and bring her back to life!'

'In her throat! She was stabbed in the throat?' Melissa's mouth became dry.

Barney passed a hand in front of his face, as if trying to erase an image too terrible to contemplate. 'They think I did it.'

'For heaven's sake, why should they think that?' Melissa tried to inject some surprise into the question despite having the same thought, the same lurking fear. Common sense warned her to make some excuse and get away, yet the notion of leaving Barney alone with his distress seemed too callous to contemplate.

'Why shouldn't they?' he said bitterly. 'Someone did, so why not me? Everyone knew how I felt towards her. I had to admit that we'd had an argument, that I lost my temper and hit her.' He stared down at his shaking hands with a bewildered expression as if unable to believe them capable of such a deed.

Melissa was dumbfounded. 'You hit her?' she echoed. 'But why?'

'I struck her in the face. My little Angy, how could I have done it to you!' Another wave of grief broke over him; he covered his face and rocked to and fro in anguish.

'Would it help to talk about it?' she asked when he was calmer. It was a stupid, trite-sounding question, like a line from a TV soap, but for the moment it was all she could think of.

He leaned back in his chair and began speaking in a weary monotone. 'On Sunday evening I called round at her flat. I was concerned about her. She hadn't seemed herself lately and I had the impression she was keeping something from me.'

'You saw her often?'

'She needed someone to keep an eye on her. She was so trusting, you see, and so sweet-natured. I was afraid that sooner or later, someone would take advantage of her.' The old-fashioned euphemism sounded perfectly natural, coming from Barney. 'It seems as if I was right,' he added, still in the same toneless voice.

'You mean, she had a lover?'

He winced, as if her bluntness hurt. 'It wasn't like her to be secretive. She was usually so open with me.'

'She was a grown woman,' Melissa reminded him gently. 'It's natural for grown women to have affairs and they don't necessarily want to tell everyone about them.'

'I know, I know, you're trying to tell me that it was no business of mine what she did. But she had no one else to look after her or to turn to if she was in trouble.'

'Is that what she told you?'

'Didn't you know? Her parents are dead and her only relatives are in Italy. Poor little soul, she was so alone. I became like a father to her. She used to call me Poppa Barney when we were on our own.'

'I see,' said Melissa thoughtfully. It could be true, of course; people's circumstances do change. Aloud, she said,

'So you went round on Sunday to have it out with her?'

Barney gnawed his lower lip. 'I said I was worried about her. I pointed out how she seemed to have changed. She just laughed and said I was imagining things. She was offhand, teasing. I felt sure she was keeping something from me. I began to get angry. She said . . . ' He broke off suddenly and turned to look at Melissa. 'Has she ever mentioned a chap called Eddie to you?'

'Eddie? Yes, I believe she did mention him once.' Melissa trawled her memory. 'I remember! She said he didn't charge her much rent, so I assumed he was her landlord.'

'She'd mentioned him several times lately. It was Eddie this and Eddie that and Eddie says . . . but when I questioned her about him she'd become evasive. I was trying to warn her about . . . possible consequences . . . if she . . . and all of a sudden . . . ' Barney's voice had become thick with embarrassment. 'She gave another silly, sly little laugh and said, "You're afraid I'm pregnant, I suppose? Well, so what if I am?" '

Melissa raised her eyebrows. 'Are you saying that Angy was having this man Eddie's baby?'

'That's what it sounded like. I couldn't believe it. I never dreamed it had gone that far . . . and all she could do was laugh.' His face was grey, his fists clenched. 'I lost my temper and hit her twice across the face . . . and then I walked out.'

'And that was on Sunday?' said Melissa. He nodded. 'When was the next time you saw her?'

'I went into the office on Monday morning. I was going to apologise but Rodney Shergold was there. He was looking at the bruise on her cheek. My signet ring must have caught it; the skin was broken.' For a moment, remorse seemed to make speech difficult. 'I was appalled to think I'd done that to her,' he finished in a whisper.

'Go on,' Melissa prompted.

'She was telling Shergold she'd walked into an open door. There was a look on his face I'd never seen before, could never have imagined him capable of. It was almost tender, and she . . . she was smiling, playing up to him. I walked out. I don't believe either of them even saw me.'

'Did you see her again after that?'

'On Tuesday afternoon, on her way to her class, chatting to a student as if she hadn't a care in the world. I didn't have a chance to speak to her. I wasn't feeling well. My stomach was upset—nerves, I suppose. I tried to phone her in the evening, to say I was sorry, but her line was engaged. When she didn't show up at college on Wednesday I got anxious and called her number several times but there was no reply, so this morning I went round there . . . and found her.'

He got up and walked over to the window. It was as if an actor had just spoken the epilogue to a tragedy and stepped back to allow the curtain to fall . . . but the play was far from over.

The door was suddenly flung open and a stout woman with a broom in one hand, a duster in the other and a plastic sack tucked under one arm marched in, glaring at finding the room occupied.

'Haven't you got homes to go to?' she demanded.

'I'm sorry, we were talking and forgot the time.' Melissa gathered up her things and took Barney gently by the arm. 'Come on, we're in the way.' Mechanically, he picked up a briefcase and a portfolio while the cleaner, grumbling to herself, began emptying the waste bins. Melissa led him downstairs and out of the building. He looked round him as if lost, blinking in the sunshine like one emerging from the dark; at the bottom of the steps he stumbled and almost fell.

'You aren't fit to drive,' said Melissa as they crossed the almost empty car park. 'Where do you live?'

'Edgebury. I don't suppose you've ever heard of it. It's in the middle of nowhere.'

'As it happens, it's not far from my village. Let me run you home.'

'You're very kind.' He sounded tired and apathetic.

'What about food? What have you got in the house?'

'Not much. I usually go to the supermarket on a Thursday.'

'I've got a chicken casserole ready to be warmed up. There's enough for two—how about sharing it with me?'

'You're very kind,' he repeated.

'Not at all.' At least, he was responding to practical suggestions and he'd be a lot better with a meal inside him. 'We can come back for your car later.'

'There's no need for that. If you don't mind running me home, I can get a lift in the morning from someone in the village. I accept your invitation to supper, if you're sure it isn't putting you to any trouble.' He recited the formal phrases like a schoolboy remembering his manners.

'No trouble at all,' Melissa said briskly, opening the car door.

You're mad, she told herself as she buckled her seat belt and switched on the ignition. This man is under suspicion of murder. He seems quiet and rational enough at the moment but he could be unbalanced. Anything could set him off; you're simply asking for trouble. Yet she was not afraid. She drove slowly towards the exit, easing the car over the humps installed by the college to discourage speeding by the Grand Prix driver manqué. Beside her, Barney sat with closed eyes, his hands resting on his thighs. His long fingers lay apart, no longer shaking but relaxed and still. She visualised them holding pencil or brush, creating images on blank paper or canvas. It was hard to imagine such hands in an act of murder.

His eyes remained closed until she pulled up outside Hawthorn Cottage and switched off the engine. He lifted his head and stared around him like someone awakened from a long sleep.

'This is where I live,' she said. Without a word, he got out of the car and followed her indoors. Iris, hoeing her vegetable plot, looked across and waved. When she'd given Barney something to eat and driven him home she'd go and tell Iris what had happened. She'd probably learn about it from the television or the local paper later on and be bursting with curiosity.

Barney ate the food and drank the wine Melissa put in front of him and thanked her politely when the meal was over. She made coffee and carried the tray into the sitting-room; he commented on the lovely view and said he would like to paint it some time. He scanned her bookshelves and asked her what she was writing just now. They began talking about books and pictures and as the evening passed, something of the torment faded from his eyes. The tragedy had not been mentioned since they left the college.

At nine o'clock Barney said that it was time he went home. It was only a short drive to Edgebury and they met no other cars in the quiet lanes. His cottage, surrounded by trees, was even more isolated than Melissa's and in the fading light the shadows had an alien, almost menacing quality. Barney opened the car door and a chilly breeze blew in. Melissa shivered.

'Will you come in for a few minutes and have a drink?' She hesitated. 'Please,' he said urgently.

Better not, warned a voice inside her head. Just say goodnight and leave. He'll be all right now, he's over the worst.

'Why not?' she said and went indoors with him.

The furniture in his sitting-room was old, the armchairs were shabby but comfortable-looking and everything appeared clean if a little untidy. There were bright curtains, a standard lamp with a design of roses on the shade, a fireplace with loaded bookshelves on either side and pictures on the whitewashed walls. On the table, among a scattering of newspapers and an empty wineglass, stood a china jug of fresh tulips. It was a welcoming room, the room of a sane and sensitive human being.

'What will you drink?' he said. She asked for a small brandy and while he got out a decanter and glasses from an antique corner cupboard she began inspecting one of the pictures, a water-colour of a Cotswold village.

'Yours?' she asked, and he nodded. 'I like it.'

'Thank you.' She took a sip from the glass he handed her and together they moved round the room, examining pictures. They were mostly landscapes but there was one portrait of a young woman with dark, glossy hair that seemed to Melissa to have been executed with a particular, loving skill. It crossed her mind that there was a resemblance to Angy in the large eyes and delicate features. She studied it for a moment or two, aware that Barney's eyes were on her.

'You like that?' he asked.

'It's a lovely portrait.'

'My wife,' he said quietly.

'Your wife?' Melissa glanced around, seeking some sign of a woman's presence that she might have missed. In the porch she had noticed a single pair of rubber boots and there had been only a man's tweed hat and raincoat on the hall stand. 'I didn't know . . . ' she began in some embarrassment.

'She died many years ago. In childbirth.'

'How sad. I'm so sorry.'

'The baby lived for two days . . . a little girl. They let me hold her.' Subconsciously, it seemed, he made a cradle of his arms and looked down at them. 'She would have been the same age as Angy.'

'Oh Barney!' Now she was beginning to understand. She took a step towards him.

'I didn't kill her,' he went on quietly. Love, sorrow and, above all, sincerity were in his face. 'I only wanted to protect her.'

Yes, I know, that's what I told Detective Sergeant Waters, she thought. I'm not sure if he believed it, not sure I believed it myself then, but I do now.

'I never told the police what she'd said about the baby,' he went on. 'I didn't want them to know she was that sort of girl.'

Despite the tragedy of the situation, Melissa could not repress a smile at his naïveté. 'Oh Barney, how do you suppose that could be kept secret? The post mortem . . . '

His shoulders sagged and he bowed his head. 'Yes, of course, the post mortem. I didn't think. You must take me for an utter fool.'

'You were shocked and confused.' Melissa put down her half-finished drink and moved closer to him. 'Look, it's getting late and you need rest. I'd better be going.'

He looked at her and there was nothing in his eyes but emptiness. 'No, please,' he begged, 'don't leave me alone . . . not tonight.'

He held out his arms and she went to him as if it was the most natural thing in the world.

NINE

A LIGHT KNOCK ON THE BEDROOM DOOR aroused Melissa next morning. There was no sense of disorientation as she opened her eyes, no groping through the mists of sleep for a landmark in an unfamiliar world. Memories of last night floated on the surface of her mind; the sheer glory of it, the peace and well-being that came after to carry her away into dreamless sleep, were still there when she awoke, obliterating all recollection of the tragedy that had brought her to Barney's house.

'Come in!' she called and he entered, dressed as usual in a sweat-shirt and jeans and carrying a glass of orange juice.

'Good morning,' he said. 'I thought you might like this.'

'Oh, lovely!' She sat up and smiled at him. His hair and beard were damp and she caught a whiff of some lightly scented soap as he handed her the glass. He picked up a saffron-yellow robe from a chair by the bed and wrapped it round her bare shoulders with slightly hesitant, awkward movements, as if half expecting some resistance, uncertain whether his solicitude would be welcome. She leaned towards him so that her cheek brushed his in reassurance.

'How did you sleep?' he asked gravely.

'Like a baby. How about you?'

'Not very well. I've been awake since four, thinking about yesterday.'

Yesterday! How could she have forgotten? The shock of that awful remembrance made her choke and splutter over the drink. Barney patted her back and she hid her face on his shoulder, overcome by remorse at the untroubled slumber that had left him to face long hours of grieving alone.

'Oh, Barney, I'm so sorry! You must think me utterly callous . . . and now I've spilt juice all over the place.' Tears of self-disgust filled her eyes as she made futile dabs at the sleeve of the robe.

'Callous? No, not you.' He kissed her gently on the brow, then got up and went over to the window. The low ceiling made his spare frame appear taller than usual, even though his head was bent. 'I forgot as well and I did sleep for a little while. Then I woke up and I remembered. You were lying there beside me, breathing so quietly, and I thought of her and how she looked when she . . . when I . . . ' His voice shook and trailed away. 'I felt so guilty,' he went on when he had regained control. 'All I could think of was that I'd struck her, marked her. I loved her so much and yet I did that to her!'

He turned from the window with one arm raised and stared down at the floor, his face contorted with emotion. For one sickening moment, Angy's blood-soaked corpse with the raw, red wound in the throat and bewildered, open eyes seemed to materialise at his feet. That's how the murderer might have stood after striking the fatal blow, thought Melissa with a shudder.

'So guilty!' he repeated sombrely, looking across the room at her. 'Can you understand that?'

'Yes, of course I understand.' She managed to keep her voice steady but her heart was thudding in her chest. The seedling doubt that last night seemed to have withered away was not dead after all. She shivered as she put down the empty glass and pulled the robe more closely around her shoulders.

'When I woke up in the night, I felt I'd betrayed her by forgetting,' he said and the words crumbled in his throat. 'And yet,' he went on after a moment, 'it wasn't being unfaithful, was it? My relationship with her wasn't like that.' He came and sat beside Melissa and took her hand. He had the same air of sad loneliness as on the previous evening when he spoke of the loss of his wife while cradling in his arms the ghost of his dead child. The sense of trust and sympathy that she had experienced then, the conviction that he was no murderer, began to revive.

'I believe you,' she said.

'Thank you.' Some of the despair faded from his eyes and the tautness round his jaw seemed to ease. He took her face between his hands and murmured, 'Thank you for last night. It was beautiful.' He appeared suddenly shy; there was nothing of the sophisticated, worldly lover about this man.

She leaned forward and kissed him on the mouth. 'It was beautiful for me too.'

After a moment, he stood up. 'I hate saying this,' he said, 'but it's gone half-past seven and I have a class at nine.'

'A class? Are you sure you can face it?'

'I have to face it.' There was a determined note in his voice that she had not heard before. 'There's hot water if you'd like a bath or shower. I'll go and make some coffee.' He picked up the glass and went out, closing the door quietly behind him.

Melissa took a quick bath, dried herself on a large fluffy towel that Barney had put out for her and helped herself from a tin of own-brand talcum powder that, with a plastic container of supermarket shampoo, appeared to comprise the entire range of toiletries in the bathroom. She squeezed some toothpaste on to one finger, rubbed it round her teeth and rinsed out her mouth, then hummed a tune as she dried her face and hands.

'Rule number one, never go anywhere without your toothbrush!' she said to herself as she wiped the steam from the mirror. Her image emerged from it like a photograph coming slowly into focus. There was a gloss on her skin and a sparkle in her brown eyes that was new and exciting . . . and dangerous.

'Watch it, girl!' she chided herself as she ran a comb through her thick dark hair. 'Don't go over the top on the strength of one night. You're no spring chicken, you know!'

The image did its best to persuade her that after last night she looked a good ten years younger. Anyway, it seemed to say, Barney's no teenager, is he?

'You don't know anything about him!' This time she actually spoke the words aloud. 'There's a little thing called a murder investigation going on, remember?'

'But he didn't do it!' pleaded the mirror.

'Prove it!' she retorted, but the only response was a radiant smile. She gave herself a jaunty salute with the comb, put on the saffron robe and went downstairs, following the scent of coffee into the kitchen.

The morning sun made a chequered pattern on the white tablecloth and a percolator bubbled on the Aga. Barney, a pottery mug in either hand, looked up as she entered and surveyed her with eyebrows raised and his head tilted in appraisal.

'You should wear that colour often. It gives a golden tinge to your eyes,' he commented.

'Thank you.' Other people, Joe included, had complimented her on her colouring but from Barney it gave her an especial pleasure.

'What would you like to eat?' He waved at an assortment of packets on a pine dresser. 'I usually have a cereal but there's an egg if you fancy one.'

'A cereal will be fine.'

'Help yourself. I've put out bowls and spoons. Here's the milk.' He took a blue jug from the refrigerator.

'Thanks.' She shook muesli into a stoneware bowl, poured milk over it and sat down. He brought two mugs of coffee to the table and took the chair facing her. His eyes had lost their haunted look and were openly studying her features.

'I haven't done a lot of portraiture,' he said, 'but I'd like to paint you one day, just as you are.'

'You mean in this?' She glanced down at the robe.

'Yes. No, on second thoughts, without it.' The tone was matter-of-fact; it was the artist who had spoken but the man looked suddenly confused as if afraid of having offended. Colour rose in his cheeks and she laughed.

'You shocked yourself!'

He gave a rueful smile. 'The fact is, I haven't had many relationships with women,' he admitted. 'After Becky and the baby died I went off and buried myself in work for a long time. When I came back into the world I felt a bit like Rip Van Winkle . . . alienated.'

'I think I know how you must have felt. I went through something similar once.'

'You did?' He poured milk into his coffee and stirred it; she was glad he made no attempt to pry. 'What made you start writing thrillers?' he asked after a pause.

'My mother-in-law packed me off to creative writing classes because she thought I was getting broody and sorry for myself. I found I was quite good at crime short stories. Then a member of the CID came to live near us and I got to know him, he gave me an idea for a novel and it sort of took off from there.'

He frowned into his coffee mug, turning it restlessly between long, thin hands. The tips of his fingers flattened and the close-cut, oblong nails grew pale under the pressure.

'Your mother-in-law? Are you . . . I assumed . . . that is, I didn't realise you were still married,' he said uncomfortably.

'I'm not. Guy died many years ago.'

'I'm sorry.' Despite the conventional formula she thought he looked relieved. An affair with a married woman, even one long estranged from her husband, would have been deeply troubling to his sense of morality.

He put down his mug, picked up a knife and began drawing indentations on the tablecloth. 'I suppose you know about police procedure?' he said.

'Yes, quite a bit.'

'How long are they going to play this cat and mouse game with me?'

She stared at him, frowning. 'What do you mean?'

'I told you, they think I killed Angy . . . but they let me go.' The tension was back, his voice jerky and staccato.

'I suppose they'll have me at the station again, asking those same awful questions until I break down and say what they want me to say. I've got no alibi for Tuesday evening. They think I've got motive, that I killed her in a jealous rage and only pretended to find her. I can't prove I didn't do it.'

'You don't have to,' she pointed out. 'They have to prove you did.'

'They'll think the baby was mine.'

'There are tests that can settle that too. You've nothing to be afraid of if you've been telling the truth.'

'If?' He looked at her with a kind of shocked despair. 'You don't really believe me at all!'

'But I do believe you.' She crushed the seedling doubt into the depths of her mind. 'And the police will eventually, when they've found the real killer. The investigation has only just started—there'll be all sorts of leads to follow up.' She made herself sound confident and well-informed, looking directly into his eyes. He looked back at her like a sick man in fear of death.

'Now listen,' she said, briskly ticking off points on her fingers. 'First, they have to build up a picture of Angy . . . her background, family, close friends and so on. Then they check up on all the people living in the house, the students in her art class, neighbours who might have seen someone calling or leaving at about the time she was killed. There'll be dozens of people they have to interview. You were the obvious starting point because you found her, but several of us have been questioned already, and fingerprinted. They sent a man to the college; even Miss Knott had to go through it. She hadn't had a fag for at least half an hour and she was a nervous wreck when she was called in!'

Very slowly, he relaxed under the barrage of reassurance; at the end he even managed a weak laugh. 'Poor old Knotty! I can just picture it!'

'Try not to brood, and don't let them rattle you.' She was on the point of revealing that Chief Inspector Harris was a friend of hers—well, perhaps not a friend, more an acquaintance and an adviser—and that she might be able to find out what other leads he was following, but decided against it. Instead, she finished her coffee and got up to take her empty mug and cereal bowl to the sink. 'Shall we wash up before we go?'

'Don't bother.' He glanced at his watch. 'We ought to leave now, if you're sure you don't mind?'

'Of course not.'

Outside, Melissa stood for a moment with her key in the car door, looking back at the cottage. Last night, in the chilly darkness, it had appeared almost sinister; this morning it sat in its woodland clearing like something from a fairy tale, with round patches of lichen making golden platters on the sun-dappled roof. The neat patch of lawn was ringed with flowers and alive with starlings on the march for food.

'It's so pretty!' she said. 'Like the Three Bears' cottage.'

Barney gave a wan smile. 'At least this Father Bear didn't gobble up Goldilocks!' It was almost as if he had read, and understood, the fear that had been intermittently nagging at her mind. 'Yes, it is lovely at this time of year.' He settled into the passenger seat of the Golf and reached for the safety belt. 'Not so much fun in winter when the track's a quagmire. First thing I did when I moved in was buy a four-wheel-drive car.' As if to ensure that no more disturbing topic was introduced, he continued to talk about cars until they reached the outskirts of Stowbridge.

'Drop me here,' he said as they joined the queue of traffic crawling towards the town centre. 'I can cut across the park and you can turn off at the lights and go straight home.'

'Right.' She pulled into the kerb and he got out. Before closing the car door, he bent down and said:

'Will you come again?'

She had prepared herself for the question—hoped for it, in fact—but at the last minute she restrained the impulse to reply with a joyful 'Yes!' Instead, she said carefully, 'Maybe, when all this is over.' He looked disappointed and she felt a twinge of regret, but the thing was done. It was better this way.

The minute she pulled up outside her own garage, the door of Elder Cottage flew open and Iris marched out, clasping Binkie in her arms. Her thin face was sharp with anxiety.

'Where've you been?' she demanded. 'Saw you go off with that bearded fellow. Never saw you come back.' She opened the garage and waited for Melissa to put the car away before resuming her harangue. 'Banged on your door this morning but no answer. Your phone kept ringing last night. Worried sick, weren't we, Binkie?'

She gave the imprisoned cat an affectionate squeeze to which he responded with a startled yowl. She bent and allowed him to slide from her arms to the ground, where he stood regarding the two women for a moment with unblinking eyes and twitching tail before disappearing through a gap in the hawthorn hedge.

'Good boy, catch lots of mice for muvver!' called Iris in her baby voice. She turned back to Melissa with an accusing look in her eyes. 'You've been up to something! Want to tell?'

'Oh Iris, it's awful! Angy's been murdered!'

'Murdered? How?'

'She was stabbed in the throat.'

'Good Lord! Don't tell me that young fool . . . no, I can't believe that. When did it happen?'

'The police think some time on Tuesday afternoon or evening, but her body wasn't found until yesterday morning.'

'Who found her?'

'Barney Willard. He's dreadfully shocked. I've told you how fond of her he was and on top of that he's convinced they suspect him of killing her.'

'The art lecturer? The oddball Sybil Bliss was talking about?'

'He's not an oddball!' Instantly, Melissa realised that her too-quick, too-sharp response had been a mistake.

Iris pounced. 'That was him you were with last night!'

'I had to take him home. He was too upset to drive his own car.'

'And you stayed.' Iris's face was a jigsaw of emotions, all of them disapproving. 'Spent the night with a man suspected of knifing his girlfriend! Need your head examined!'

'She wasn't his girlfriend. He thought of her as his daughter. Truly, Iris.' Briefly, Melissa related the story. Iris listened in silence but her expression was wary and sceptical. 'I didn't intend to stay,' Melissa insisted, 'and I'm sure he didn't plan it either. It just happened, and I'm glad it did. And he didn't kill her, I know he didn't!' Who am I trying to convince, she asked herself, Iris or myself?

'Hm.' Iris was still unpersuaded. 'So who d'you suppose did?'

'I've no idea at the moment, but I have a hunch the police are going to find out things we never suspected about dear little Angy.'

'What makes you say that?'

'Several reasons but I want time to think . . . and I must get some work done. That was probably Joe on the phone last night, wanting to know what's happened to the script I promised him. Why don't you come for supper this evening?'

'Will do. What time?'

'Say about seven.'

Melissa was on her way to her study when the telephone rang.

'Gloucestershire Constabulary here,' said a female voice. 'I have Detective Chief Inspector Harris for you . . . you're through.'

'Melissa?'

'Hullo Ken! What can I do for you?'

'About the Caroli girl. I understand from Waters that you know something of her background.'

'A little. I told him everything I could think of.'

'I'd like to come round and see you. I think you may be able to help us further.'

'If I can. When would you like to come?'

'Now, if it's convenient.'

'Sure. I'll be here.'

TEN

AT FIRST GLANCE, IT MIGHT HAVE BEEN thought that Detective Chief Inspector Kenneth Harris was squatting unsupported, like a meditative idol, in Melissa's sitting-room. His broad frame almost concealed the small but sturdy upright chair—it had to be sturdy to support all that solidly-packed flesh and muscle—on which he sat. One red hand lay like an enormous starfish on his knee and the other held a notebook to which he referred from time to time while Melissa repeated her account of the sensational episode at the Ravenswood College of Art the previous July.

When she had finished he made a few amendments with a pen that looked as flimsy as a straw in his massive fingers, and said, 'You're sure it was in the throat that this fellow Lawrence slashed the picture?'

'Quite sure.'

'Did you know that Angelica Caroli died from a stab wound in the throat?'

'Yes, I had heard.' The episode that had at the time seemed melodramatic and ridiculous now took on the ominous quality of some ancient saga of vengeance. Yet surely, in real life, no one would be so utterly stupid . . .

Harris interrupted her train of thought. 'Can you describe this fellow Lawrence?'

So they were considering Rick as a possible suspect. That could mean Barney's fears were groundless . . .

'I'll do my best,' she said, a shade too eagerly. 'It was nearly a year ago and it all happened very quickly,' she added, aware of the interest in the small, penetrating eyes that never left hers. It crossed her mind, as it had done before during their acquaintance, that anyone with a guilty secret would have to be pretty insensitive not to feel uncomfortable under that unwavering stare.

'Just take your time,' said Harris impassively.

Melissa put her hands over her eyes and sat for a few seconds in fierce concentration. Little by little she recalled the handsome young artist on the platform: receiving his trophy from Iris; kissing her hand and making her blush and simper; delivering his speech to the appreciative assembly; mutilating his creation before their eyes.

'He wasn't very tall. Five foot seven or eight perhaps and on the fleshy side—he'll run to fat in a few years. I got a general impression of rather flamboyant, typically Italian good looks—dark eyes, olive skin, black hair.'

'Long or short?'

'His hair? Oh, quite short, with tight curls close to the head.'

'Any beard or moustache?'

'Definitely no beard. I don't think he had a moustache . . . no, I'm pretty sure he was clean-shaven. He had a very . . . ' she searched for the right word, 'romantic sort of appearance. He could have modelled for a piece of Roman statuary.'

Harris took a sheet of paper from his briefcase and passed it to her. 'Is that anything like him?'

Melissa studied the sketch with mounting excitement. 'Yes! I don't think the mouth is quite right but . . . yes, it looks very like Rick Lawrence.'

Questions boiled in her brain but she had the sense to wait, to allow Harris to release in his own good time whatever information he was prepared to give. He was a man who did not like to be pushed; the formula, 'we ask the questions', might have been coined expressly by him.

'Two witnesses saw a man in the neighbourhood of the house where the victim lived at about six o'clock on the Tuesday evening,' he said. 'Our artist produced that sketch from their combined descriptions.'

'Then it must be Rick Lawrence! He found out where
she was living and came down here and stabbed her the
way he stabbed her portrait!' Keeping her voice level was
not easy and she paid no heed to the voice of logic that
asked whether anyone, even a jealous, fiery-tempered Latin,
would do anything as obvious as that in cold blood.

' "Found out", you say.' Once more, Harris broke into
her thoughts. 'Didn't Lawrence know the girl was living in
Stowbridge?'

'She was afraid to let him know where she was. That's
why she never returned the ring—in case he managed to
trace her.'

'She told you she was afraid of him?'

'Yes. She said he had a very hot temper. Looked at
from his point of view, she had treated him rather badly
but she saw herself as the victim of a family conspiracy
to make her marry someone she didn't love. She made it
sound perfectly plausible. Incidentally, she kept referring
to him as "Ricardo" and she seemed very proud of her
Italian ancestry.'

'When did she tell you all this?'

'The first time I met her, the day I took my first writers'
workshop back in September.'

'She confided in you on a first acquaintance?'

'I recognised her from the portrait and expressed surprise
at seeing her at the college. When she realised I'd witnessed
the picture-slashing, and had met Lou Stacey, she chattered
away as if we were old friends.'

'Lou Stacey.' Harris consulted his notes. 'The girl you
met at the prize-giving?'

'That's right. She and Angy were friends before all the
upset over Rick. Lou had already told me the story of the
so-called engagement but she put all the blame on Angy
for the way she jilted Rick.'

Melissa looked again at the drawing, willing it to be the
clue that would lead to the real killer and exonerate Barney.
'It looks as if he managed to track her down, doesn't it?'
she said, trying to sound matter-of-fact. 'I wonder if he was

hoping to win her back and knifed her when she refused him, or whether he intended all along to kill her out of revenge at the insult to his pride.'

Harris held out a hand for the drawing and returned it to his briefcase, giving no sign of having heard her speculative remarks.

'So she left home, being especially careful not to let the rejected lover know where she'd gone. You suggested there might also have been a rift with her relatives in London?'

'Lou said they were very upset but she was pretty sure it would blow over.'

'That seems to have been the case. We found letters in Italian from an address in Chalk Farm signed "Aunt Rosina"; we had them translated and they're quite affectionate. Just general chat, though, nothing significant. According to neighbours, the aunt and uncle have been on holiday in Italy but they're expected home tomorrow.'

So, thought Melissa, Angy had been lying to Barney when she told him she had no family in this country. She remembered the happy picture that Lou had somewhat acidly described: exuberant Uncle Vittorio and emotional Aunt Rosina rejoicing over the betrothal of their adored niece. Soon they would be asked to identify her body.

'They'll be heartbroken,' she said sadly. 'First the engagement falling through, then Angy leaving home . . . and now this.'

'They were happy about the proposed marriage, then?'

'Oh yes. They were involved in planning the party that caused all the trouble.'

'So they might have hoped for a reconciliation?'

'It's possible. Perhaps Rick got Angy's address from them.'

'That's something we have to check on. What about the Stacey girl? Would you say she was jealous of Angy?'

'Not so much jealous as angry . . . on Rick's behalf. She thought his life had been blighted for ever. You know how girls over-react at that age.'

'So you could say Lou had a grudge against Angy?'

'She certainly felt very strongly at the time,' agreed Melissa, seeing in her mind's eye a vision of the distracted girl, shoulders bowed, eyes streaming, nervous fingers tugging at her hair as she railed against her former friend. But surely not a murderess?

Aloud, she said, 'That was last year. She's had plenty of time to cool off.'

'Presumably she could have got hold of Angy's address?'

'Quite easily, I should think. She was living with the Carolis.'

'But she'd have been unlikely to encourage any further contact between Lawrence and Angy?'

'I'd say it was the last thing she'd want.'

'Hmm.' Harris referred again to his notes. 'According to Barnaby Willard's statement, Angy claimed she had no relatives in this country. At the time, we hadn't checked on next of kin but we now know it wasn't true. Can you suggest any reason why she should lie to Willard?'

'To gain his sympathy, perhaps. The poor little orphan syndrome. And then, as head of the art department, he was in a position to help her. Perhaps she asked him to use his influence with Doctor Shergold to let her replace the art teacher who was sick.'

'Shergold. The head of the department where they both worked?'

'That's right. As his secretary, she'd have known about the vacancy as soon as it arose.'

'So you think she was using Willard?'

'I didn't say that.' It dawned on Melissa that the questions were taking an uncomfortable line.

'Perhaps it had occurred to him that he was being used,' Harris said smoothly. 'That would have upset him, wouldn't it? No one likes to feel they've been taken for a ride.' It was as if he had taken her by the shoulders and forced her to look at something she did not want to see.

'If you're suggesting that would give him a motive for murdering Angy, I simply don't believe it!' she declared, altogether too vehemently for an objective opinion.

Harris's eyes never flickered. 'I'm suggesting nothing,' he said blandly. 'Just considering possibilities.'

'Barney isn't the vengeful sort,' she declared, sounding more confident than she felt. 'He might flare up if something upset him but he wouldn't kill anyone, least of all Angy.'

'On his own admission, he "flared up", as you put it, enough to do her actual bodily harm last Sunday,' observed Harris. 'Or didn't he bother to mention that to you?' One corner of his mouth kinked but it was hard to tell whether the cause was amusement or contempt.

'If by "actual bodily harm" you mean a small bruise on the cheek, yes, he did, as a matter of fact!' she retorted, falling straight into the trap. Not once had there been any reference to contact between her and Barney since the murder.

The kink deepened until it was almost a grin. She gritted her teeth and dug her nails into the arms of her chair.

'So presumably he told you what the quarrel was about?' Harris began drawing an elaborate design of circles on a blank page in his notebook. His tone was deceptively casual.

'He said she'd changed and when he tackled her about it, she just laughed. I gather she'd been seeing a lot of someone called Eddie who I think owns the house where she lives.'

'Eddie Brady,' Harris confirmed, without taking his eyes from his doodling.

'Is that his name?' Harris looked up and appeared about to say something. Melissa waited but he merely shrugged and wrote something in a margin. 'Anyway,' she continued, 'Barney had the impression that this Eddie had some kind of influence over Angy and he didn't like it. I suppose she taunted him and he just lost his temper and lashed out at her. He was full of remorse about it and I'm sure he'd never have gone back and attacked her in cold blood.'

'How well do you know him?' The small eyes seemed to be dissecting her. She felt her cheeks grow warm and it was an effort not to look away.

'We've been colleagues since last September and we've become quite friendly.' She knew that her voice did not sound natural but there was no visible reaction on Harris's lumpy features. 'He came back to the college in a dreadful state after finding the body. You really gave him a hard time,' she went on, suddenly angry on Barney's behalf. 'He's terribly sensitive and he was devastated at what had happened.'

'So he poured it all out to you.' Harris shifted his massive frame on the chair as if to make sure it was evenly distributed. 'Perhaps you remember something that might help us?'

'He didn't kill Angy!' She had never meant to betray her partisanship so openly but the damage was already done. 'Honestly, Ken, he's far too kind and gentle a soul and he worshipped that girl. She was like a daughter to him. Besides, isn't it obvious now? Rick Lawrence is the killer—he must be!'

'A daughter?' Harris's eyebrows lifted and his lips pursed. Again, he had totally ignored part of what she said.

'Yes, didn't he tell you?' she said impatiently.

'He told us very little. It made us curious to know what he was trying to hide.'

'He was trying to protect her reputation. Oh, I know this sounds like old-fashioned chivalry but he really did think of her as his daughter. His own little girl died in infancy— she'd have been about the same age—and his wife died giving birth to her.'

'So you're telling me that Angelica Caroli was a substitute for the child he had lost?'

'Yes.'

'Men have killed their daughters before now,' Harris pointed out. 'Just as a lover will murder a faithless mistress, if a daughter he idolises should fall off her pedestal . . . '

'I don't believe it!'

'You don't believe Angelica Caroli was the sort to fall off her pedestal?'

'I don't believe Barney Willard is capable of murder. As to Angy, I'm beginning to believe she's capable of

quite a lot. She lied to him about her family and . . . '
Just in time, she checked herself from referring to the
possibility of Angy's pregnancy. She had not been officially told and it would do Barney's case no good if the
police knew he was aware of it and had said nothing
to them.

'And?' said Harris. Frantically, Melissa tried to think of
something to fill the gap.

' . . . and Doug Wilson was always throwing out innuendoes,' she said, praying that it sounded convincing. 'Hinting
that Angy was "no better than she should be" as they used
to say, as if he knew something.'

'Wilson? Ah yes, the English teacher. Fancies himself a
real young stallion, doesn't he?'

'You could say that. It used to enrage Barney when he
hinted that Angy might have been unchaste.'

'Do you think she was "unchaste"?' Harris seemed to
find the word mildly amusing.

'It wouldn't surprise me.' Melissa was shocked at the
vitriol in her voice. 'She had certainly slept with Rick
Lawrence . . . she as good as told me so. And she wasn't
short of admirers. As Lou put it, the best cherries always
fell into her mouth. She had this facile, ingenuous way with
her, all soft and pliant. I think she hated confrontation so
she'd always say or do what was easiest and caused the
least hassle at the time.'

'Would it be fair to say that in spite of being on friendly
terms with her, you didn't really like her very much?'

'I certainly didn't *dis*like her, but I don't think I would
have trusted her very far,' Melissa admitted. 'She had a kind
of felinity.' Lou's comment came back to her: 'Cats take
what they want and then walk away.' Whatever it was that
Angy had taken this time, someone had seen to it that she
didn't walk away.

Harris put his notebook to one side and drew a folder
from his briefcase. 'I thought you might be interested in
these,' he said. He went over to a small table on which
Melissa kept magazines. 'May I?' He cleared a space and
laid out a series of crayon portraits.

'Good heavens, that's me!' Melissa picked up one of the drawings and stared at it in astonishment. It was signed 'AC' in an elaborate monogram. 'Are these Angy's? They're very good . . . but I've never sat for her.'

'Apparently none of her subjects did. They were all done from memory. A very talented girl, it seems.'

Melissa ran her eye along the row of sketches. 'There's Barney . . . Rodney Shergold . . . Doug Wilson. This is Sybil Bliss who comes to my writers' workshop. The lad with the earring is one of her art students, I think.' Harris nodded confirmation. 'I don't know him,' she added, picking up the last sketch.

'That's Eddie Brady.'

'Oh, so that's what he looks like.' The face was clean-shaven, with high cheekbones and an unsmiling mouth. A lock of straight hair fell across a high, unlined forehead; overhanging brows gave a brooding expression.

As before when Eddie's name was mentioned, Harris seemed about to say something and then changed his mind. He gathered up the sketches and put them away.

'We found them in her flat.' He took out a second folder. 'Here's the PM report. Knowing your professional interest in these matters, I thought you might be interested in the gory details.' He ran his eye down the typewritten sheet. 'She was killed by a single blow with a kitchen knife, struck from above, some time on Tuesday afternoon or evening as near as can be determined. The blow severed her windpipe and the actual cause of death was asphyxia. She choked on her own blood.'

'How absolutely horrible!' Melissa put a hand to her mouth and swallowed hard.

'At least it was quicker than bleeding to death. The pathologist reckoned two minutes, and of course, she'd have lost consciousness before that. As it was, she managed to reach the telephone and get the receiver off. Not that it would have done her much good even if she had managed to call 999. She wouldn't have been able to speak.'

'There must have been an awful lot of blood.'

'There was . . . well spread around too. We think she was stabbed in the kitchen; the trail leads from there into the bed-sitting-room. On the way past she must have fallen against the bathroom door. There's blood and her finger-prints down the panels and on the handle. From there it seems she staggered and crawled over to the bed, where she finally collapsed.'

'Barney said he'd called her number on Tuesday evening but it was engaged.'

'It would be, wouldn't it?'

'But the receiver must have been put back some time before he rang on Wednesday evening because he heard it ringing.'

'If he's telling the truth. He insists it was in place when he got to the flat and found her yesterday morning. He used it to call us.'

'So either the murderer replaced the receiver once Angy was dead, or he came back later and did it, or someone else came to the flat and did it but didn't report finding her body.' Suddenly, the adrenaline began to flow. The logical side of her brain had taken over, the way it did when she was devising puzzles for Nathan Latimer to resolve. For the moment, Barney was forgotten.

'Gets complicated, doesn't it?' said Harris, with an unex-pected grin that put her in mind of a Toby jug. 'Just to add to our problems, security in that house is non-existent; the front door is left open all day and the last one in at night locks up . . . if they remember. The flats have individual locks but, would you believe, the one on Angy's front door is defective and only functions if the door is slammed really hard.'

'So anyone could have gone in and out?'

'Right.'

'What about the other tenants? Didn't they hear any-thing?'

'We're out of luck there as well. Eddie Brady lives in the basement and was away on a two-day residential course for social workers. Went to the training centre straight from the office on Tuesday and didn't get back until late yesterday.

There are two other flats in the house; one's just been vacated and the people in the other one are on holiday. Angy lived right at the top, in a converted attic.'

'And she was all alone in the house?'

'Except for her killer, yes.'

'What about people going in and out? Workmen or someone delivering things?'

'No luck so far, but my men are combing the area for more witnesses.'

'What else does the PM say?'

'Nothing that helps us very much. She was a healthy young woman and the only time she'd consulted her doctor since coming to Stowbridge was for a sore throat last January. Not a virgin but no evidence of recent sexual activity or assault, so we're not looking for a rapist.'

'No sign of pregnancy or recent termination?' Melissa tried to sound detached and clinical.

'Definitely not. She was menstruating.' Harris shot Melissa a searching look before putting the papers away. 'Does that surprise you?'

'Not especially. I just wondered.'

'Are you sure you didn't have another reason for asking?'

'What reason would I have?'

'You might be thinking that her relationship with your friend Willard wasn't as innocent as he'd like you to believe.'

'I wasn't thinking anything of the kind!'

'All right.' Harris stood up and moved towards the door. 'I'm sure you'll let us know if you think of anything else that might help.'

'Yes, of course. Would you care for something before you go? Coffee, or a drink?'

'No thanks, I've already stayed longer than I intended.' At the front door he said, 'Be careful, Melissa. Don't take any risks.'

'What's that supposed to mean? You don't suppose *I'm* a potential victim?' She tried to sound flippant but he did not smile.

'I think you know what I mean but if you insist I'll spell it out. Our enquiries are at an early stage and we have totally open minds. No one has been eliminated. No one,' he repeated with what she considered quite unnecessary emphasis. 'Do you understand?'

'If you're warning me against Barney Willard . . . '

'He had motive and opportunity and he hasn't been entirely straight with us.'

'But I told you . . . '

'Perhaps I'll be more inclined to believe his story when I hear it directly from him.'

Melissa felt a surge of outrage on Barney's behalf. 'You're not going to put him through all that trauma again?' she pleaded. 'He's heartbroken over Angy's death. And what about Rick Lawrence? Surely he's got a much stronger motive . . . and he was seen near Angy's flat at the crucial time.'

'You know enough about police work to be sure that we'll follow every lead, but I don't have to remind you that Lawrence may have a perfectly sound alibi and that the man seen by witnesses could be an innocent look-alike.' The put-down was made gently enough but once again, Melissa felt foolish at having revealed her feelings so easily.

'I understand,' she said lamely. 'I appreciate your concern for me.'

He opened the door of his car, put his briefcase on the back seat, then took off his jacket and laid it on top. He did all this slowly and deliberately, the way he always seemed to do everything. There must be times when he moves quickly, Melissa thought, trying to imagine him in hot pursuit of some villain.

His eyes met hers above the roof of the car. 'Remember now, don't go sticking your neck out,' he said in a low voice, although there was nothing but a solitary cow within earshot. 'Once a man has killed, for whatever reason, he'll do it again if he has to.' He got into the car and started the engine before she could reply.

ELEVEN

'I WONDER IF THEY'VE ARRESTED RICK LAW-rence yet?' remarked Melissa during supper. She had spent the first part of the evening putting Iris in the picture and was aware that her relief that the heat should by now be off Barney had not escaped notice.

Iris, helping herself to vegetable curry, raised her eyebrows.

'You seem pretty sure he did it,' she said.

'Of course he did it.'

'May simply have been calling on an old friend.'

'Old friend? After the way Angy treated him?'

Iris waved a dismissive fork. 'You sound like that clown-faced child—what was her name? Lucy something or other.'

'Lou Stacey. But surely . . . '

'Be rational. All that hoo-ha was nearly a year ago.'

'He could have been nursing a grudge, brooded over it, then at last found out where Angy was and gone after her.'

'Unlikely. Might have growled around for a week or so, then gone back to work.'

'You sound very sure.'

'Self-centred lot, we artists. Get absorbed in our work. Can't be bothered to waste time over difficult relationships. Quite capable of anything in the heat of the moment, though.' Iris jabbed her fork in Melissa's direction. 'Remember that, before you get too carried away over lover-boy,' she warned.

'You're as bad as Ken Harris!' said Melissa impatiently. 'I won't have people hinting that Barney is a murderer.'

'Only thinking of your own good.' Iris put a hand over
Melissa's wrist and gave a disarming grin. 'Don't want you
topped. I might get undesirable neighbours!'

Melissa laughed, her momentary annoyance forgotten.
'All right, I'll be careful.'

Iris pushed aside her empty plate and refilled their glasses with elderflower champagne. 'Good vegetarian supper,
Melissa. You're learning!'

'Glad you enjoyed it. Thanks for bringing the wine.'
Melissa took their plates to the kitchen and fetched the
dessert. When they had finished eating she sat back and
picked up her glass. 'One thing that puzzles me,' she said,
'is the way Angy seems to have changed her attitude to
Barney. And why let him think she was pregnant when it
wasn't true? She must have known it would upset him and
she told me more than once how much she hated seeing
people unhappy.'

'So she made an exception in his case.'

'Yes, but why? He'd been good to her. He probably
recommended her for the job in the Art Department. He'd
have done anything in the world for her.'

'Bored with having him hanging around looking pi?'
speculated Iris, swirling her glass and watching the bub-
bles streaming in sparkling columns to the surface of the
wine. 'Or he'd been pestering her to marry him? Could
have figured the baby yarn'd shock him into dropping
her.'

'He didn't want to marry her. He thought of her as his
daughter.'

'So he told you. Could have been lying.'

'He wasn't lying.'

Iris, fiddling with the stem of her glass, looked across the
table with a troubled expression. 'Wish you'd stop kidding
yourself. You hardly know the man. He admitted he lost his
temper and slapped her. Could have picked up the knife and
struck out in a blind rage.'

'That's what he thinks the police have been trying to get him to admit.'

'Without knowing about the baby story,' Iris pointed out. 'Wait till they hear that.'

'They won't get it from Barney. I'm the only one that knows and he never meant to tell me.'

'But you're going to tell them.'

'Me?' Melissa looked aghast.

'Yes, you,' said Iris drily. 'Not going to withhold vital information, are you?'

Melissa shifted uneasily. 'You're asking me to betray a confidence?'

'Suppose it comes out? Your policeman chum'll be pretty miffed if you've been holding out on him.'

Melissa sighed. The thought had already occurred to her. A vision of Harris loomed into her mind, his burly frame engulfing the chair beneath him and the occasional smile crumpling his rough-hewn features. He wouldn't smile if . . . Normally, the thought of being under his inquisition while in possession of a guilty secret would make her shiver and yet, at this moment, for some unaccountable reason, it struck her as hugely comic.

'Go bananas, wouldn't he?' she chortled. 'But I'm not telling him, and that's that!'

Iris shrugged and picked up the wine bottle. 'Suit yourself. Just trying to help. Have some more bubbly? Last bottle till we make this season's brew.'

'Thanks.' Melissa drained her glass and held it out to be refilled. From being utterly downcast, she felt suddenly buoyant and free from care.' 's gorgeous,' she said happily. 'Got a t'rrific kick.' She stood up; the room swayed a little and she grabbed hold of the table until it steadied itself. 'Le's leave this lot and go in the sitting-room . . . don't like shitting . . . *heeheehee* . . . sitting among dirty dishes.' She led the way, still tittering. Iris followed, carrying the bottle. They had just sat down, Melissa in an armchair, Iris on the floor as usual, when the telephone rang.

'Oh, get stuffed!' said Melissa. Then it occurred to her that it might be Barney and she leapt out of her chair.

'Watch it! Nearly spilt your drink!' said Iris reproach-fully.

Joe was on the line. 'Mel! Where have you been?'

Stupid man. Stupid question. 'Here, of course. Wha's the problem?'

'I tried most of yesterday to get you. I rang in the evening as well, quite late . . . '

'Wasn't here then.' Melissa directed a beatific smile at the ceiling.

'So I gathered. I wasn't worried then . . . '

'Sh'd think not. I'm a big girl now. Go out by myself quite often.'

' . . . but when I read in the paper about the murder . . . '

'You were *sooo* worried you waited till now to call me.' Melissa took a mouthful from her glass and gave a gentle hiccough. 'Oops . . . manners!'

'I've been at meetings all day and I've only just seen the report,' said Joe, sounding huffy. 'Mel, are you sure you're all right? You sound strange.'

'Never felt better!' said Melissa dreamily.

'It's just that, not knowing where you were, and then reading about the murder . . . '

'You thought the big bad wolf might have got me!' Melissa let out a high-pitched hoot. 'Poor old Joe!' She took a noisy swallow of elderflower champagne. 'I'll tell you what I was doing.' She dropped her voice to an exag-gerated whisper. 'I was grilling number one suspect . . . *aaawll* night long!'

There was a five-second pause before Joe spoke again. When he did, there was a cool, slightly acid note in his voice. 'Mel, you've been drinking. You sound distinct-ly . . . '

'Oh, I am!' Melissa interrupted proudly. 'As a newt!'

'I'll speak to you tomorrow,' said Joe and hung up.

Melissa put down the phone and went unsteadily back to her chair. 'Silly ol' fusspot!' she said gleefully, trying to picture Joe's face.

'Shouldn't have said that!' said Iris, looking disapprov-ing again.

'Why not? Not my minder. None of his business where I spend my nights.' She held out her empty glass. 'More elderbubbly, please!'

Very deliberately, Iris got up and walked out of the room, carrying the bottle. 'No more tipple for you tonight!' she called over her shoulder. 'Cup of tea'll sober you up. I'll make it.'

'Don't want to sober up,' said Melissa sulkily as she followed Iris into the kitchen. She slumped into a chair and watched as her friend bustled about. Her brief surge of elation had subsided like a spent firework and she felt weary and depressed. She had the beginning of a headache, her eyes were smarting and her mouth trembled. She sniffed and swallowed hard.

'None of that!' Iris commanded. 'Big girls don't cry.'

'I'm so worried!' Melissa faltered.

'About Barney Willard?'

'He's so kind, so gentle . . . I'll never believe . . . '

'Now you listen to me!' Iris planted two mugs of tea on the table, sat down opposite Melissa and grabbed both her hands. 'You took one hell of a chance last night. Don't do it again, not until this is cleared up. D'you hear me?'

Melissa nodded miserably.

'Promise?'

'I promise.' Tears escaped in spite of her efforts and she released one hand to grope for a handkerchief. 'I feel such a fool!' she gulped.

'Nervous reaction. Perfectly natural!' Iris gave her other hand a consoling pat. 'What you need is sleep. Drink your tea and get to bed.'

'Thanks, Iris. You're a good friend.'

Ignoring Melissa's feeble protests, Iris insisted on clearing the supper things from the table and loading the dishwasher before going home. It was nearly eleven by the time they said goodnight. Melissa waited in her own front porch until she heard Iris's door close, then switched out the exterior light and stood for a few minutes in the dark, letting the peace of the Cotswold night quieten her tired brain. A soft breeze lifted her hair and soothed the ache in her head. She thought of Barney and wished she could be with him—not just to make love, but to give the comfort and support that he must surely need.

She had just finished locking up when the telephone rang.

'Melissa? I hope I'm not disturbing you?'

'Barney! I was thinking about you. How are you feeling?'

'Terrible. The police have been here, asking more questions. After they'd gone I drank several whiskies and then crashed out in a chair. I've just woken up and I feel like hell.' He sounded distraught; before she could utter another word, he burst out, 'Melissa, Angy lied to me!'

'What about?' she asked, but already she had guessed.

'About the baby. It wasn't true! Why would she lie to me like that?'

'I don't know, Barney. Who told you this?'

'That Inspector Harris suddenly asked me if I had any reason to think that she might have been pregnant. I said I hadn't—I remembered what you said about motive—but I don't think he believed me. He went on and on, and when I asked him if it was true, he said it wasn't. I was shattered. I didn't know what was going on . . . and then he asked me all over again whether I'd thought she might be having a baby, and if so, if it could be mine.' His words were punctuated by intervals when his self-control seemed to be at breaking-point.

'Barney, listen to me!' said Melissa urgently. 'Did you admit that she'd hinted . . . ?'

'No! That's what I can't understand. If it wasn't true, what put the idea into the man's head?' Suddenly, his voice grew harsh. 'You've been talking to the police—you told them! Melissa, how could you?'

If he had shouted at her, screamed abuse down the phone, she could have understood and endured it. It was the resignation, the sense of betrayal in the final, sad little question, that made her throat contract.

'Barney, I promise you I never breathed a word about what you told me. It's true!' she insisted, sensing rather than hearing his disbelief. 'DCI Harris told me what was in the post mortem and she definitely couldn't have been pregnant.'

'Why should he tell you? What's it got to do with you?'

'Don't be angry, Barney. I've known Ken Harris for a long time. He helps me with police procedure and stuff for my novels.'

'That doesn't explain . . .'

'Look, he came to see me as part of the murder enquiry and while he was here he told me about the PM report, purely because he knew I'd be interested—professionally, I mean.' Put like that, it sounded clinical and heartless and she hurried on, 'I checked that Angy wasn't pregnant but I never let on about what you told me.'

'You must have said something to make him suspicious.'

'I promise you I didn't. All I can say is that my mentioning it might have put it into his head and he decided it was worth following up.' There was a long silence. 'I'm sorry, Barney. You'd have found out, sooner or later.'

He sighed heavily. 'All right, I believe you. What I can't understand is why she should say those things. She must have known how upset I'd be. Anyway, what difference does it make?' His voice took on a dead quality; it was the voice of a man who was past caring.

'I think,' said Melissa gently, 'that you have to face up to the fact that there was a side to Angy that you never saw. None of us really knew her.'

'Yes, I suppose so.'

'Was that all the police wanted?'

'No, there was something else. They asked if I knew a young artist called Rick Lawrence. At least I was able to give them some help there.'

'You know Rick Lawrence?'

'I met him on Monday. A friend of mine is helping some youngsters to mount an exhibition in Cheltenham and this guy Lawrence was helping him.' There was a pause. 'You sounded surprised. Do you know him too?'

'Not exactly but I know of him. Didn't Angy ever mention him?'

'Not that I remember.'

'Perhaps she referred to him as Ricardo Lorenzo.'

'You mean the maniac who slashed her portrait?' Barney's voice seesawed in astonishment. 'Is that the same man?'

'Yes. It seems that someone answering his description was seen near Angy's flat the day of the murder.'

'My God! He must have found out where she was living and gone there to kill her!' The seesawing became wilder, ending in a thin note of anguish.

'You mustn't jump to conclusions,' said Melissa. 'We don't know for sure that he did it.'

'But it's obvious, isn't it?'

'He could have had some other reason for going to see her.'

'Like what?' He sounded hostile.

'A little matter of a ring,' said Melissa cautiously.

'Ring? What ring?'

'Didn't Angy tell you . . . ?'

'She told me that fellow Ricardo had beaten her and she ran away to hide from him. The poor little girl was terrified of him. He must be the killer!'

'That was my first reaction and it does seem the most likely but . . . '

'Of course it is.' Like a weak radio signal, his voice wavered, faded and then grew strong again. 'If I could get hold of him I'd choke him with my bare hands! But why were the police wasting their time talking to me when they should be out looking for him?'

'They'll find him soon enough, don't worry. They have to follow every possible lead.'

'Yes, I suppose so.' The deadness had come back into his voice. She longed to put her arms round him and soothe his hurt.

'Try not to brood,' she said, thinking how banal and useless the words sounded. 'Go to bed and get some rest.'

'May I call you tomorrow?' he said.

'Of course . . . any time. Goodnight Barney.'

'Goodnight Melissa.'

TWELVE

MELISSA SLEPT LATE AND AWOKE WITH A splitting headache. Grumbling to herself, she put on her dressing-gown and tottered downstairs, filled a kettle and rummaged in a drawer for aspirin.

After a cup of strong coffee and a slice of dry toast, she contemplated the day ahead. She normally did this quietly in bed before getting up and almost invariably began with an early breakfast followed by three or four hours' work on her current novel. This morning, having forced herself to her study, still wearing her dressing-gown and clutching a second cup of coffee as if it were attached to a lifeline, she began searching among her papers for the output of the previous day. It came as a mild shock to realise that there was none. Today was Saturday and she had not written a word since Thursday morning.

Ruefully, she recalled her pleasure at the way the book, after a difficult patch, had begun to develop. She had been reluctant to put it away, wishing she had no other commitments so that she could continue with the next chapter and looking forward to getting down to work again the following morning. And all the time, she thought as she sat at her desk nursing the remains of her hangover, Angy had been dead in her little one-room flat, alone and open-eyed, lying where she had fallen with the knife in her throat and her lifeblood flooding her lungs. With her vivid imagination, Melissa could visualise the scene and it sickened her. How much worse must the recollection be for Barney, who had seen the hideous reality?

She got up and opened the window. The sky was clear and the sunlight had a brilliance and intensity that made her head reel. She winced and shaded her eyes. It was no good, she simply couldn't concentrate. The best thing she could do was take a shower, get dressed and go out for some fresh air.

By the time she was ready it was almost ten o'clock. Normally, she would have been up for several hours and written a couple of thousand words. Today threatened to be a write-off as far as work was concerned, but perhaps she could recoup some of the lost time later on. She was about to leave the house when the telephone rang.

'How are you this morning?' asked Joe.

'Fragile, thank you. Iris's elder brew is not for the faint-hearted.'

'Serves you right for overdoing it.'

'Your sympathy is just what I needed. What can I do in exchange?'

'Mel, just how involved are you in this murder?' He sounded hesitant, embarrassed almost. She vaguely remembered saying something rather foolish and provocative last night. 'I mean,' Joe stumbled on, 'you aren't doing anything . . . silly, are you?'

'Silly?'

'Dangerous, then. You said something about "number one suspect".'

'Oh, that.' Damn, why did I have to go and let that out? Aloud, she said, 'I was a bit tight . . . just talking nonsense.'

'I hope you're not taking any risks.' An authoritative note had crept into his voice and Melissa felt a stab of resentment. First Harris, then Iris, and now Joe, all telling her what to do.

'Did you ring to give me a lecture or have you got something you want to discuss?' she asked impatiently.

'Don't take offence, Mel. I'm only thinking of your safety. You have been known to get yourself into scrapes.'

'Well, I'm not in a scrape this time, so stop fussing.'

'All right, all right!' Now he was getting irritable with her. She'd have to be more discreet in future. 'The reason I rang last night is that I had a message from your publishers,' he went on. 'A girl called Louise Stacey has been on to them, asking how she could contact you. They wouldn't give her your address, of course, but promised to refer to you through me.'

'Did she leave a number?'

'Yes, do you want it?'

'Please.' He dictated a London telephone number and she wrote it on her pad.

'Do you know this girl?' he asked.

'I've met her.'

'Any idea what she wants?'

'It could have something to do with Angy's murder. They used to be friends.' Melissa made herself sound casual but the curiosity that Lou's call had aroused was breaking through her lethargy.

'Does she know you're connected with the college?'

'I've no idea. I'll give her a call and find out.'

'Remember what I said. Don't go getting involved in anything dodgy.'

Melissa restrained a sharp retort. 'I'll remember. Was that all you called to say?'

'More or less. How's the book going?'

'It's been buzzing along quite well lately but the mur-der—the real murder, that is—has thrown me rather badly. I expect I'll get back to it quite soon.'

'Would you like me to come down?'

'What for?'

'I could help take your mind off the unpleasantness.' The signals were unmistakable. Alarm bells rang; some quick thinking was called for.

'Weren't you saying something a few months ago that too quiet a life was bad for a writer's creativity? Now something exciting has happened, you want to dull the effect!'

'Meaning, you don't want me to come?'

'Not this weekend, Joe. I must get down to some work.' She adopted a brisk, businesslike tone. 'I'll be in touch when I've got something to show you.'

There was a short silence before he said, 'Sure, good-bye then,' and hung up. Immediately, Melissa dialled the number he had given.

Lou answered in a voice distorted by stress. When Melissa gave her name, she burst out in mingled relief and fear, 'Ms Craig, the police are looking for Rick!'

'Yes, I know,' said Melissa.

'You know? But how . . . ?'

'I do some tutoring in the college where Angy worked. I was there the day her body was found.'

Emotion overwhelmed Lou for several seconds. When, at last, she managed to speak, the words fluttered out so faintly that Melissa had to strain to catch them. 'Ms Craig, I need your advice.'

'I'm listening. Just take your time.'

'I'd rather not . . . not on the phone. Someone might . . . could I possibly come and see you? It must sound a bit of a cheek,' Lou rushed on as Melissa hesitated, 'but I don't know who else to . . . '

'Was Rick at Angy's flat last Tuesday?' Melissa interposed.

'Yes.' It was hard to believe that a monosyllable could convey so much terror.

'Then why do you want to talk to me?'

'I thought that you . . . being a crime writer . . . you know about the police and things . . . you could tell us what to do.'

'I think you already know what you should do.'

'You mean, Rick should give himself up? But he didn't kill Angy! She was dead already!' The words rang with the passionate, unreasoning conviction of a girl in love. 'Ms Craig, please!' she implored again, 'let me come and talk to you!'

It was, of course, Melissa's plain duty to end the conversation without arousing the girl's suspicions and immediately pass the telephone number to the police. Well, so she would, she assured her conscience, after hearing what Lou had to say. 'I hardly see what I can do, but come if you want to,' she agreed. Fifteen love to writer's curiosity.

'Oh, Ms Craig, thank you!' Relief all but swamped the words. 'How will I reach you?'

'The trains run from Paddington. How long will it take you to get there?' Melissa checked herself from asking the obvious question; the girl might fear betrayal if she wanted to know her exact whereabouts.

'I don't know. Half an hour perhaps.'

'Hold on a minute.' Melissa rummaged in a drawer and dragged out a timetable, glancing at the clock. 'There's a train at eleven—you should be able to catch it. Get a ticket to Stowbridge and I'll meet you at the station.'

'You're so kind. Ms Craig, you won't tell anyone?'

'I won't tell anyone you're coming to see me,' Melissa promised, 'but if you have any important information, the police will have to know. You do understand that, don't you?'

'Yes, but I want to talk to you first.' The words struggled out through a tangle of sobs.

'You be on that train,' said Melissa. She cut short the stumbling thanks and put down the phone. So much for her intentions of doing some work. Never mind, this was more exciting. She'd have to organise something for lunch though, instead of making do with a sandwich. First, however, she'd take the walk she'd promised herself. It would help to clear her head in readiness for whatever Lou had to say.

Leaving the cottage, Melissa climbed the stile and made her way along the footpath which led past the church to the village. In the far corner of the churchyard, a woman was tending a grave; she bent over the stone urn to arrange fresh flowers, then stood quietly with bowed head and folded hands. Soon, thought Melissa sadly, it would be the turn of Uncle Vittorio and Aunt Rosina to stand sorrowing over the grave of their niece. Such a waste of a young life.

Outside the church, she was surprised to see Snappy, tethered to a drainpipe. He had at last accepted her as a friend and began whining and wriggling with pleasure as she approached. Stooping to pat him, she glanced into the porch. The inner door stood open and through it she caught sight of Eleanor Shergold sitting in one of the pews. Melissa felt a pang of remorse. The murder must have been a severe shock to her and she would no doubt be deeply concerned over its effect on her husband; she should have gone to see her yesterday, or at least telephoned. She tiptoed across the aisle and sat down beside the motionless figure.

Eleanor was staring at the altar. She did not turn her head when Melissa entered and for a moment it seemed that she was unaware of her presence. Melissa touched her arm; still she did not move but as if a tap had been opened, tears spilt from her eyes and began streaming down her face. She made no attempt to wipe them away and one by one they dripped from her nose and chin on to the hands that lay folded in her lap. It was as if a statue had started to weep.

'All this must be terrible for you,' said Melissa in a hushed voice. She fished a paper tissue from her pocket and held it out. 'Here, take this. It's quite clean.'

Her words seemed to break a spell. Eleanor stifled a groan, put her hands over her face and began quietly sobbing. Melissa slid an arm round her and patted her on the shoulder.

'There now . . . it's all right . . . it's all right,' she soothed.

With her face still hidden, Eleanor began shaking her head violently from side to side. 'They . . . think . . . Rodney . . . did it!' she gasped between sobs. 'Oh dear God, what shall I . . . what shall we do?'

'Rodney? Oh, surely not!'

'They've been questioning him. He's quite ill with worry, and the reporters have been pestering him. A detective came to the house and took some of his clothes . . . it's like a nightmare!' She reduced the tissue to a pulp and Melissa, searching her pocket, managed to find another.

'Listen, Eleanor,' she said gently, 'you have to understand how the police work. They question everybody very closely, just to make sure that they find out every tiny detail that might be useful. It doesn't mean . . . '

With more violent shakes of the head, Eleanor began demolishing the second tissue.

'They suspect Rodney! I know they do . . . they took his fingerprints!'

'They've taken all our fingerprints. It's just routine, honestly. Everyone associated with Angy has to be checked—her colleagues, her friends, the students in her art class . . . '

Eleanor lowered her hands and turned to stare at Melissa, an expression of bewilderment on her blotched and swollen face. 'Her students? They think it might be one of them?'

'Not necessarily. It's just for comparison with prints they might find in her flat—on the murder weapon, for example. Once they've eliminated someone, the prints are destroyed.'

Eleanor was clearly unconvinced. 'It's terrible to think of Rodney being suspected,' she whimpered.

'I'm sure you're wrong. As a matter of fact, they're already looking for someone else.'

Hope blended with the fear in Eleanor's ashen face. 'I know they've been questioning Mr Willard but he was the one who found her.'

'No, not Barney. Someone else, an ex-boyfriend of Angy's.'

'A boyfriend?' The look of bewilderment returned, as if Eleanor had difficulty in grasping the significance of what Melissa was saying.

'It seems she jilted him, which might be a motive.'

'Of course, there has to be a motive, doesn't there?' Eleanor was beginning to calm down; she stopped crying, dried her eyes and patted her hair with quick, fussy movements of her small, white hands. 'They couldn't really think a man in Rodney's position would have a motive for killing a little secretary, could they?'

If it wasn't so tragic, it would be laughable. Eleanor's devotion to her husband amounted almost to veneration. It did not seem to occur to her that he might suffer from any of the normal masculine weaknesses.

'I'm sure it'll be all right,' Melissa repeated. 'Try not to worry.'

'You're very kind.' Eleanor's eyes still betrayed anxiety but she had regained her self-control.

From outside came the sound of impatient whining.

'I think Snappy's getting restless,' said Melissa. 'Hadn't you better see to him?'

'Yes, of course.' Eleanor put on her gloves and stood up.

'Are you going home? I'll walk with you if you like.'

'You're very kind,' Eleanor repeated mechanically and followed Melissa from the church like a submissive child.

Rodney Shergold was cutting his front lawn when they reached Cotswold View. He glanced up as they approached and gave Melissa a distant nod without interrupting his progress up and down the small patch of grass. As the two women were saying their goodbyes he came to the end of his task, switched off the motor-mower and headed with it towards the narrow gate at the side of the house.

'I'll leave you to do the edges, Nell,' he called over his shoulder. 'We'll have coffee when I've finished the back.'

'Yes, dear,' said Eleanor. With a brief, tremulous smile at Melissa, she trailed meekly behind him.

As Melissa passed Tanners Cottage on her way home, Dudley Ford was pretending to trim his already immaculate front hedge while shooting glances up the lane from beneath the brim of his panama. No doubt he had observed her talking to the Shergolds and was itching for the chance to find out what she knew. She would have hurried on after an exchange of greetings and comments on the splendour of the morning but he moved forward to take a snip at a dandelion growing on the grass verge and contrived to block her path.

'Dreadful business, this murder!' he observed as he straightened up, red in the face and breathing heavily. He leaned towards Melissa with an air of great confidentiality. 'A CID johnny called on us, asking if we could say what time a certain person came home last Tuesday. We were able to help him ... we can see their house from our bedroom and we just happened to be looking out of the window at the time, don't you know.' His fierce little eyes swivelled towards Cotswold View. 'We've been wondering,' he lowered his voice and gave a sly grin, 'whether there was any hanky-panky going on?'

'It was probably just part of their routine enquiries,' said Melissa briskly. 'They check up on everyone's movements for elimination purposes.'

He was not to be put off. 'Never can tell with these quiet, donnish chappies . . . and having a homely little body like that for a wife . . . I understand the poor young lady was quite a beauty?'

'She was a very lovely girl and it's been a great shock to us all,' agreed Melissa. 'Excuse me, Dudley, I have to meet someone at the station.'

'Of course. I mustn't detain you!' He raised his panama, all correctness and courtesy. As Melissa turned to go, she saw Harriet Yorke approaching. Anxious not to be further delayed, she merely nodded and waved but before she was out of earshot she heard Ford's voice boom out a greeting. The Yorkes lived next door to the Shergolds and might have gleaned some scraps of information that he could wheedle out of Harriet. What a busybody the man was!

THIRTEEN

LOU HAD ALLOWED HER COAL-BLACK HAIR TO to grow into a softer, more feminine style that flattered her small features. She was wearing little or no make-up, so that for a moment Melissa did not recognise her. It was her air of nervous tension that set her apart from the other passengers as she jumped from the train at Stowbridge, searching the platform with a fraught expression that only partially lifted when she caught sight of Melissa.

'Oh, Ms Craig!' she exclaimed, rushing forward with outstretched hands as if afraid Melissa would vanish if she did not lay hold of her. From the way her mouth twitched, it was plain she was on the verge of breaking down. Melissa took her by the arm and piloted her through the booking hall. When Lou got in the car, the bulky jacket that she wore over her washed denim skirt got in the way of her seat belt and her movements as she struggled to fasten the buckle were jerky and nervous. Melissa had barely turned the key in the ignition when she began to speak in a brittle, staccato voice.

'Ms Craig, I don't know what to do! I've told Rick to go to the police but he won't and I'm so afraid . . .'

'I can't concentrate on what you say while I'm driving,' said Melissa gently. 'It's only a short distance.' Lou bit her lip but took the hint and settled quietly into her seat. 'And by the way, suppose you start calling me Melissa? I'm not terribly keen on Mizz.'

The minute they were indoors, Lou burst out, 'I suppose, because you saw Rick stab Angy's portrait, you think he killed her!'

'Why don't you just sit down and tell me the whole story from the beginning.' Melissa led the trembling girl to the sitting-room and sat beside her on the window-seat. 'What about a drink, or some coffee? Have you had anything to eat today?'

'I don't want anything.' There was desperation in Lou's eyes and she clutched at Melissa's arm while words poured from her mouth like water from an overflowing vessel. 'He was there but he didn't do it! I know he stabbed the portrait but he'd got over all that and he never killed her . . . he did it out of sheer unhappiness and frustration . . . but that was months ago . . . you must believe me!'

'Look, I can't make any sense of all this, so try and calm down,' said Melissa.

Lou withdrew her hand, leaned her head against the wall and stared out of the window as if trying to pull her thoughts together. She had abandoned the huge earrings for dainty gold studs and wore a fine gold chain round her neck. For a split second she seemed to metamorphose into Angy . . . Angy with dead eyes wide open and blood gushing from the terrible wound in her throat. Horror crept into the room and settled beside them like a crouching beast.

'I don't know where to start,' Lou mumbled.

'Just tell it the way it happened and try not to get sidetracked,' said Melissa, thinking that this could take a long time. Workwise, the day was already a write-off and in any case she was eager to know what the girl had to say. It might help to clear Barney. The police would have to know about this visit, of course; her conscience persistently reminded her that she should have informed Harris already but she silenced it by telling herself that a few hours would make no difference. It wasn't as if Rick was a dangerous psychopath who might kill again, she reasoned, and Lou had as good as agreed that after their talk she would tell them what she knew.

'After the bust-up I didn't see Rick for several weeks,' Lou began. 'Then I ran into him again. He'd left home. His parents were furious over the engagement business. They felt they'd been made fools of . . . and the ring is some sort of family heirloom and his father went on as if it was all Rick's fault that Angy had made off with it.' Lou began fulminating at the injustice of it all.

'Never mind whose fault it was. Just stick to the facts,' said Melissa, trying not to sound impatient.

'All right, I'll try.'

The story, told with mounting bitterness, was a classic example of a well-intentioned action leading to tragedy. Rick had gone to Cheltenham to help some friends to set up an art exhibition and Lou had gone with him. She had found out from Angy's relatives that she was living in the area and had secretly taken the opportunity of getting in touch with her. Her main motive was simple: to retrieve the ring and thereby enable Rick to make peace with his family. As Lou's story progressed, however, it emerged that she had been living with Rick for several months and had high hopes of becoming engaged to him herself.

Angy had professed to be delighted to hear from her, had invited her to her flat but refused point-blank to hand over the ring. Instead, having been assured that Rick no longer had any violent feelings towards her, she earnestly pleaded that she had long been awaiting an opportunity to return it in person and apologise for causing so much distress. With every evidence of cordiality and goodwill, she invited them both round for supper the following evening.

By the time she reached this point in her narrative, Lou's eyes had hardened, her nostrils were flaring and her small-boned hands were gripping her knees like talons. She reminded Melissa of an angry young hawk.

'She sat there wearing her cat-at-the-cream expression and saying how lovely it would be for all three of us to be together again!' Lou spat out the words as if they had turned rancid in her mouth.

'Did you think she was trying to get him back?' asked Melissa.

'I didn't know what to think. Angy always played up to a man . . . any man. She just couldn't help it. Even though she once told me she didn't really care much for men, she said it was fun to see the way they reacted to her. I could imagine her in her sexiest dress and her most alluring perfume, cooking pasta the way Rick liked it. I was afraid . . . '

'That he'd realise he was still in love with her?' suggested Melissa gently.

Lou nodded miserably. 'I made excuses, said I thought he'd be too busy and so on, so she said, "Well, just pop round for a drink then." She was quite determined to get Rick there and there was no way she was going to give the ring to me. I even thought of trying to grab it from her but she put it away in the drawer where she kept it and stood in front of it. I wasn't going to fight her for it but I was so angry I could have killed her.' Lou's hand flew to her mouth. 'Oh my God, what am I saying? I didn't mean that, honestly!'

'All right, I believe you!' Melissa patted her hand. 'Tell me what you did then.'

'I went back to the house. We were all staying with some friends of Steve's—that's the man who's organising the exhibition; Rick shares a studio with him in London. They hadn't come in yet so I started getting some food ready and tried to make up my mind what to tell Rick. Already I was wishing I'd never been to see Angy, even though I knew how much being estranged from his family had hurt him and it would mean a lot to him to get the ring back.' Lou put her hands over her eyes. 'Oh, if only I'd let well enough alone!'

'Now, let me get this straight,' said Melissa. 'You went to see Angy on Monday afternoon and told Rick that evening about the invitation for Tuesday, right?' Lou nodded. 'How did he react?'

'He was very surprised, but over the moon about the ring.'

'Did he agree to accept Angy's invitation?'

'Yes, but he said he'd go on his own. I had to stay behind to cook supper for the others.' Lou's heightened colour betrayed her embarrassment, as if she could read Melissa's unspoken disapproval at this example of male chauvinism.

'How did he get there?'

'Steve lent him his car.'

'And what time did he arrive?'

'He thinks it was a few minutes after six.'

'Where were you when he left?'

'At the house—he dropped me off on the way. Steve and the others were still working and I began getting the meal ready. Oh, if only he'd let me go with him!' Without warning, Lou began beating her forehead and moaning; plainly she was on the verge of hysteria.

Melissa grabbed her wrists. 'Now stop that, you're not rehearsing Ophelia! What time did Rick get back?'

'A little before seven.' Lou's voice, her hands, her whole body shook uncontrollably. 'He walked in looking dreadful, like a ghost. He collapsed into a chair and began to cry . . . it was ages before he could say anything. There was blood on his hands and I thought he'd had an accident. I found some brandy and it steadied him a bit . . . and then he told me he'd been to Angy's flat and found her dead.'

For several seconds the two women sat staring at one another, unable to speak for thinking of that awful scene. Melissa broke the silence.

'Why didn't he phone the police?'

'He said he was going to. He actually picked up Angy's phone . . . it was off the hook and covered in blood as if she'd tried to use it to call for help. Then he got scared. Angy had been stabbed in the throat and that's exactly what he'd done to her portrait . . . he was afraid that would all come out and everyone would think he'd done it.'

'So what did he do?'

'He says he can't remember exactly but he thinks he may have tried to pull out the knife. Then he lost his nerve and rushed out of the flat and came back to the house to find me.'

Leaving his fingerprints all over the place, thought Melissa. Aloud, she said, 'Didn't you try to persuade him to call the police?'

'Of course I did. I argued and pleaded . . . I even went to the phone to call them myself and he snatched it away from me. He was so angry, I thought he was going to hit me.'

'He's got quite a temper, hasn't he? Isn't that why Angy was afraid of him?'

'He was in a panic . . . he hardly knew what he was doing! He'd never really have hurt anyone.'

'So what did you do?'

'We checked his clothes for bloodstains . . . there weren't many but he told me to wash his shirt and handkerchief while he had a shower. I did that, and then I went to sponge his jacket. I felt something hard in his pocket and I took it out . . . it was the box with the ring in it!' Lou shook her head as if unable to believe what she was saying.

'He had the ring in his pocket? Are you telling me that after finding Angy's body he was too scared to stay and call the police but still found the nerve to go rummaging around her flat?'

'He didn't rummage around! I'd already told him where she kept it . . . and he was afraid that if he left it there it'd be traced back to him. Anyway, it belongs to his family, doesn't it?' The girl's voice took on a whine as she flew yet again to the defence of her man.

Melissa bit back a scathing comment but she could hear the icy edge in her voice as she said, 'So you helped him to clean up. Then what?'

'Rick insisted we go home straight away. Nothing I said could make him change his mind. Luckily the others still weren't back so he made me write a note saying we'd been called to London on some family matter and we took the next train from Cheltenham station.'

'How did you get there?'

'By taxi.'

'And where's Rick now? Back at the flat?'

'No, at the studio. Steve's due back tomorrow evening . . . he'll have to leave before then but I can't think where he'll go.' Lou's voice trailed into silence; she was played out, too exhausted even to weep. Under its crown of smooth black hair, her face had the colour and texture of wax.

'I think perhaps you should have some food before we talk any more.' Melissa got to her feet. 'There's some lunch ready in the kitchen.'

'I'm not hungry,' protested Lou.

'Well I am, I'm ravenous,' declared Melissa. 'And you won't be much help to Rick if you starve yourself, so at least have a sandwich and a cup of coffee.'

Reluctantly, Lou dragged herself upright and trailed behind Melissa. After some coaxing she struggled with a minuscule portion of chicken salad and half a slice of bread, all the while gazing at Melissa with the eyes of a frightened child.

'They're going to arrest Rick, aren't they?' she said. 'He'll be charged with murder.'

'That depends on whether they believe his story,' said Melissa. There was no point in glossing over the situation. 'He's going to have to answer some pretty tough questions.'

'They've got to find him first,' muttered Lou defiantly.

'I'm afraid they'll do that all too easily. The taxi-driver will probably remember picking you up, people on the train may have seen you . . . and of course they'll question your friends.'

'Steve wouldn't give him away.'

'I don't think you can count on that. It's a killer they're after, not a burglar or a car thief.'

'And you . . . you're going to ring the police the minute I've gone, aren't you?' Suddenly hostile, the girl leapt to her feet and snatched up her handbag. 'I thought you'd help us! I should never have come . . . just let me call a taxi and I won't bother you any more!'

'Now don't go flying off the handle.' Melissa put out a restraining hand. 'The police are going to find Rick without any help from me—they may already have found him— and they're going to want to talk to you as well. You're a material witness . . . you talked to Angy the day before she was killed. You realise that, don't you?'

'Yes, I suppose so,' said Lou in a dull voice. She stood with hunched shoulders, a pathetic picture of defeat and despair. 'But Rick didn't kill Angy, he swears he didn't and I believe him. Somebody else must have done it. I thought perhaps you . . . you know about crime and detection and that sort of thing . . . ' Her eyes were fixed on Melissa as if in quest of a miracle.

'Is that what you had in mind when you talked about my helping you? My dear girl, I'm a writer, not a private investigator. Besides . . . ' Melissa broke off, trying to think of a tactful way of stating the brutal, unpalatable truth. 'You may be convinced of Rick's innocence, but it's asking a lot of me.'

'I know he's innocent!' Despite her misgivings, the passionate sincerity in the girl's declaration of faith struck a chord. Hadn't she, Melissa, expressed just such a sentiment? But if Rick wasn't the killer, what did that imply for Barney?

'When he's angry, he acts the fool—you saw what he did to the portrait—but he wouldn't kill anyone. And he wasn't angry when he went to see Angy, he was happy. He thought everything was going to be all right . . . '

'Something might have happened between them to make him lose his temper.'

'It didn't! She was already dead when he got there!'

'So he says, but there's going to be a lot of circumstantial evidence against him.'

'It isn't fair! Someone else killed her and Rick's going to get the blame!'

'He was very foolish not to tell the police right away. There may still be time before they get to him . . . why don't you have another go at persuading him? Is there a phone at the studio? You can call from here if you like.'

'Thanks, but it wouldn't be any good. He wouldn't even answer the phone.'

Standing there in her denims and her cotton T-shirt, she

looked like a lost, lonely child. Melissa stood up and put an arm round the thin shoulders.

'Where are your parents, Lou? Why don't you go to them?'

'They're in the States,' Lou muttered. 'My Dad works there.'

'Really? So does my son.' There was no response but the rigid stance seemed to soften a fraction. 'He works for an oil company. Look at me, Lou.' Melissa took the girl by the shoulders. 'Do your parents know about this trouble you're in?'

Reluctantly, Lou met her eyes. 'No,' she whispered. 'They're on vacation in Hawaii at the moment. I haven't spoken to them for nearly two weeks.'

'Haven't you any other relatives?'

'Only my young brother. He's in Germany with the army.' Her voice wavered and her face crumpled. 'I know I said horrid things about Angy but she was my friend and I . . . ' A spasm of violent weeping threatened to tear the slight young body apart. Melissa took the girl in her arms and gently stroked her head until she became calmer.

'I keep thinking of her, lying there in all that blood,' Lou moaned between her sobs. 'Rick's so frightened! He didn't kill her but he'll go to prison just the same. What can we do? Please help us, Melissa . . . please!'

'Sit down again for a while.' Melissa pushed her gently into a chair. 'Listen, I've been thinking. You told me you had a bit of a chat with Angy before you asked her about the ring.'

'Yes.'

'I want you to try and remember everything the two of you said, right from the beginning. What time did you get there, by the way?'

'Soon after two o'clock. She finished at the college at one but she had some shopping to do.'

'And you said her reception was friendly?'

'Oh yes. She said, "Lulu, how lovely to see you!" and kissed me on both cheeks.'

'So what then?'

'She was making herself a sandwich in the kitchen and we went in there first while she ate it and made coffee for both of us.'

'Did you notice any knives lying about?'

Lou screwed up her eyes. 'Yes,' she said after a pause. 'Now you mention it, there was one of those wooden blocks with about six knives sticking out of it.'

'Where was it?'

'Next to the cooker, I think ... yes, it was. She had quite a few gadgets. She enjoyed cooking, especially Italian things.'

'And what did you talk about?'

It was plain that Lou's recollection of everything prior to Rick's discovery of the body had been blurred by shock but under Melissa's gentle probing, details began to emerge. Angy had asked most of the questions at first ... about Lou's job with a fashion magazine, former acquaintances at college, recent visits to Uncle Vittorio and Aunt Rosina. She had spoken affectionately of them and shown Lou a postcard from Italy where they were spending a holiday.

'Hm. Nothing very significant so far,' Melissa commented when Lou paused for further thought. 'Tell me about the ring. Is it an antique, by the way? You said it was an heirloom.'

'It's a garnet in a heavy gold setting ... a gorgeous, blood-red stone.' Lou looked down at her left hand with a wistful expression, as if picturing the jewel on her own finger.

'And you say she kept it in a drawer?'

'That's right, in a cabinet next to her bed. It was in a leather box with a crest on it.'

'And you asked her to give it to you so that you could return it to Rick. Was that before or after you'd had your chat?'

Lou scowled. 'After. I think she'd guessed what I'd really come about and was sort of savouring it, waiting to see how I'd approach the subject. She was so sure of herself, so self-satisfied!' Like a fire that has been damped down but not extinguished, anger smouldered in Lou's eyes.

'Now don't get worked up again. Did she talk about herself at all? Her job, her friends, people she worked with? What about boyfriends or lovers?'

'I got the impression that she had several on a string.' Lou frowned. 'Now, how did that come up?'

'Perhaps,' suggested Melissa in a flash of inspiration, 'she showed you sketches of them!'

'That's right. How did you know?'

'I've seen them. I told you, I tutor at the college.' It would be bad psychology to tell Lou that she had been shown them by the police.

'I remember now!' Suddenly, Lou came alive. 'I'd been asking why she'd taken a clerical job when she'd had an art training and she said it was all she could get at first but after a while she'd managed to wangle this daytime class.'

'Wangle? Is that the word she used?'

'Yes, I'm sure it was. Some man at the college had arranged it for her . . . she more or less admitted she'd worked on him.'

'What do you mean, worked on him?'

'She said, "I showed him a bit of leg and he came running." Then she said something like, "The poor sap's been a bit of a pain since. I'll have to do something about him but you know how I hate scenes." ' Lou's eyes flared in her pale, pointed face. 'Oh, Melissa! Do you suppose he's the one who killed her?'

Cold fingers clawed at Melissa's stomach. 'Let's not jump too far ahead,' she said in a voice that was not quite steady. 'Did you see a picture of this man?'

'I don't know . . . I might have. She had this portfolio of crayon portraits. She asked me what I thought of them. They looked good . . . she was very talented, you know.'

'Yes, I thought so too. Think about those portraits, Lou. Did you see them all? What did Angy say about them?'

Lou made a helpless little gesture. 'I can't remember.'

Melissa's mouth had dried out and a pulse was vibrating like a pneumatic drill somewhere near her navel. 'You can . . . you must!' she insisted. 'Concentrate! You're an artist; use your visual memory. Picture that portfolio lying on the table . . . '

Lou pressed her hands to her eyes. 'They were just heads . . . men and women. There was one who looked familiar. Of course!' She looked up and stared at Melissa in sudden recollection. 'It must have been you! I remember Angy saying, "She's one of the tutors at the college." '

'Go on,' said Melissa quietly. 'If you can remember that, you can remember the others if you try.'

'She was picking them up at random and saying things like, "This boy's in a wheelchair but that doesn't stop him giving me the eye," or, "This is the college stud but he cuts no ice with me." '

Doug Wilson, no doubt, thought Melissa, and young Godfrey Mellish who had been so firmly put in his place by Barney.

'There were two of women in her class. One she said was new this term and quite talented, and the other did "twee little flower paintings".'

Poor Sybil, how hurt she would be to hear that. Still, Iris had encouraged her.

'You're doing splendidly,' encouraged Melissa as Lou fell momentarily silent. 'What about the "poor sap who'd become a bit of a pest"? Did she point him out?'

'He could have been one of several.'

'Can you describe any of them?'

'There was one with a beard . . . ' Barney, of course, 'and a po-faced one with glasses . . . ' Despite her anxiety, Melissa's lips twitched at this description of Rodney Shergold, 'and one she called "Eddie". I had the feeling she rather liked him.'

'So the "poor sap" she was going to have to "do something about" could have been either Po-face or,' Melissa swallowed a hard lump swelling in her throat, 'the one with the beard.'

'I guess so.'

'Can you remember which one?'

'Sorry.'

'Please, try!'

'Honestly, I can't.'

Lou sat back in her chair and closed her eyes. She looked utterly spent; there was nothing to be gained by pressing her further.

With an effort, Melissa sifted mentally through all she had just heard. Was Rodney Shergold the 'poor sap'? Supposing he'd agreed to let Angy take the art class in return for her favours? If he'd become too demanding, and 'doing something about him' meant ending the relationship, that could well have been a motive for killing her. Dudley Ford had his suspicions and the police seemed to have been doing a pretty thorough job on him . . . but Doug Wilson believed that Shergold lacked the nerve and she was inclined to agree with him. 'So what about Barney, then?' a voice whispered in her head. Barney, enraged by Angy's taunts, had just as much motive and was a far stronger character . . .

She felt exhausted. Every nerve had been strained in the effort to prompt Lou's memory but what she had learned could do little to prove Barney's innocence. On the contrary, said the voice, it could do his case untold damage. But surely, she reasoned, once they catch Lawrence, the police will demolish his story . . . the story that he and Lou have cooked up together. Perhaps this was all a conspiracy between them . . . they were trying it out on her first. Rubbish, said the voice, you're getting as hysterical as Lou . . .

'The police will have those sketches,' she told Lou. 'You could find yourself going through all this again.'

Lou opened her eyes and sat up, looking bright and determined. 'I don't care what they ask me if it helps them find the real killer. It must have been one of those men Angy sketched . . . the one she was talking about packing up. I think it was the man with the beard.'

'You mustn't say that if you aren't sure!' said Melissa sharply.

'No, of course not. I'll think about it on the way home.'

'And you'll get in touch with the police and tell them what you've told me?'

'I . . . I'll have to speak to Rick . . .'

'You asked me for my advice, and that's it.' Melissa glanced at the clock. 'If you want to catch the four o'clock train, we'd better be leaving.'

FOURTEEN

WHEN MELISSA RETURNED FROM TAKING LOU to the station, Iris was working in her garden. She looked up and waved as the Golf drove past and when Melissa had put it away and locked the garage door, she rammed her fork into the ground and strolled over for a chat.

'Just had a load of muck delivered,' she announced with a complacent nod in the direction of a sinister-looking mound at the bottom of her vegetable patch. 'More than I need. Want some?'

'Yes please, if you can spare any,' said Melissa. It was a timely reminder that her own garden needed attention and in any case, mechanical tasks like digging and muck-spreading might have a therapeutic effect on her emotional system.

'Wanted sheep but got cow, and it was promised weeks ago,' Iris complained. 'Well-rotted, though. Should be okay.'

Melissa gave a wry smile. The provenance of a manure heap seemed of limited importance beside the problems presently exercising her mind.

Iris scrutinised her, eagle-eyed. 'You all right?' she asked. 'You look tuckered.'

'I am. I've just had a visit from Lou Stacey.'

'The girl you drove off with just now?' Melissa nodded. 'Thought she looked familiar. Quite presentable without the warpaint! What did she want with you?'

'You're not going to believe this!'

'Something to do with that crazy young boyfriend, I suppose.'

119

'She's convinced he's innocent of Angy's murder and she only wants me to play detective and find the real killer! According to her, Rick Lawrence is caught in a web of circumstantial evidence. While he languishes in gaol, the real murderer will go free unless I unmask him!'

'Could be right,' said Iris, her eyes still fixed on Melissa's face.

'You aren't serious! You think I should . . . ?'

'Of course not. Stay out of it. But if circumstantial evidence is all they've got . . .'

'You wait till you hear the whole story. Come in for a cup of tea?'

'Sure. Just go in and clean up.' Iris retreated behind her cottage, reappearing a short while later at Melissa's front door. She listened in silence to the story of Lou's visit, seated straight-backed and cross-legged on the floor.

'I feel desperately sorry for the poor kid,' said Melissa when she had finished. 'She's got no one of her own to turn to in this country, but the notion that I can help her to clear Rick is so fantastic it isn't true. She'll just have to face up to the fact that he's guilty, I'm afraid.'

'Think so?'

Melissa stared at her friend in dismay. 'You mean, you believe their story?'

'You want it to be him, don't you?'

Melissa shifted uncomfortably. 'I don't know what you mean.'

Scorn at the feeble prevarication glittered in Iris's eyes. 'Yes, you do. If Rick didn't do it, we come back to your lover-boy, don't we?'

'Iris, you're hateful! I know Barney didn't do it!'

'More likely him than Rick Lawrence.'

'How can you say that?'

'Be logical, like your detective character . . . Norman Thingummy.'

'Nathan Latimer,' Melissa corrected frostily.

Iris brushed aside the interruption with a wave of a hand. 'What was the motive?'

'Revenge, of course. She'd hurt his pride . . . brought about a rift with his family . . . '

'Forget the wounded pride. Soon consoled himself with his old flame, didn't he? And getting the ring back would solve the family problems.'

'Suppose Angy changed her mind about letting him have the ring?'

'Knew where she kept it. He'd just have taken it.'

Melissa shook her head. 'She'd have tried to stop him. She was quite a determined little thing under that gentle exterior.' Suddenly, it all seemed clear. 'Yes, that must have been it! He went to take the ring from the drawer . . . there was a struggle . . . he picked up a knife . . . '

'The knives were in the kitchen.'

'So he went and fetched one.'

Iris's grin was a mixture of pity and condescension. 'Be your age! Hefty young chap like that could have swatted her out of the way with one hand!'

Melissa had to admit that was true. 'But there could have been an argument about something else,' she pleaded, reluctant to abandon her theory altogether. 'Something that brought all the old resentment and tension and violent feelings back to the surface.'

Iris clasped her ankles and rocked gently to and fro, shaking her head. 'Don't believe it.'

'How can you be so certain?'

Iris shrugged. 'Just doesn't smell right. Not a nice type, not good enough for Lou . . . but not a murderer.'

'So what's your theory?' snapped Melissa in exasperation. 'No, don't bother telling me. I know you think Barney did it.' She got up and began slamming the tea-things on to a tray.

Iris stayed where she was, a troubled expression on her face. 'Never said that. Only that he was the more likely of the two. Could have been someone else. This chap Eddie, for example. She might have had other irons in the fire as well. Bit of a slut, if you ask me.'

'Don't let Barney hear you say that,' Melissa murmured

with a faint smile. She put down the tray and went back to her chair. 'It appears that Eddie has a cast-iron alibi. I did wonder about Rodney Shergold, though.'

'Shergold?' Iris screwed up her face in amusement and disbelief. 'You serious?'

'When we were waiting to be questioned by the police, Doug Wilson was saying that Rodney had been making a play for Angy and hinting that he might have got somewhere.'

'Wilson? The randy English teacher? Just trying to stir things for Shergold, more likely.'

Melissa grinned. 'Maybe. There's no love lost there. But it's possible, you know. Remember what Lou said. And I've told you before that I've noticed an atmosphere in the office now and again. Incidentally, I met Eleanor this morning and she's scared out of her wits that the fuzz suspect her beloved.'

Iris gave an unfeeling cackle. 'Serve him right if they do. Teach him a lesson. Sorry for Eleanor, though, poor little rabbit.'

'The way things look at the moment, Barney Willard and Rick Lawrence are rivals for the role of chief suspect. At the moment, the odds would seem to be on Rick but . . . ' Melissa gave a sigh. Iris, her common-sense unclouded by emotional involvement, had forced her to face reality. 'I'd give a lot to know what forensic evidence they've found.' A lock of hair had fallen across her face and she raked it back wearily with her fingers. 'It's so frustrating. I wish I could do something!'

'Like what?'

'Oh, I don't know. Maybe Lou's notion wasn't so crazy after all. I might turn up something the police have missed.'

'Something to clear Barney and nail the killer?' suggested Iris, looking alarmed. 'Forget it, Melissa. Your job is writing about crime. Leave the real thing to the professionals. Must be going now.' She rose gracefully to her feet and made for the front door, with Melissa following. 'Thanks for the tea.'

'You're welcome. Thanks for listening.'

'And stay out of trouble! Stick to writing and gardening.' The grey eyes were serious and the mouth and chin set in a stern line.

'You sound like Joe!' taunted Melissa.

'Now there,' said Iris with unusual gentleness, 'is a nice man. Much safer bet than an artist!' Her features relaxed into an impish grin. 'Oh, and by the way, you'll be telling your policeman friend about Lou's visit?'

Melissa sighed. 'I know I should, but I hate the idea. It seems like a betrayal of trust.'

'Don't be wet!' Iris snorted. 'You of all people. Suppose he finds out about it from some other source?'

'Like who?'

'Like Lou. They'll question her, you said so.'

'I suppose you're right,' said Melissa resignedly. 'If Ken Harris thought I'd withheld information . . . '

'Wouldn't make you flavour of the month, would it?' Iris gave her a pat on the shoulder. 'Do your duty. Get on that phone right away. Promise?'

'Oh, very well.'

Iris departed and Melissa went disconsolately to the telephone and called police headquarters. As she acknowledged the formal expression of thanks for the information she had given, she consoled herself with the near-certainty that they knew most of it already. She trailed wearily into the kitchen to clear away the tea-things, her thoughts turning to Barney. When the telephone rang and she heard his voice on the wire, her spirits soared.

'Oh Barney, I've been thinking about you so much!'

'That's nice. I've been thinking about you, too.'

'How are you?'

'Surviving. May I see you?'

'Yes, of course.'

'How about meeting for a meal this evening?'

'I'd love to.'

'Where would you like to go? Do you like American food?'

'Do I? It's wickedly fattening, but once in a while . . . '

'There's a new restaurant in Stowbridge called the May-flower. It's opposite the library.'

'I know it.'

'Meet me there at seven?'

'I'll look forward to it.' Melissa put down the phone and ran upstairs, singing.

When Melissa arrived at the Mayflower American restaurant, Barney was waiting near the entrance—a tall, distinguished figure in a well-fitting fawn suit with a paisley cravat tucked into the neck of his light red cotton shirt. He wore a sombre, brooding expression that relaxed into a half-smile as he caught sight of her, sending a surge of electricity round her nervous system. Careful now, she warned herself, this is not the time to get carried away . . .

'I hardly recognised you in that sharp gear!' she teased him.

'Would you rather I turned up in my paint-stained jeans and smelling of turpentine?' He smiled again, fleetingly, and her pulse gave another blip as he took her arm and led her through the entrance.

The place was fitted out in dark, polished wood in the style of the twenties. A huge ceiling fan turned slowly above an open area in the centre, which was laid out with bentwood chairs and marble-topped tables for the bar customers. The dining tables were tucked away in high-sided compartments like old-fashioned church pews. With the modern embellishment of piped music to smother conversation it was, Melissa reflected as they sat down, an ideal setting for meetings between lovers . . . or spies or plotters of stings or heists. For a moment, her crime writer's instinct took over and she made a mental note to jot down a description as soon as she got home.

A jolly young waiter with a Gloucestershire accent and the stars and stripes emblazoned on his apron lit the candle lamp on their table and gave them each a menu. When he had retired with their order and the drinks waiter had served them with lime daiquiris, Barney planted his elbows on the table and leaned towards Melissa.

'Haven't they arrested Lawrence yet?' he demanded. 'Why hasn't there been anything in the papers? No photograph, not even an artist's impression or a description. People won't know who to look out for.'

'The police won't name anyone publicly until they're sure it's the right person.'

'You've got friends in the local CID—can't you find out what's going on?' he pursued. His face was flushed and his eyes glittered.

'Ken Harris has promised to keep me up to date with the press briefings . . . ' she began.

'Press briefings!' He made a scornful gesture. 'I can read the papers for myself.'

'They don't necessarily print every detail they're given,' she said. 'As soon as I hear anything definite, I promise I'll let you know.' Already, she had decided against any mention of Lou's visit and Rick's claim to have found Angy's body. Things were too uncertain and it would be wrong to raise false hopes.

'You mentioned something last night about a ring,' he said.

'Surely you noticed the antique ring with the garnet that Angy used to wear?'

'Of course. It was a family heirloom and she was very fond of it. What did it have to do with Lawrence?'

'Everything. It was *his* family heirloom. He gave it to her as an engagement ring and when she took off, she never sent it back.'

'And that's why he killed her? To get back a miserable ring? If that's the sort he is, it's no wonder she was terrified of him!'

For a moment, he reminded Melissa of Lou in his haste to defend a loved one, but she had seen how his knuckles whitened on hearing the story and guessed what he must be thinking. Little by little, he was getting to know the true Angy.

She reached out to cover one of his hands with her own. It felt like ice. 'You're cold,' she said. 'You aren't ill, are you?'

He rolled his hand over so that hers rested in his palm. 'I haven't had much food today. I'll soon warm up in here.' He gave her fingers a brief squeeze, then released them and began drumming on the table.

'Do try to relax,' she urged.

'How can I, when the brute who killed Angy is still free?' He took a gulp from his drink and began fidgeting with the cutlery. 'The sooner they get him, the sooner she can be laid to rest.' There was a catch in his voice; he was on a knife edge and for a moment Melissa feared he would break down. 'Forgive me,' he said, pulling out a handkerchief and brushing it across his eyes and nose.

'It's all right, I understand.'

'Yes, I think you do.'

'I lost someone dear to me, very suddenly.'

'You did?'

'My son's father, in a road accident. I thought my world had come to an end.' She hesitated. Knowing Barney's standards of morality, she wondered if she was being wise, but it was best to be honest. 'I was two months pregnant and my parents said I'd brought shame on their house and they kicked me out.'

'That was inhuman!' Barney stopped short in the act of lifting a spoonful of clam chowder to his mouth. There was no disapproval in the exclamation, only a shocked concern for her. 'Whatever did you do?'

'I was lucky. Guy's parents looked after us—Simon and me.'

They finished their first course in silence. Barney appeared to be mulling over what he had just learned; several times he looked searchingly at Melissa across the table. The flame of the candle in its amber glass shade threw shadows that accentuated the dark rings under his eyes.

The waiter removed their empty plates and brought huge portions of southern-fried chicken. Melissa declined Barney's offer of wine and asked for mineral water.

'Living out in the sticks, I can't afford to lose my license.'

'How very sensible. I'll join you.'

By mutual consent, it seemed, they spoke for the rest of the meal of anything but the one topic that was on both their minds. It was Barney who returned to it first, dribbling cream into his coffee and watching it swirl into a spiral on the surface.

'How long do you think the trial will last?' he asked. When Melissa did not immediately answer, he made an impatient movement with one hand. 'You know about these things. You must have some idea.'

'It's impossible to say. Quite often, the police ask for a remand to give them time to make further enquiries, assemble their evidence and so on. And then it can be several weeks after committal before the trial takes place.' Melissa concentrated for a moment on the unnecessary task of stirring her unsweetened black coffee. 'Of course,' she continued, avoiding his eye, 'all this is on the assumption that he's going to be charged.'

'Whatever do you mean?'

She flinched at the outraged disbelief in Barney's expression and it took some courage to say what she had to say. It was only fair to forewarn him that Rick's arrest, let alone his trial and conviction, were by no means a foregone conclusion.

'I mean that without evidence, they can't bring a charge.'

'You mean, they'll let him go? He'll get away with it? That's monstrous!' He glared at Melissa as if holding her responsible for this potential miscarriage of justice.

'There may be evidence—I don't know. But if there isn't, if he can convince them he's innocent . . . '

'Innocent? Are you crazy?' He was becoming agitated and his voice was getting louder.

'Shsh! People will hear!' she warned.

'I tell you, he did it!' he said in a frantic whisper. 'He must have done it. His family declared vendetta or whatever they call it!'

'You have to admit, that does sound a bit far-fetched and melodramatic.'

'Italians *are* melodramatic!'

'Sometimes, yes, but I can't help wondering if it's likely

that a young man on the brink of a successful career and maybe planning marriage to another girl would . . . ' Melissa broke off. What she was doing was unbelievable. It was Iris, throwing doubts on Rick's guilt, who had cast her in the role of the devil's advocate. Once again, the thought that if not Rick, then possibly Barney was the killer, returned to torment her. The indirect reference to Lou had been a mistake; if he picked it up and she had to admit she knew more than she had told him, he'd never trust her again.

Even so, it was plain from the mixture of resentment and hostility on his face that her words had wounded him. 'You think I killed her, don't you?' he hissed, his voice barely audible.

'No, Barney, of course I don't!' She reached out to him but he drew his hand away and sat back, distancing himself from her. Across the table, his eyes reflected the candle flame; the twin images seemed to grow and generate a searing heat of their own.

'I find that hard to believe,' he said stiffly. His face had grown hard as flint, the skin taut and bloodless. He signalled to the waiter; during the brief ceremony of settling the bill, handing over a tip and saying yes thank you they'd had a lovely evening and enjoyed their meal, his avoidance of her eye was constant and deliberate.

'Where did you leave your car?' he asked as they stepped on to the pavement. His tone had the same finality as the sound of the door closing behind them.

'Just round the corner.'

'I'll walk you there.'

'There's no need.'

He gave a bitter laugh. 'Perhaps you don't feel safe with me in a side street!'

'Oh Barney, please! You're getting it all wrong. I never meant to imply . . . '

'Forget it. No one would blame you.'

They reached the spot where the Golf was parked. He put out a hand for her key, unlocked the driver's door and held it open while she settled into her seat.

'I'll see you around,' he said, dropping the key into her outstretched palm and slamming the door.

She wound down the window, trying to think of some way of putting things right. All she could think of was, 'Thank you for a lovely meal.'

'Sure,' he said and turned away.

Depression clamped itself round Melissa's head and shoulders and the meal she had enjoyed so much lay like a stone in her stomach as she drove home. She put away the car, quietly locked the garage door and stood for a few moments looking out over the valley. A steady breeze sent shreds of cloud tumbling across the face of the moon. She closed her eyes and inhaled through her mouth, tasting the freshness, letting it play round her head and soothe its ache like a splash of cool water.

She leaned on the fence, wrapped her coat more closely round her body and tried to assimilate something of the tranquillity of the night, but all she could think of was the hurt in Barney's eyes and the stiffness of his voice. She hated herself for doubting him. Iris might be right in implying that Rick was the innocent victim of circumstantial evidence coupled with his own cowardly refusal to go to the police . . . but Rick's innocence did not automatically confirm Barney's guilt.

She hurried indoors and went to the telephone. Trembling slightly, she dialled Barney's number. He answered immediately, as if he had been standing by the instrument.

'Barney, it's Melissa.'

'Yes?'

'I'm sorry if you got the wrong impression . . . '

'Was it the wrong impression?'

'Yes, it was. Barney, please listen. I'm not sure whether I believe Rick Lawrence killed Angy or not but I am sure that you didn't, truly I am.' A gush of tears took her by surprise, swamping the last few words.

'You mean that?' Instead of being wooden, his tone had become hostile. Melissa pressed blindly on.

'Of course I do. I was only trying to warn you that things aren't always cut and dried. We don't know everything.'

'What you're saying is, there could be more than one person who hated Angy enough to do that to her. You're making her sound like some kind of monster.'

And you're making a hash of this, Melissa. It's hard enough for him to accept Angy's shabby treatment of Rick, her lies about the ring and her deceit in letting him think she was carrying another man's child. Now you're suggesting that's only the tip of an iceberg.

'Is that what you're saying?' he persisted.

'Barney, it's a wretched, miserable business and I can only guess what it's doing to you. I haven't got any answers. All I can say is that whatever happens, I do believe in you.'

'Thank you, Melissa,' he said quietly and this time she knew she had reached him. 'That helps a lot.' There was a pause before he added, 'I'm sorry about the misunderstanding.'

'I'm sorry too.'

'I'll keep in touch.'

'Yes, please do. Goodnight, Barney.'

She put down the receiver and was on her way upstairs when the telephone rang. It was Lou—frantic, almost incoherent, reporting that Rick had vanished along with his passport, that the police had been to see her and had asked hundreds of questions. She was sorry . . . terribly sorry . . . but she'd had to tell about her visit to Melissa . . . she hoped it wouldn't mean trouble for her. The end of the message disintegrated into sobs which no amount of soothing words could stem.

Thank goodness for Iris, thought Melissa as she plodded wearily up to bed, for insisting that she cover herself by reporting Lou's visit. Presumably they'd now be watching the docks and airports. Ten to one, they'd have Rick Lawrence by the morning.

The next day was Sunday. There was nothing on the seven o'clock news; she listened again at eight and nine but still there was no mention of the hunt for Rick Lawrence. It was a relief when Iris called for her to go to church. All the regular attenders were there: the Yorkes, glossy as newly-painted furniture; the Fords, sending darting glances round the congregation to see if anyone was missing; the Shergolds, sitting in their usual place near the door in the pew where Melissa had come upon Eleanor the previous day, Rodney with his normal air of self-importance that might or might not be hiding an inner anxiety, his wife pale and twitchy as she pulled off her gloves to turn the pages of her hymnbook.

The one o'clock news included a brief statement that a man had been detained early that morning while attempting to board a cross-Channel ferry at Dover and was helping police with their enquiries into the murder of Angelica Caroli, found stabbed in her Gloucestershire home the previous Thursday.

On Monday evening it was reported that the man detained the day before had been released without charge. Detective Chief Inspector Kenneth Harris, in a radio interview, announced that another line of enquiry was being pursued. He appealed to any member of the public who had been in the neighbourhood of the deceased's home at the critical time to come forward.

A joyful Lou called Melissa to thank her for her kindness and to say that Rick was now reconciled with his parents. No, he hadn't actually said anything about getting engaged yet. The poor darling had been through a lot and couldn't be expected to . . . well, she was sure Melissa would understand how he must be feeling.

Melissa murmured some banal phrases of encouragement and put down the telephone with a feeling of desolation. For Lou, the future held almost certain disillusion; for Barney, the shadow of suspicion; for those who had loved Angy, the anguish of uncertainty. And meanwhile, a ruthless killer still lurked in the darkness.

FIFTEEN

MELISSA RANG BARNEY'S NUMBER BUT THERE was no reply. He should be home by now; there was no evening class on Monday. She tried again an hour later with the same result. After some hesitation she called Ken Harris's home and was told by his wife that he had not yet returned. Her imagination went wild; she pictured Barney seated in a hard chair in a dingy police interview room while the detective probed and bullied and cajoled, plucking away at the outer layers of his mind, stripping it down to its sensitive core, implacable in his search for signs of weakness or guilt. He would use whatever insight into Angy's true nature that he had gleaned from Rick and Lou to undermine the pure, unsullied image that Barney was dedicated to preserving. She spent the evening trying to work, with limited success.

At ten o'clock, Harris rang back. 'Sorry I was out when you called,' he said affably. 'What can I do for you?'

'I've been trying to contact Barney Willard.' That was foolish, she thought, laying yourself wide open.

She detected some irony in Harris's voice as he replied, 'We haven't arrested him, if that's what you're worried about.' There were sounds of swallowing and the rattle of a cup in a saucer. 'I did pop round for a chat with him earlier this evening and I thought he seemed a bit jumpy. Perhaps he's gone to the pub to steady his nerves.'

'So he's still under suspicion?' Melissa's heart descended into her stomach and lay there, throbbing like a muffled drum at a funeral.

132

'He's one of several people who may be able to help us with our enquiries.'

'Oh please, Ken, spare me the jargon. Why did you let Rick Lawrence go? He had a long-standing grudge against Angy . . . surely he's the obvious . . . '

'Sometimes,' Harris said blandly, 'things are almost too obvious.'

Immediately, she grasped his implication and was outraged. 'Are you suggesting that Barney made up his mind to kill Angy and cold-bloodedly chose a method that would throw suspicion on someone else? He wouldn't do a thing like that! It's monstrous!'

'I'm not suggesting anything. We're simply proceeding with our investigations.'

'Oh please, Ken, what have you got on Barney?'

'You know very well that I can't give you that sort of information,' said Harris, his gravelly voice unusually gentle. 'But here's something I'd like you to think about. Of all the ways to commit a murder, isn't it a strange coincidence that Angy was stabbed in the throat, just like she was in the portrait?'

'Not if the same man carried out both attacks.'

'You heard the reports. We've eliminated Lawrence from our enquiries.'

Melissa felt as if she was falling through layer after layer of despair. 'I won't believe Barney killed Angy!' she declared.

'Now look here, Melissa!' A note of impatience, anger almost, had entered Harris's voice. 'I want you to promise me you won't see Willard alone again until this case is cleared up. Do you hear me?' he went on as she remained silent.

'If you're so sure he killed Angy, why don't you arrest him?' She hadn't meant to shout, and the rage and frustration in her own voice shocked her.

'At the moment, there's insufficient evidence to arrest anyone,' said Harris quietly, 'and if I thought you were keen on any of the other men in this case, I'd be saying the same thing about them.'

Damn you, Kenneth Harris, thought Melissa, for making me doubt Barney all over again. Aloud, she said miserably, 'All right, I promise.'

'Good girl. I'll keep in touch.'

'Thanks, Ken. Goodnight.'

She put down the receiver and stood for a moment with her hand resting on it, her head bowed and her thoughts in turmoil. Then, feeling utterly defeated, she went mechanically through the routine of locking up the cottage for the night and plodded upstairs. In the bathroom, her woebegone face stared at her from the mirror. She scowled in disgust at the sight of her drooping mouth and reddened eyes.

'You look a fright!' she said aloud. 'You've been making a fool of yourself, dripping around like some lovesick teenager. Ken's right. Iris was right. You're old enough to have known better.'

She cleaned off her smudged make-up, filled the bath and had a long soak. Tomorrow she really must settle down to serious work on her novel; time was slipping past, her deadline was approaching and if she didn't get on with it she'd have Joe making agitated phone calls and coming down to visit. She didn't want to see Joe or anyone else; she wanted to close her mind to the outside world and crawl back into the safe, controllable environment of her imagination. As she lay down in bed and put out her light, she forced herself to recall the latest chapter, completed a few days before, and fell asleep mulling over the next.

When she awoke next morning it was raining. That should please the farmers—and Iris; for a couple of weeks or more it had been dry and unusually mild and the land was thirsty. She stood at the open kitchen window with her early cup of tea clasped in both hands, listening to the swish of the falling water and watching it gather in tiny globules on the tips of the leaves of the apple tree like crystal drops on a chandelier before sliding with a slow, regular inevitability on to the grass. The air was cool and pure; she felt an urge to be out in the rain, to smell and taste it, let its cleansing freshness wash over her. She dressed quickly, put on rubber boots and a waterproof, and set off along the footpath leading to Benbury Woods.

Half a mile or so along the valley bottom, the path converged with another which led down the hill from the village. Someone was approaching, clad like Melissa herself in waterproof and wellingtons. A small brown dog scurried out of the undergrowth, pulled up at the sight of another human, then rushed towards her. It was Snappy, a squirming bundle of wet fur and muddy paws, greeting her with excited yaps while his mistress uttered a torrent of ineffectual commands and reproaches.

'It's all right, I'm only wearing old clothes,' said Melissa reassuringly as the dog hurled itself at her legs. 'You're out early, Eleanor. I thought I was the only one mad enough to go walking in this weather.'

Eleanor smiled and pushed a sodden lock of hair under her hood, which was pulled close to her face by a drawstring. 'Yes, dreadful isn't it,' she agreed. 'Still, the farmers need it, Rodney says, and the garden . . . '

Compared with the near-despair that she had shown during their recent encounter in the church, her manner was almost jaunty. Perhaps she'd heard on the college grapevine that Barney had been getting an undue amount of visits from the police and was rejoicing that the heat was off her beloved Rodney. Well, that was natural; only a short time ago, when Rick Lawrence was the quarry, Melissa had felt exactly the same.

'I take it you and Rodney are feeling better?' she commented as they strolled side by side.

Eleanor's eyes sparkled. They were pure jade, like a shallow sea on a clear day, the eyes of a water-nymph set in a pale, pudgy face above a dumpy body encased in rubberised nylon.

'Oh yes, much better, thank you. Things are still very difficult for Rodney, of course.' Eleanor seemed anxious not to lose sympathy. 'It's not nice, is it, having one of your staff suspected of murder. And then, not having a secretary, you know, he even has to do his own typing! It's too bad, really. He tries to do a couple of hours' work on his book before going to the college. I get up to cook his breakfast and there's no point in going back to bed . . . ' She ended on a slightly peevish note.

Melissa did not reply. Her sympathy had evaporated; she felt sickened by the self-centred attitude of the Shergolds. A girl had been murdered and their sole concern seemed to be its effect on their own convenience.

'Of course, everyone kept saying how beautiful she was but she couldn't really have been a very *nice* girl,' Eleanor went on, her small mouth a prissy rosette of distaste. 'All those men coming to her flat . . . '

'*All* those men?'

'Well, there was that young man they arrested and then let go, and Mr Willard, of course, and who knows how many others? Girls like that simply ask for trouble, don't you agree? Rodney says . . . ' She broke off to pick her way round a patch of mud. 'I do so hate getting my feet dirty, even when I'm wearing wellies, *khikhikhi*!'

'Has Rodney solved the murder yet?' asked Melissa, making little effort to keep the sarcasm from her voice. It was, however, completely lost on Eleanor.

'Oh, he's sure it was Mr Willard who killed Angy, and I agree with him.' Of course you do, you haven't got an independent thought in your head, reflected Melissa crossly as Eleanor prattled on. 'Such a strange-looking man, I've always thought . . . *khikhikhi* . . . my father always told me not to trust men with beards. Silly isn't it?'

'Very silly.' With an effort, Melissa twisted her mouth into something she hoped was a smile. 'I think I'll have to be going back now. Hearing about Rodney's book has reminded me that I've got to get down to work on mine.'

'How is it coming on? Have there been any more murders lately?' Eleanor turned her head to peer at Melissa, her doughy face alight with a morbid curiosity. 'I expect you're finding this real-life mystery quite useful for a plot, aren't you?'

'Not particularly.' Melissa was shocked at the lack of sensitivity and promptly made up her mind to use Eleanor as the model for a future victim. In her present mood, it would relieve her feelings to devise a sticky end for her. 'So long for now, Eleanor.' She turned and headed for home. Snappy bounded after her for a few yards, then scampered away to follow his mistress.

Melissa glanced back for a moment and watched her plodding stolidly on her way. In her shapeless garments, she had the silhouette of a Russian 'Babushka' doll, the type that held a number of smaller dolls within its hollow wooden shell. Irritation melted into pity. However many prettily-painted Eleanors might lurk inside that dumpy frame, the combined influence of an overbearing father and a domineering husband would ensure that they remained securely locked away.

Back indoors, she brewed coffee and ate a hasty breakfast before settling down to work. She unplugged the telephone and disconnected the doorbell, resolutely shutting herself off from the world as she manipulated her characters like pieces in a board game, reading their thoughts, putting speech into their mouths, controlling their destinies. Playing God with them, no less, someone had once said to her. The hours passed and she worked on, taking hurried meal breaks and firmly rejecting all thoughts of listening to the radio or reading the newspaper.

At five o'clock she got up from her desk. She was stiff and tense in every muscle but she had done her first good day's work since the discovery of the murder. She spent the evening rereading the day's output and went to bed moderately satisfied. The plot was working and the characters had played their parts as she intended. She fell asleep with her mind determinedly focused on plans for the next chapter.

The following day was Wednesday and Gloria, the extrovert young matron who 'did' for both Melissa and Iris, arrived to do her weekly stint of housework. She came bustling into the kitchen, exuding good humour and exotic perfume as she took off her jacket and put on her overall. 'You've had your hair done differently,' Melissa remarked. Gloria's huge brown eyes sparkled as she twisted her head this way and that to give a better view of the elaborate blond topknot from which floated multi-tinted spiral streamers.

'D'you like it? My Stanley says it makes me look like a film star!'

'Very becoming,' agreed Melissa. 'It really suits you.'

'Ooh, thanks. Any special jobs this morning or just the usual?'

'Just the usual, please. I'll be in the study if you want me.'

'See you presently then!'

'Dreadful business about the murder, innit?' Gloria remarked as they shared their coffee break in the kitchen.

Melissa suppressed a sigh. She had hoped to dodge the subject but might have known that Gloria's boundless interest in all things morbid and sensational would make it impossible. 'Yes, dreadful,' she agreed. 'I suppose you've been reading all about it in the papers?'

Excitement sent the topknot quivering. 'We got inside information!'

'Really?'

'You know my Stanley's showroom?'

Melissa nodded, concealing a smile as she pictured the ramshackle building where Gloria's husband operated his used-car business.

'Well,' continued Gloria between swallows of coffee, 'the lady what polishes the cars for him has got a sister what does cleaning at Stowbridge Tech.' She paused to crunch a ginger biscuit.

'Oh, yes?'

'Laura—that's Jean's sister, see—was talking about the murder with the other cleaners during their tea break.'

'I can imagine,' murmured Melissa. The entire college must have been humming with gossip and speculation.

'Some of them reckoned one of the teachers—some arty chap with a beard—might have done it, but Laura don't think so.'

So far, Melissa had been only half listening. Now, she gave the conversation her full attention. 'She doesn't?'

Gloria shook her head, sending the streamers aswirl. 'She reckons it were that chap she worked for, the one what lives

in one of the new houses here in Upper Benbury.' Gloria
was from Lower Benbury herself, commuting to her various
jobs in a red Ford Escort supplied from her Stanley's stock
of 'genuine, low-mileage, used cars'.

'You don't mean Doctor Shergold?'

' 'sright.'

'Whatever makes her think that?'

'Laura's a bit of a nosey parker,' Gloria continued,
draining her mug and drawing the back of her hand across
her mouth. 'She were doing his room one evening and she
noticed he'd left his cupboard open. She had a peek inside,
and what do you think she found?'

Gloria paused for dramatic effect and Melissa shook
her head.

'I've no idea!'

Gloria leaned forward and dropped her voice to a hoarse
stage whisper. 'A jacket!' she announced. 'Reeking of
fancy perfume! Laura reckons,' she continued, a salacious
gleam in her toffee-brown eyes, 'old Po-face—that's what
they all calls him cos he never smiles—had been having
it off with that sekertary for weeks. She reckons he's a
two-coat man.'

'Has she told the police about it?' asked Melissa, wondering if 'two-coat' could be local dialect for 'two-faced'
and thinking that it might well be a suitable epithet for
Rodney Shergold.

'Not she. Avoids the coppers like the plague since they
done her Jimmy for joy-riding in a borrowed car.' Plainly,
Gloria well understood this point of view. 'Anyway,' she
added with a shrug, 'the jacket might not be there now. It
were weeks ago Laura found it.'

Melissa played thoughtfully with her empty coffee mug
and reflected on what now seemed the certainty that Rodney
Shergold had been having an affair with Angy. Still, the
idea that they could have had the kind of torrid relationship
that leads to murder was another matter. From what she
knew of him, the man simply didn't have the character, or
the guts.

From what she knew of him. That didn't amount to much

and most of it was second-hand, picked up from his wife's artless prattle and staff-room gossip. Maybe, as Gloria had hinted, there was another side to his nature, carefully hidden from the outside world, a side that was capable of strong passion and sudden violence. There were plenty of people around who were not what they seemed. Crime writers would be lost without them.

Gloria's round face was pink with excitement. She loved a bit of gossip and this morsel must seem particularly juicy. She should not be encouraged to share it with too many people.

'I do hope,' said Melissa, trying not to sound censorious, 'you won't go spreading this around the village. There's probably nothing in it and it would be dreadful to cast suspicion on an innocent person.'

'Ooh, don't worry, I won't say nothing to no one else round here,' promised Gloria. 'Only you, cos you're into this sort of thing with your books.' Admiration shone in her luminous eyes. 'I'll bet you could find some clues the coppers have missed.'

'I think that's most unlikely,' said Melissa, wishing it could be true. It would be good to make Ken Harris admit that for once he had suspected the wrong man.

Gloria's expression became pensive. 'I do hope it wasn't that arty chap. Laura told her sister he's a real nice gentleman, not like old Po-face, he's a real pain in the backside she says . . . '

'You really shouldn't speak of Doctor Shergold like that,' said Melissa firmly. 'I think it's time we got back to work, don't you?'

Obediently, Gloria slid her ample bottom from her stool. 'Ooh my, is that the time!'

After Gloria had gone home, Melissa ate a sandwich before driving into Cheltenham to do some shopping. She was back at her car, stowing her purchases, when someone called her name. It was Sybil Bliss, laden with bulging plastic carrier bags.

'Oh Melissa, what a piece of luck! I was going to ring you. Have you got a minute?'

'Of course.' Melissa glanced at her watch. 'Why don't we go and have a cup of tea?'

'Super idea! I'll just dump this lot in the car.'

They found a café a short distance from the car park.

'Shall I pour?' said Melissa when the waitress brought their tea.

'Oh no, let me!' responded Sybil eagerly. Her movements as she set the inverted cups upright on their saucers and manipulated milk jug, teapot and hot water jug were precise and just a little fussy. 'There we are! Do you take sugar?'

'No, thank you.'

'Have a scone? They're simply *smothered* in butter, and there's jam and cream too. I'm afraid your friend Miss Ash wouldn't approve!' Iris had given Sybil a severe lecture on the dangers of eating animal products of any kind.

'Never mind, she'll never know, will she?' said Melissa. They chuckled and helped themselves, exchanging guilty glances like naughty schoolgirls.

'Have you done anything more with your flower pictures?' Melissa asked.

Sybil's smile faded. 'Not yet. As a matter of fact, I was going to have a chat with Angy, you see, at this week's art class, but of course . . . ' She bit her lip and played with her teaspoon. 'It's terrible, isn't it? Such a lovely girl! Whoever would want to kill her?'

'I'm afraid the police suspect Mr Willard,' said Melissa.

'Oh no, I *can't* believe that!' Melissa looked up in surprise at the earnest ring in Sybil's voice. 'I know he had a rather possessive attitude towards her—I told you about that time he came into her class, didn't I?—but from the way he looked at her, you'd have thought she was the most perfect and precious thing on earth to him. I can't think he'd ever hurt her.'

'Not even if he found out she was less than perfect?'

Sybil shook her head, sending her wings of hair swinging across her chin. With two forefingers she tucked them behind her ears.

'I wouldn't have thought so. It'd be rather like having a

lovely picture that you thought was a genuine old master and then being told it was a fake. You'd be very disappointed, even angry, but it would still be beautiful. You wouldn't destroy it, surely?'

'Some people might.' Neither Harris nor Iris, Melissa reflected, had expressed any such view. 'I suppose it's a matter of temperament.'

'Well, I'm sure the police will find out they're making a mistake.' Sybil appeared entirely confident in her assessment of Barney's character and Melissa felt warmer towards her by the minute. 'Maybe she was carrying on with someone they don't know about. There's that chap Eddie, her landlord.'

'I'd thought of that . . . in fact, she once mentioned Eddie to me. Said he didn't charge her much rent for her flat. I remember at the time wondering why. What do you know about him?'

'Nothing really, except that last week Angy showed us a sketch she'd done of him. It was with some others. She was good at heads—she'd done several of us, from memory. There was one of Mr Willard, and the head of department, I can't remember his name . . . '

'Doctor Shergold?'

'Yes, that's right. Now I come to think of it, there was one of you.'

'Yes, I know, I've seen the drawings,' interrupted Melissa. She ignored the question in Sybil's face; she could tell her about Harris's visit some other time. 'Did she make any comment about this man Eddie?'

Sybil frowned, absent-mindedly twirling a strand of hair round her fingers.

'So far as I remember, she just said something like, "That's Eddie who owns the house where I live." The police will have interviewed him, surely.'

'Yes, I suppose so.' Yes, of course they had. Harris had mentioned that the owner of the house was a social worker. He'd been away at the time of the murder but if, as seemed likely, he'd been having an affair with Angy . . . suppose he was married and his wife had found out, and taken the opportunity while her husband was absent to do away with her rival?

'I mustn't keep rattling on like this!' Sybil's voice, apologetic and embarrassed, interrupted the wild onrush of Melissa's thoughts. 'I'm quite forgetting what I wanted to ask you.'

'Yes, you said you were going to phone me.' With an effort, Melissa hauled her mind back from its helter-skelter ride.

'Yes. It was just that I and the others in the class—at least, the ones who turned up yesterday, a lot of people didn't bother—anyway, we felt it would be nice to send some flowers and a card or something to her relatives. We could all sign it . . . '

'What a nice thought! I'm sure they'd appreciate it. They live in London but I can get their address for you.'

'That would be so kind. There's one other thing. As I said, not everyone was there yesterday and I don't know how to contact the others. Is there any way I can get hold of their addresses?'

Melissa was touched by the look of gentle compassion in Sybil's eyes and thought what a thoroughly nice person she was, despite the odd bout of histrionics.

'No problem,' she assured her. 'I'll get them from the register tomorrow. Will you be at the workshop?'

'Oh yes, of course. I do so look forward to it.'

'That's good.' Melissa glanced at her watch. 'I'd better be going. I like to get home before the rush hour.'

'Me too.' They paid their bill and strolled back to the car park. As they reached it, a white Ford Fiesta heading for the exit drew up alongside them, waiting for a gap in the traffic. Eleanor Shergold was at the wheel with Snappy in the back. Melissa waved and Eleanor wound down the window.

'Hullo, Melissa,' she said. The bright April sun was full in her eyes and she shaded them with one hand. Recognising his friend, Snappy jumped up at the window and barked.

'Hullo, Eleanor!' Melissa glanced over her shoulder and gestured to Sybil, standing behind her. 'Can you spare a moment? I'd like you to meet a friend of mine.'

'Down, Snappy!' said Eleanor ineffectively. She peered beneath her hand at Sybil, then jumped as an impatient hoot sounded behind them. She glanced in her mirror and fumbled with her gear lever. 'Some other time!' she said hastily, looking thoroughly flustered. She edged the Fiesta forward, found the road clear and let the clutch in with a jerk. The following car, a Volvo with a fat, red-faced man at the wheel, shot out on her tail.

'Well, really! The manners of some people!' commented Sybil as they made their way to their cars. 'I'd have made him wait!'

'That was Doctor Shergold's wife,' explained Melissa.

'You mean the head of our department at college? Isn't she the one you tried to persuade to come to our art class?'

'That's the one.'

'She seems a very nervous lady.'

Melissa shrugged. 'She's been so conditioned by her husband that she instinctively kowtows to any man who says "boo" to her.'

'I didn't realise he was that sort. Of course, I've only set eyes on him a couple of times.'

'Eleanor told me her late father was Principal of Brigston. Rodney was a lecturer there and they cherished hopes of a chair for him but unfortunately Daddy died before he could wangle it. Reading between the lines, I suspect that Rodney has never quite forgiven either of them.'

'You mean, he married her just to further his career?'

'Well, it wasn't for her looks, was it?' said Melissa with a grin. 'No, that was catty of me. She's not a bad sort but there are times when I could shake her.'

'How absolutely dreadful to be so downtrodden.' With her key in her hand, Sybil stood by her car, her mobile features working overtime to register shock and disapproval. 'Poor woman!'

'Oh, she seems happy enough, living in his shadow,' said Melissa. 'She's got him on a pedestal.' She moved towards her own car, parked a few yards away. 'See you tomorrow!'

SIXTEEN

ON THURSDAY AFTERNOON, MELISSA ARRIVED at the college to find Barney alone in the staff room. She greeted him warmly but he responded with a perfunctory nod and immediately got up to leave.

'What's the hurry?' she asked. 'It's only half-past one and you haven't finished your coffee.'

'Got some things to set up. I'll take it with me.' Avoiding her eye, he scooped up his portfolio, briefcase and half-empty mug and went out. Ken Harris again, thought Melissa angrily. He was so sure that Barney was his man, even though the evidence against him wasn't strong enough to arrest him, that he'd had the cheek to warn him off. Once he had his teeth into something he was like a bull terrier; you'd have to wrench his jaws apart to make him drop it . . . or produce some equally strong evidence to blow his case to bits. 'Well, so I will,' Melissa informed the empty room through gritted teeth. 'You just wait, you mutton-headed copper!'

She found her own register in its usual place and then took from the 'Tuesday' pigeonhole the one marked 'Line Drawing and Water-colour'. As she opened it, a faint breath of perfume escaped. Angy had moved in an aura of musk and here it was, clinging to the papers she had handled so many times. Was this the perfume that an inquisitive cleaner had detected on Rodney Shergold's jacket?

At the back of the folder was a neatly typed list of names and addresses which she photocopied before going downstairs to Rodney Shergold's office. He was on his feet, gathering up books from his desk. He glanced up as she entered, gave a curt nod and began hunting through some papers with jerky, impatient movements.

'I wish they'd hurry up and find me another girl,' he muttered irritably. 'It's most inconvenient having no one to keep things in order.'

'I'm sure it must be.'

If he noticed the heavy slice of sarcasm that Melissa laid on the words, he paid no heed. He picked up his jacket from the back of his chair and dragged it over his shoulders. 'I'm lecturing in the main building this afternoon. Was there something you wanted?'

'I was wondering if you could give me Angy's address?' she said casually. She could, of course, have obtained it from the Bursar's secretary but was interested to see if the question brought any reaction. She was not disappointed; if a firebell had gone off within a yard of his car, he could not have appeared more shaken.

'Wh . . . what makes you think I would know that?' His sallow face turned a dull pink and his voice, never particularly strong or resonant, became a querulous squeak.

Melissa received his alarmed stare with an innocent smile and a careful blend of honey and vinegar in her voice as she replied, 'I thought, as she worked for you, you'd be bound to have a note of it . . . but never mind, I can always ask Mrs Ellis. Oh, excuse me, Doctor Shergold.' She raised a finger and he gave a nervous start. 'Did you realise you have a smudge of chalk on your lapel?'

'Huh? Oh, er, thank you.' He brushed blindly at the front of his jacket.

'No, the other one!'

But Rodney Shergold, normally so dapper and careful of his person, was not interested in chalk smudges; his one desire was to escape from further conversation with Melissa. With a sulphurous glance at her, he grabbed his books and papers and rushed out.

'Well,' Melissa murmured aloud as she listened to his footsteps pattering through the hall, followed by the slam of the outer door, 'there goes a man with a guilty secret. Now, I wonder . . . ' She glanced round the room and her eye fell on the desk where Angy used to sit. It had been cleared of papers; the typewriter was covered and the chair pushed firmly into place. The police would have been through every drawer with a toothcomb in their search for clues; there was nothing to be gained there. But the cupboard in the corner, behind Rodney Shergold's desk, was for his personal use. Perhaps the police hadn't searched in there; if not, they could have missed a vital clue after all. Melissa dumped her register and handbag on a chair, marched round the desk and tried the cupboard door. It was locked.

'Bother!' she muttered. She glanced at her watch; in ten minutes her class was due to start. She tried the door again, then pulled open the top drawer in Shergold's desk. It was only two or three inches deep, more like a tray divided into sections containing a neat arrangement of pins, paperclips and other small office requisites. In one of the compartments lay a key. A little hesitantly and with an ear cocked for approaching footsteps, she picked it up and tried it in the cupboard lock. It fitted and the door swung open.

It was a narrow wooden cupboard with a shelf at the top and a rail below. The shelf and the floor were piled with books, boxes and folders stuffed with papers. She picked up a dusty-looking volume at random and flipped through the pages. It contained reprints of some papers presented to a local antiquarian society—probably research material for the book on neolithic burial mounds. She dropped it back on the pile.

Hanging from the rail was an empty coat-hanger. Remembering what Gloria had said, Melissa took it down and sniffed it, hoping to detect some tell-tale trace of scent, but there was nothing. Well, it had been a forlorn hope at best. Disconsolately, she relocked the cupboard, replaced the key and went slowly upstairs to her classroom.

It was inevitable that the previous week's tragedy should colour the contributions to the writers' workshop. With few exceptions, they were meditations on death, bereavement and the uncertainty of the human condition. Sybil had composed a poem about dead flowers, each quatrain ending with the line 'And the spent petals fall, one by one, to the ground', which she read aloud to a receptive audience, a note of melancholy in her voice and a trace of moisture dimming her eyes.

By four o'clock Melissa's spirits were at rock bottom. Normally, she thoroughly enjoyed her Thursday afternoons; today, she was thankful when the session was over and the aspiring authors trooped out, clutching their masterpieces and chanting their thanks.

Only Sybil Bliss lingered behind. 'You look tired,' she said. 'Would you care to come round to my house for a cup of tea? I only live a couple of streets away.'

Melissa accepted without hesitation. She felt jaded and in need of emotional uplift. Iris had an American cousin staying with her and had been too busy dragging him round every art gallery and stately home in the country to have time for her. In any case, she had recently shown a disconcerting facility for mind-reading. The last thing Melissa wanted at the moment was for Iris to find out that she was planning to probe into the circumstances of Angy's death. Sybil would be a far more sympathetic companion.

'I do feel a bit drained,' she admitted. 'By the way, I've got that list of addresses you wanted.' She took out the photocopy and handed it over. 'The last one's a bit indistinct. I think it must have been added later by someone using a dud typewriter ribbon.'

Sybil scrutinised the list. 'That's Delia Forbes. She only joined the class at the beginning of this term.'

'I'll check it in the Bursar's office. I have to go over to hand in my register now there's no one here to take charge of it.' A pathetic little shade hovered for a moment at her elbow, reminding her of her other errand. 'And I want to get Angy's address. I know she lived in Tranmere Gardens but I'm not sure of the number.'

'It's number twenty-two. Now, how do I know that?' Sybil's brow wrinkled. 'I've never been there myself. Oh yes, I remember! I overheard her telling Delia.' Her eyes rounded with curiosity. 'Were you planning to go round there?'

'I thought I might have a word with Eddie Brady.' Melissa heaved a sigh. 'I'm not sure what good it can do but I've been thinking over what you said about Barney Willard. I don't think he killed Angy either. Perhaps there's something the police have missed.'

Sybil's face glowed. 'Are you going to do some detective work? Could I help, do you think? I'm a great fan of your Nathan Latimer!'

'Why not? Two heads are better than one.'

'How *super*! Shall we talk about it over that cup of tea?'

'Yes, let's. I'll just drop this register in to Mrs Ellis and double check that address. See you outside the main gate.'

Ten minutes of easy walking brought them to Sybil's house. It stood on a corner, at the end of a terrace of four which had, Sybil explained as she put her key in the front door, replaced a large Victorian dwelling. The sitting-room was on the first floor, above the garage, with a picture window overlooking a small park. The place was comfortably and tastefully furnished, with some good ornaments and pictures and several vases of fresh flowers.

'Do make yourself at home,' said Sybil hospitably and bustled off into the kitchen. When she returned with a tea-tray, Melissa was on her feet admiring a portrait of a handsome, grey-haired man that hung above the stone fireplace.

'My late husband,' said Sybil. She stood for a moment beside Melissa, looking up at the portrait. 'We'd only been married five years when he died. We had to wait a long time because I had my mother to look after and she was rather difficult.'

'I'm so sorry.'

'He had cancer. We took up painting after we found out. It was something quiet that we could do together.' Sybil's expression, which had become momentarily sad, softened into a tender smile that was wholly natural. 'He'd always been keen to try but never seemed to have the time. He wasn't very good at it, but we both enjoyed it very much,' she added wistfully. 'I've kept on going to classes ever since.'

'And you are very talented,' said Melissa.

'It's kind of you to say so. Do sit down.' Sybil placed a small table at her elbow and poured tea into dainty china cups. 'No sugar . . . that's right, isn't it?'

'Mmm.' Melissa sipped gratefully. 'Just what I needed. I thought today's class would never end!'

'It was rather depressing, wasn't it? But I suppose it was only natural that people should feel affected by what happened.'

'I checked Delia Forbes' address, by the way. Mrs Ellis looked out her enrolment form for me. Her writing wasn't all that easy to read but I think it's correct.' Melissa handed over a slip of paper. 'Talking of addresses, you mentioned that Angy gave hers to Delia.'

'That's right.'

'Have you any idea why? Was Delia going to visit her?'

'She might have been. She was very taken with those drawings we were talking about. Maybe Angy had offered to show her some more of her work, or lend her a book or something.'

'What's Delia like?'

Sybil thought for a moment. 'About my age, I suppose. Dark curly hair . . . glasses . . . ' Her pointed face rounded into a smile. 'I'm not much of a detective, am I? I'm usually too absorbed in my work to spend much time looking at the other students.'

Melissa's brain was nibbling away at an idea. 'Can you remember when it was that Angy gave Delia her address?'

'Oh, quite recently. Let me think . . . yes, it was the last time we had a class.'

'Then it must have been the day Angy was murdered! This could be very important, Sybil. Suppose Delia had become friendly with Angy and gone to her flat that afternoon. She'd have been one of the last people to see her alive.'

Sybil's eyes grew round. 'My goodness, so she would! The last I saw of Angy was a few minutes after the class ended. I'd popped into the library to get a book renewed and when I left the college building I saw her walking along the road on her own.'

'Delia might have followed later. Did you tell the police?'

'About Angy giving Delia her address? I don't think so. No, I'm sure I didn't. It'd gone right out of my mind until just now. A policeman came to call on me that Thursday evening, after Angy's body had been found, asking what time the class ended and where I went afterwards . . . that sort of thing. Oh, and he asked if I'd ever seen Angy having any kind of disagreement with anyone and I had to tell him about that little contretemps with Mr Willard and young Godfrey Mellish.' She sighed heavily. 'Poor Mr Willard, I don't suppose that helped him very much.'

'I don't suppose you were the only one who mentioned it,' sighed Melissa. 'And the police will have spoken to Delia herself by now, so we can't expect to find anything new there.'

'Never mind!' said Sybil briskly. 'When do you propose calling on Eddie Brady?'

'Why not now, if you've got time? It's not far, is it?'

Sybil was already on her feet, her eyes shining. 'Just round the corner from the college. Isn't this *exciting!*'

Number twenty-two Tranmere Gardens was a double-fronted house in the Regency style which bore all the familiar signs of having seen better days: peeling stucco, blistered paint and sagging gutters. Behind a low wall, a ragged hedge squatted like a moulting hen over a clutch of empty drink cans and discarded crisp bags; a couple of unkempt evergreen trees, grown to roof height, screened the house from the road and severely restricted the amount of light reaching the dingy windows.

Sybil and Melissa mounted what had once been an imposing flight of steps flanked by tall white pillars and peered at the labels alongside the row of bell-pushes in a corroding brass frame affixed to the wall beside the front door. One was blank, two were roughly printed with unfamiliar names and the top one read 'Caroli' in artistic capitals.

'Not much help, is it?' said Sybil, frowning.

'Hang on, I've just remembered,' said Melissa. 'He lives in the basement flat.'

As they descended the steps, a battered car turned into the drive and pulled up in a corner of the small courtyard. The driver, a slight figure in a tweed jacket and grey flannel trousers, got out and looked across at the two women before turning to rummage behind the front seat and extract a bulky briefcase and an armful of files. The glance was sufficient for identification.

'That's him!' said Melissa. 'Excuse me,' she called, 'aren't you Mr Brady?'

A pair of deep-set, greyish-brown eyes stared from beneath a high forehead and strongly-marked brows. Their expression was guarded and none too friendly, and the response to Melissa's question was a jerk of the head that plainly said, 'What if I am?'

'We recognise you from your portrait,' said Melissa. There was no softening in the defensive manner.

'The one Angy Caroli did of you,' added Sybil.

'You knew Angy?' It seemed to Melissa that the expression had become a shade less hostile. The voice had a curious quality, husky and high-pitched as if uncertain whether it was a light tenor or a throaty mezzo-soprano. The face, too, was intriguing, its strong lines accentuated by severely cropped hair and a skin smooth and ruddy as an apple.

'We knew her from college,' Sybil was explaining. 'I was a student in her art class—I'm Sybil Bliss—and this is Melissa Craig who teaches creative writing.'

'Eddie Brady.' A slim hand shook each of theirs in a powerful grip. 'Angy's spoken about you both. Come to think of it, she did your heads as well, didn't she?' They nodded, relieved that the ice was broken. 'What can I do for you?'

'I don't know if you've heard, but it rather seems that the police suspect one of the lecturers at the college of killing her,' said Melissa.

Eddie Brady looked from one to the other and said, 'I think I know the one you mean.'

'We both know the gentleman concerned and we're not very happy about the way things are going so we're making a few enquiries of our own.'

'Mrs Craig's a crime writer. She knows a lot about detection and things!' explained Sybil, evidently thinking this would impress.

Melissa smiled and shook her head. 'Oh, I'm no Sherlock Holmes! It's just that Mr Willard is a friend . . . and the police do make mistakes sometimes. We understand you knew Angy quite well and we thought you might be willing to help us.'

An extraordinary change came over Eddie Brady's face. Grief welled into the deep-set eyes and the reply, when it came, was unsteady and uttered through tightened lips. 'I've told the fuzz all I know.'

'Please. It won't take long.'

'Oh, all right. You'd better come in.'

The sitting-room of the semi-basement flat was overfull of shabby furniture and littered with books and papers. Eddie Brady dumped the briefcase on the floor with the heap of folders on top, took off the tweed jacket and threw it into a corner, and dragged two chairs from under the cluttered table.

'Have a seat. How about some tea?'

Melissa sensed rather than saw Sybil's nervous hesitation as they sat down. 'Actually, we've just had tea, thank you,' she said.

'Oh, well, mind if I do?'

'Not at all.'

'Shan't be a tick.'

'Well!' murmured Melissa as the door closed. 'That's something I hadn't thought of.' The haircut would have won the approval of an army officer and similar clothes could be seen in the windows of men's outfitters in any high street, but the body inside them was unmistakably female.

'Oh, dear!' whispered Sybil in some alarm. 'I've heard about such people, of course . . . '

'Shh!' murmured Melissa, smothering a grin. Plainly, Sybil was about to have her horizons widened. After a few minutes, the door reopened and Eddie returned with a mug of tea, drew up a third chair and sat down. 'Mm, that's better!' she said after a few mouthfuls. She found a stained beer-mat and put down the mug, which bore the legend, 'When God made man, she was only joking' in spiky black letters. 'Right, now!' She sat leaning forward in her chair, her hands planted on her thighs so that her elbows jutted outwards. 'How can I help you, ladies?' Outwardly, she had recovered her composure but her eyes were watchful as well as sad.

Conscious of Sybil at her side, tense as a patient in a dentist's waiting-room, Melissa took the plunge.

'How well did you know Angy?' she asked.

Eddie scowled. 'If you've come here to pry . . . '

'Please.' Melissa put out a hand. 'I don't mean to offend. We want to find out who killed her. Surely, you want that too, if you were fond of her?'

'Fond?' Eddie made a harsh sound that could have been intended as a laugh but sounded more like a cry of pain. She grabbed her mug of tea, gripping it in both hands and staring down into it with an expression of such misery that one could almost imagine the dead girl's face reflected in the surface of the liquid.

'I'm sorry, I didn't mean to distress you,' said Melissa softly.

Eddie put down the mug and pulled a man-sized handkerchief from her trouser pocket. Angrily, she dashed away the tears that had gathered in her eyes. It was several moments before she regained her self-control.

'I fell in love with her the minute I saw her,' she said at last.

'When was that?'

'Last summer. She came here looking for somewhere to live. She'd seen the card I put up in a local shop, advertising the top flat. She was like a waif . . . alone, anxious, scared.'

'What was she scared of?'

'A man, of course!' Eddie's lip curled. 'He'd beaten her, bullied her into an engagement she didn't want. I took her in, looked after her, helped her get settled. Then these other creatures started pestering her.'

'Creatures?'

'Men from the college. She used to tell me about them. There was that bearded artist, Poppa Barney she called him. He was constantly interfering in her life, lecturing her, ordering her about. I tried to get her to give him the elbow but she would always say, "but Eddie, he means well and he's so kind". Kind!' Another mirthless bark. 'He slapped her around as well, did you know that?'

'I know he hit her once, just before she was killed. He never had a chance to speak to her again and he'll never forgive himself. Did she tell you what the quarrel was about?'

'She did!' A faint, sardonic smile softened the harsh lines of Eddie's face. 'We had a good laugh about it once she'd got over the shock. "At least," I said to her, "he won't bother you any more, now he thinks you're having my sprog. Now all you've got to do is get rid of your Wednesday afternoon creep and start planning your own life." '

'Who was the Wednesday afternoon creep?'

'Her boss—Shergold, his name is. She wheedled him into letting her take the art class . . . for a consideration, of course.' Eddie mimed an attack of nausea. 'It was that Barney who put the idea of teaching into her head. Ironic, isn't it?'

'And Shergold came to see her regularly?'

'Like I said, every Wednesday afternoon. I don't know how she put up with it but she felt obligated. She was like that.' Eddie gave a fond, sad smile. 'Soft as a mop. "He's so repressed, Eddie," she told me after the first time. "I felt so sorry for him." Sorry! I'd have kicked his balls in!'

Sybil made a faint tutting noise and shuddered, as if she had just discovered an unpleasant insect on one of her flowers. Melissa frowned, shook her head and put a finger to her lips but Eddie appeared not to have noticed.

'Did you ever meet either of these men?' Melissa asked.

'I never met Barney but I caught sight of the other one once, scuttling across the yard like a nervous rabbit. Looked a right little prat!' Eddie's lip curled. 'He used to sneak out of college wearing a spare jacket so's no one'd know he was missing. Rush round here every Wednesday afternoon, have it off with Angy and rush back. She hated it, I know she did.' Every word was coated with a gritty layer of disgust. 'She just couldn't bring herself to tell him to sod off.'

So that, thought Melissa in a flash of enlightenment, was what Gloria had meant when she called Shergold a two-coat man. That coat-hanger had once held the spare jacket—but where was it now?

'Yes, that fits in with everything I've heard about her,' she told Eddie. After a pause, she said, 'And you were hoping that one day she'd give up seeing men altogether and have a steady relationship with you?'

'So what's wrong with that?' Eddie glared and clenched her fists. 'She was halfway there already . . . and I'd have looked after her.'

Impulsively, Melissa leaned across and put a hand on the bowed shoulder. 'Yes, I'm sure you would,' she said gently.

The gesture of sympathy was almost too much for Eddie. Her features buckled and she put a hand over her eyes. 'I was sure she'd come to love me in the end, if I could just be patient,' she whispered.

Sybil was increasingly and audibly restless and Melissa was becoming irritated; she had no business to make her disapproval so obvious. It might be better to leave before there was open unpleasantness but she was reluctant to go now. She had the feeling that if she could get Eddie to go on talking long enough, there was a chance that something significant would emerge. It was, she knew, wholly irrational; her common-sense kept reminding her that Eddie must already have been closely questioned by the police.

There was, however, one point that might not have been raised. 'Did Angy ever mention a woman called Delia Forbes?' she asked.

Eddie put down her empty mug with a thump and glared. 'Who's Delia Forbes?' she demanded.

'One of her students,' said Melissa. 'We think Angy may have invited her round to her flat last Tuesday. Mrs Bliss overheard her giving her this address.'

'I don't believe it! She's never been involved with another woman!' Eddie's jaw set and her hands gripped the edge of the table. Her breathing had become agitated.

Sybil at last found her voice. 'You needn't worry,' she said prissily. 'Delia Forbes is a decent married woman, not one of your sort!'

'And what the hell's that supposed to mean?'

Sybil flinched at the aggression in Eddie's manner but she held her ground. 'I mean, she wouldn't be capable of . . . ' her mouth became a tight bunch of disgust, 'your . . . unnatural practices.'

'You sanctimonious cow!' Eddie was on her feet, leaning across the table with one hand raised. Her face was scarlet. 'Think you're so bloody superior just because you happen to be straight!'

Sybil leapt from her chair, sending it toppling sideways on to the floor. 'Don't you dare touch me!' she hissed. 'Are you coming Melissa? I'm not staying here another minute!'

'You're dead right!' Eddie marched to the door and yanked it open. 'There's the way out . . . piss off!'

Looking as if there was a dead cat in her path and leaving as much space as possible between herself and Eddie, Sybil marched out of the room. Drawing aside her skirts, thought Melissa sadly. She just can't cope with this sort of thing.

Eddie stood holding the door-knob, her face twisted in a ferocious glare. 'What are you waiting for?' she snarled at Melissa.

'Please, let me stay another minute or two,' said Melissa quietly. Outside, they heard Sybil's shoes clattering up the stone steps. 'She's really a very kind person but she's led a completely sheltered life and . . . '

'Don't bloody patronise me!' Eddie's stance was still aggressive but her grip on the door-knob slackened.

'I'm not patronising you. Your relationships are nothing to do with me. All I'm after . . . '

Eddie swallowed and gnawed her lips, blinking ferociously. 'We've got as much right to love as anyone.'

'Of course you have; we all have. Barney Willard loved Angy too but we both know it wasn't her body he was after and I can't believe he would ever have hurt her. I want to help him and the only way I can do that is try and find out who really killed her. You were in love with her . . . won't you help?'

'Don't see what I can do.' Eddie gave the door a shove and returned to her chair. She spun it round and straddled the seat, laid her forearms along the back and sank her head on them. 'Any one of them could have done it, couldn't they?' she mumbled, her face hidden. 'And in the end, what difference does it make? She's dead, that's all I can think of.'

'If they charge the wrong man, it'll make a difference to him!' said Melissa drily.

Eddie raised her head. 'So what's your theory?'

'I haven't got one, but I have a hunch that Delia Forbes may be involved in some way. Not in that way!' she added hastily as Eddie jerked her head up like a watchdog at the sound of an intruder. 'She joined the art class at the beginning of this term and I believe Angy was quite impressed with her talent.'

'Ah, that one!' Comprehension and relief softened the hard set of Eddie's features. 'Now I know who you mean. Angy never mentioned the name, or if she did, it didn't register.'

'You met her?'

'No, but I saw a sketch of her.'

'Ah yes, Angy's portrait sketches.'

'She'd been working on them for quite a while. They were all done from memory and she was quite pleased with them. It was only the other day that she showed them to me. She kept them all in a portfolio; the fuzz took it away.'

'Yes, I know, I've seen it. I remember the one of you. It was very good—they all were, as far as I could tell. There was one of a young man in her class that I'd never met but . . . wait a minute!' Melissa sat bolt upright. Signals were flashing in her brain.

'What's up?' demanded Eddie. 'Have you thought of something?'

'Please, let me think!' Melissa closed her eyes and gnawed her thumb as she struggled to nail down the clue that fluttered moth-like in her memory. 'Those sketches . . . can you remember how many there were and who they were of?'

Eddie cocked her head on one side and pursed her lips. 'I think so. I went through them a second time with the copper who came round here.' She straightened up and began ticking off on her fingers. 'There was me, there was you and your holier-than-thou friend.' Her mouth contorted in a sneer. 'Then there was the beardo-weirdo,' Melissa winced at this pejorative reference to Barney, 'and the Wednesday creep. That's five. There were eight altogether. Angy counted them as she was putting them away.' Eddie wrinkled her brow. 'There was that randy English teacher . . . '

'Doug Wilson! I'd totally forgotten him! Did Angy ever talk about him?'

'Now and again. Earthy type, she used to say, but it was all talk with him and he never gave her any trouble that she told me about.' Eddie shook her head and added wistfully, 'I think she would have told me.'

'She never went out with him?'

'Don't think so. She said he asked her once or twice but she turned him down and he soon got the message.'

'That's six. What about the other two?'

'The disabled lad in her class. She took a lot of pains with him. It was because she felt so sorry for him but your Barney didn't like it . . . huh! And the last one was of that Delia woman . . . but now I come to think of it, it wasn't there when the police brought them round.'

'Are you sure?' asked Melissa. The signals were flashing furiously; was this the breakthrough she was after?

Eddie nodded, frowning. 'I never noticed at the time. I must have been too upset.'

'I saw those sketches too, after Angy was killed. All the ones you've mentioned were there except the one of Delia Forbes.'

'So?'

'Angy took her portfolio of sketches to show the students at her art class on Tuesday afternoon, the day she was murdered. I know the one of Delia was there then because Sybil saw it. Sybil also heard Angy giving Delia her address so it's reasonable to assume that she was expecting a visit from her some time. Let's suppose Delia did come here that afternoon. Maybe Angy gave her the sketch of herself as a present?'

'She wouldn't do that!' shouted Eddie, pounding the back of her chair with her fists. 'She'd never part with any of her stuff . . . she wouldn't even let me have the one of me!' This time, grief was too much for her. Tears rolled unchecked down her face and her shoulders shook. 'I might get hold of it when the Bill have done with it,' she gasped between sobs. 'It'd be something to remember her by.'

'I daresay her aunt and uncle would let you have it,' said Melissa, aware that this might be unlikely but feeling impelled to give some comfort to a fellow human being in so much distress.

Eddie lifted her head. Her face was blotchy and her eyes swollen. 'You think it's important, the portrait of Delia being missing?'

'I'm not sure. Maybe it was there after all and we both missed it. It was there on Tuesday, it was there on Monday when Lou Stacey came to see Angy . . . '

At the mention of Lou's name, Eddie's face darkened. 'Angy never told me she was coming here. I got to hear about it from the police.'

'But you knew about her relationship with Lou and Rick?'

'Rick? You mean that brute she ran away from? Yes, of course I did.' Eddie's knuckles whitened as she gripped the back of her chair. 'Angy and I had supper together on the Monday evening but she never said that girl had been here, or that Rick was coming to see her.' Once more, the strong features threatened to disintegrate but she held them bravely in place. 'I could have arranged to be there when he called . . . none of this would have happened if I'd been there to take care of her.' She gave the back of her chair a despairing slap, got up and began pacing to and fro, jerkily shaking clasped hands. 'Why the hell didn't she tell me?'

'It was obviously something she wanted to handle on her own,' Melissa said gently. 'In any case, weren't you going to be away on a course or something?'

Eddie swung round and glared. 'What do you know about that?'

'Only that you couldn't help the police very much because you'd been away for a couple of days,' said Melissa.

'The course was in Bristol and I went there straight from my office during the afternoon,' said Eddie and there was a kind of hasty defiance in her tone. 'I could have arranged to set off later if I'd known. She should never have had to face him by herself.'

'You're forgetting one thing,' Melissa pointed out. 'Rick claims that Angy was already dead when he got there and he's obviously managed to convince the police that his story is true. DCI Harris says he's been eliminated from the case.'

'Ken Harris? You know him?'

'Yes. Do you?'

Eddie shrugged. 'Our paths cross from time to time, when we have a client in common. He's okay as coppers go.' She picked up her empty mug and got to her feet, her self-control apparently restored. 'Sure I can't get you any tea? I'm going for a refill.'

'No thanks.' Melissa stood up. 'I don't suppose you'd let me see Angy's flat?' she asked.

Eddie hesitated. 'It's probably a bit of a shambles. I got the woman who comes in to clean the hall and stairs to go up and wash off the floors but I haven't been up there myself since the fuzz left. Couldn't bring myself to.'

'I'll go up on my own if you'd rather not.'

'If you think it'll do any good.' Eddie rummaged in a china bowl of oddments on the mantelpiece and handed

Melissa a bright new key. 'I had the lock changed after . . .
it happened. The old one was worn and didn't always shut
properly. I'd been meaning to do it for days and I keep
asking myself whether it was my fault her killer got in.'

'Don't blame yourself. It's pretty certain it was someone
she knew and she'd have let him—or her—in anyway.'

It was the first time that the possibility of the murderer's
being a woman had occurred to Melissa and the realisation
came as a shock. Eddie was staring at her with eyes as hard
as granite but all she said was, 'You'll have to go in at the
front door. It's right at the top.'

'Thanks. I'll only be a minute or two.'

The interior of the house was very much like the outside.
The woodwork, once painted white but now faded to a
dingy cream with a grey deposit in the crevices, was
chipped and scuffed and the pattern of leaves and flowers on
the stair carpet had long since been reduced to a brownish
blur. Doors with tarnished locks and dog-eared name cards
attached with drawing-pins indicated the entrances to the
individual flats.

At the top of the final flight of stairs was a single door.
Like the key which Eddie had given to Melissa, the lock
was new and there were marks where the paint had been
disturbed. Would it have made any difference, Melissa
wondered as she turned the key, if that lock had been
changed earlier? Probably not, but the possibility would
haunt Eddie for a long while.

Melissa felt a faint sensation of queasiness as she pushed
open the door. It led into a tiny vestibule with doors on all
three sides. The one on the left was half open, revealing a
narrow kitchen, little more than a passage with a sink and
draining board under a window at the far end, a cooker,
refrigerator, a small table and a wooden chair on one side
and on the other a laminated work-surface with cupboards
and drawers below and a run of shelves above. All the
fittings were shabby and well used, probably obtained
through the 'small ads' column in the local paper. There
was a row of bright enamel saucepans, an Italian coffee
pot and two or three painted ceramic jars on the shelves;

Melissa bent down to peek into a cupboard and saw an array of packets and tinned foods and several types of pasta in glass jars. In another cupboard were two or three bottles of Italian wine.

The police who had occupied the flat while they made their searches had left plenty of traces of their stay. Mugs containing the congealed remains of tea and coffee stood in the sink, on the draining-board was an ashtray filled with cigarette butts and the smell of stale tobacco smoke hung in the air. The place had a seedy atmosphere totally out of keeping with Angy's flower-like freshness.

Ken Harris had said she was stabbed in this room. What had she been doing when the killer struck? She had been expecting a visit from Rick Lawrence; if Lou's predictions were correct she would have changed from her working clothes into something more alluring and put on fresh make-up and perfume to receive him. Melissa wondered if the police had taken this into account and what Angy had been wearing when her body was found. It might be insignificant. She pulled a notebook from her handbag and wrote 'query clothes' on a fresh page.

In their search for fingerprints, the detectives had been liberal in their use of grey aluminium powder and little or no attempt had been made to remove it. The cleaner had evidently taken her instructions literally and limited her activities to washing the blood off the floor, which was covered in a hideous, embossed vinyl. Melissa stared at it and then glanced again round the little kitchen, trying to picture Angy's last moments.

On the work-surface, several well-defined areas clear of the ubiquitous dust showed where items had been removed for further examination. One was large and rectangular; Melissa guessed that it was here that Angy had kept the wooden block of kitchen knives that Lou had mentioned. Iris had a similar block in her kitchen; once Melissa remembered being asked to hand her one of the knives. She recalled how she had steadied the block with one hand while pulling at the handle with the other, and how smoothly the blade had slid from its slot. Was this what the murderer had done, leaving fingerprints which were by now enlarged and recorded and locked away at the police station, waiting to be produced at the trial? Whose trial would it be? Someone who had called on Angy, found her groomed and perfumed and ready to receive a rival, and been moved to uncontrollable violence by the belief that she had been unfaithful? With a shudder, Melissa returned to the hall.

The door facing the entrance turned out to be a bath-room. The fittings here also looked as if they had been in service for a long time—probably salvaged from a demo-lition site. There were traces of police activity here as well—more grey dust mingled with Angy's musky talc. Sadly, Melissa closed the door—like the floors, washed clean of Angy's blood—and went into the bed-sitting-room.

It was a largish room under the roof, with a dormer window let into the sloping ceiling and a second window which, like the kitchen, overlooked the garden of the house next door. The furniture was sparse: a circular table and two chairs; a plain bookshelf crammed with books about art and artists. Under the window was an easel and a stool and beside it a battered chest of drawers. The bed was at the far end and next to it was a small cabinet on which stood a lamp and a telephone . . . the telephone through which the dying, terrified Angy had tried to summon help. The floor was bare as if a carpet had been removed, no doubt for forensic examination. In a kind of bemused horror, Melissa imagined the ugly pattern of stains that must have formed as the lifeblood flowed remorseless-ly away.

On the window-sill, wearing like everything else its grey veil of powder, a white china vase held the remains of half a dozen tulips. Denuded heads on pale green drooping stems hung like mourners at a graveside over the ring of faded scarlet petals that lay on the painted wood. The recurring line of Sybil's poem came back to Melissa's mind, the poem about dead flowers that she had written in memory of a beautiful girl, savagely cut down. Without realising it, she spoke the words aloud: 'And the spent petals lie, where they fall, on the ground.'

'That's very moving,' said a voice at her elbow. Melissa spun round, almost petrified with shock, to see Eddie standing behind her.

'You frightened the daylights out of me!' she gasped. 'I never heard you come in.'

'Sorry.' Eddie took a couple of steps forward, her eyes fixed on the dead flowers. 'I bought her those the day before she died, so's she'd think of me while I was away.' She gathered the faded petals together with cupped hands, lifted a couple between her fingers and then let them fall. 'Who wrote the poetry?' she asked gruffly.

'Oh, er, one of my students.' It would have been tactless to reveal that Sybil was the author.

Eddie nodded abstractedly. 'I had to come sooner or later and I thought it'd be easier with someone else here.' She stared about her, grimacing. 'What a pigsty they made of it! You should have seen the way Angy kept it . . . like a new pin. I used to tease her about being so house-proud and she'd tell me how her Aunt Rosina brought her up to do everything just so.'

Teaching her all the domestic arts, Melissa reflected, in the hope that she'd one day end up a housewife and mother in the true Italian tradition. Eddie would have to be pretty discreet about her relationship with Angy if she wanted to persuade Aunt Rosina to hand over that sketch as a keepsake.

Eddie's gaze ran on round the room, taking in, as if seeing them for the first time, the stool and easel, the framed reproduction Leonardo drawings on the walls, the low divan bed. The Florentine lace cover was rumpled and she walked over and bent down to straighten it. 'I can see the copper on night duty made himself comfortable,' she muttered resentfully.

'I'd better be going,' said Melissa. She felt awkward at intruding on private grief. 'Here's the key. Thank you so much for letting me in and everything.'

'Don't suppose it's been much help.'

'You never know.'

A glint of sardonic humour appeared unexpectedly in Eddie's eyes. 'Tell your friend I'm sorry I offended her sensibilities!'

Melissa grinned back at her. 'Thanks. I will!'

SEVENTEEN

SYBIL'S EXPRESSION WHEN SHE OPENED THE door in response to Melissa's ring was a blend of dignity and embarrassment. 'So you managed to escape unscathed!' she commented as she led the way up to her sitting-room.

Behind her back, Melissa smiled at this shot at appearing worldly-wise. It struck her as comical, so soon after the expressions of revulsion and outrage on coming face to face for the first time with sexual deviance.

'It occurred to me,' Sybil continued as she waved Melissa to a chair, 'that . . . that person might have had a motive for killing Angy.' She herself sat on the couch and settled her skirts primly around her legs in what struck Melissa, in a flash of impish humour, as a symbolic gesture of respectability and self-protection.

'You mean Eddie?' she responded in surprise. 'Whatever gave you that idea?'

'We have to consider all possibilities, don't we?' Sybil gave a knowing smile as if to imply that in the interests of justice she was prepared to face up to this bizarre, extremely unpleasant but undeniable phenomenon. 'I'm quite sure she's capable of violence, and with her unfortunate ah . . . ' Sybil groped for a word and after some hesitation came up with, 'tendencies . . . yes with her ah peculiar tendencies, it would be a sort of *crime passionnel,* wouldn't it?'

Melissa shook her head. 'I'm not saying Eddie's incapable of violence but in this case I think you're on the wrong track. According to Ken Harris, she has a cast-iron

167

alibi. She was in her office all Tuesday afternoon and went straight off for a couple of days on some residential course.'

'People do sometimes manage to leave their offices without anyone noticing.' Sybil was not going to abandon her theory without a fight and, thinking of Rodney Shergold and his spare jacket, Melissa could not dismiss the idea out of hand.

'Supposing she slipped out during the afternoon, perhaps to go home for something she'd forgotten?' Sybil continued eagerly. 'She might have gone up to see Angy and found Delia Forbes there . . . '

'Playing sex games with Angy on the bed? You're not serious!'

Sybil's jaw dropped. 'Really, Melissa, that's quite disgusting! I'm surprised at you!' It hadn't taken much to disturb the woman-of-the-world pose.

'I can't believe that finding Angy having a cup of tea with a middle-aged housewife would have incited Eddie to commit murder,' said Melissa flatly. 'Anyway, the police will have checked everyone's movements very carefully and if Eddie had left her office during Tuesday afternoon I'm sure they'd know about it.'

'So really, we haven't achieved anything by going to visit that per . . . to visit Eddie?'

'One interesting fact emerged after you'd gone.' Melissa told Sybil about the missing sketch. 'So far as we know, the police aren't aware of its existence. In spite of what Eddie said, it's possible that Angy gave it to Delia but if Eddie's right, then it looks very much as if Delia—or someone else—took it. But why? And how did she manage to do it without Angy knowing? Eddie said she was very meticulous about counting the sketches as she put them away.'

'Let's ask her?' suggested Sybil. 'I've looked up her number.'

'Could do.'

Sybil picked up the telephone and dabbed at the buttons with a well-scrubbed finger. 'Funny,' she said after a moment, 'I'm getting the unobtainable tone.'

'Try again.'

Sybil tried again, with the same result. 'The line must be out of order. Never mind, I'm going into Cheltenham tomorrow to the library. I'll call round and see her . . . it's only just round the corner. If she's out, I'll leave a note.'

'Fine.' Melissa stood up and moved towards the door. 'I think I'll be going now. I'm going to have a word with Chief Inspector Harris this evening.'

Sybil's eyes sparkled. 'You will keep me posted, won't you? This is really quite exciting!' Her face grew sad again. 'You know, I do so hope Angy wasn't really like that. I hate to think of her and that . . . and that Eddie . . . '

'I'm beginning to think that under the charming exterior, our Angy was quite amoral,' said Melissa thoughtfully. 'If Eddie was going to offer her security, she might have gone along with it.'

'But it's horrible!' Sybil wrinkled her nose as if she had suddenly detected a smell from the drains. 'If that's what was going to happen, then the girl's better off dead!'

'You can't mean that!' exclaimed Melissa, appalled.

'Oh yes, I do!' Sybil's features set in a blank mask of prejudice.

There was no point in arguing. Melissa descended the stairs to the front door with Sybil following. 'I'll give you a call if I learn anything interesting from Ken Harris.'

'Oh yes, please do!'

When Melissa got back to the college it was after half-past five and the car park was almost empty. The rush-hour would be at its height, with long tail-backs at the busiest junctions; she resigned herself to a tedious journey home. Approaching a set of traffic lights where she normally went straight on, and where the queue ahead seemed to stretch into infinity, she realised that only a few cars were waiting to turn left into the Cheltenham road. On an impulse, she joined them.

It was six o'clock when she reached the outskirts of the town and the traffic had dwindled to a trickle. She found a parking space near the Queen's Hotel and strolled across Imperial Gardens where a few tourists were admiring the spring flowers and chestnut blossom in the Promenade. Ten minutes of easy walking brought her to the cul-de-sac where Delia Forbes lived.

It was almost like turning the clock back a couple of centuries. The tiny Regency houses had no doubt been listed to spare them the attentions of developers; from the state of the paving stones and the grass-studded cracks in the roadway, it seemed that the town council too had passed them by. Yet the houses themselves were trim and well maintained, with bright varnish, window-boxes, polished doorknockers and newly-painted railings. There were a couple of trees on the pavement and between them one or two cars were parked. A blue Mini arrived and began manoeuvring into the limited space remaining as Melissa picked her way along the uneven path and knocked on the door of number three.

Almost immediately, the ground-floor window of the house next door flew up and the head of an elderly woman popped out between the curtains like a character in a Punch and Judy show. Beneath a halo of white hair, her face had the texture of a withered apple.

'She's away!' the apparition announced.

'Oh dear!' Melissa was nonplussed. 'Have you any idea when she'll be back?'

'Eh?' A shrivelled hand made a cupping gesture. 'You'll have to speak up!'

Melissa approached the railings which separated the house from the path. 'When . . . will . . . she . . . be . . . back?' she shouted.

'Went this morning. Back in a day or two!' the old woman croaked. Her face lit up and she waved to someone behind Melissa. 'Evening Miss Matthews!'

'Evening Mrs Rogers!'

Melissa swung round. A young woman who had evidently just got out of the Mini was approaching. She walked briskly, carrying a manila file in one hand and a bunch of keys in the other. She was smiling at the old woman in the window;

she nodded to Melissa as she climbed the two or three stone steps leading to the house.

Mrs Rogers leaned out. 'Thought you were never coming!' she grumbled. 'Been expecting you since Thursday!'

'Today *is* Thursday!' Miss Matthews gave Melissa a sidelong glance as she inserted a key in the lock of Mrs Rogers' front door.

'Excuse me, do you live here?' asked Melissa.

Miss Matthews shook her head. 'I'm a social worker,' she explained. 'I call round and see her once a week to make sure she's got everything she needs. She manages pretty well on the whole but she's a bit vague. I'll be glad when the neighbour gets back from Australia.' She jerked her head towards number three.

'Australia?' echoed Melissa in bewilderment.

Miss Matthews nodded. 'Visiting her daughter. Mrs Rogers misses her dreadfully. She's awfully good about popping in to see her. The poor old lady loves a bit of company and her legs are bad so she can't get out much.'

'I don't understand,' said Melissa. 'Mrs Rogers said Mrs Forbes went away this morning and . . . '

'Oh, don't take any notice of that!' said Miss Matthews with a grin. 'She's been saying that since last November . . . I suppose it's wishful thinking.'

'Last November! There must be some mistake! I'm talking about Mrs Forbes at number three.'

Miss Matthews nodded. 'That's right. Nice woman.'

'Are you going to stand there gossiping all day?' demanded Mrs Rogers peevishly. 'It's me you're here to see!' She treated Melissa to a baleful glare.

'Just coming.' Miss Matthews opened the door and stepped inside. 'You could put a note through her letterbox if you want to contact her,' she suggested. 'I believe someone comes in to pick up the post from time to time.'

'You don't happen to know . . . ' began Melissa but the door had already closed. Simultaneously the window slammed shut and there was nothing but a quivering of curtains where Mrs Rogers' face had been.

Melissa walked back to her car, trying to make sense of this new development. Obviously, the Delia Forbes who had been attending Angy's art classes and whom she suspected of having taken one of the sketches, was not the Mrs Forbes who inhabited number three Regency Terrace. Yet the address was correct; maybe there was a relative—a sister-in-law or another daughter perhaps—living there . . . but in that case the phone should still be working and there would be no need to arrange for someone else to come in to pick up the post. It was all very strange.

The day had been cool and overcast with intermittent drizzle but now the sky had begun to clear and the dappled clouds made a patchwork of blue and pale grey with a hint of hazy gold. When Melissa reached home, Iris, in slacks and a baggy sweater, was leaning on her gate studying the sky as if assessing the prospects for tomorrow's weather. She waved as the Golf drove past.

'Had a good day?' she called as Melissa closed the garage door after putting the car away.

'Not bad. It's nice to get a glimpse of the sun, isn't it?' Melissa strolled across, leaned against Iris's fence and closed her eyes, listening to the bleating of young lambs and the chuckle of a solitary starling on the roof. 'Oh, isn't this peaceful!'

'Something on your mind?'

'Sort of.' Melissa opened her eyes and glanced round. 'Your cousin gone home?'

'Gone to London for a couple of days.' Iris yawned, stretched and pushed up one sleeve to scratch an arm. 'Not sorry to have a break. Nice fellow but visitors upset the routine.'

'He's coming back then?' Melissa felt no particular interest in the man's movements but it was comfortable standing here, chatting to Iris about things totally unconnected with the death of Angy and the attendant anxieties and problems. She felt disinclined to go indoors and start preparing a solitary supper.

'At the weekend. Staying till Wednesday, then back to the States. You must have supper with us . . . Sunday any good?'

'Yes, I'd like to.' Melissa pulled her sagging weight from the fence. 'I suppose I'd better go and sort out something to eat for this evening.'

'You look tired,' said Iris critically. 'Come and have a nut burger with me.'

Melissa hesitated, considering the rival attractions of a grilled lamb chop cooked and eaten in solitude and a nut burger in sympathetic company.

'With fried onions and mushroom sauce,' tempted Iris.

The lamb chop would keep until tomorrow. 'Thanks, that'd be lovely.'

'That was really delicious,' said Melissa, laying down her knife and fork.

Iris grinned at her over the rim of her glass of mineral water. 'Nearly turned it down in favour of some filthy meat dish, didn't you?' she said, a hint of malice in her eyes. 'You'll find your brain works much better on my kind of diet.'

'Maybe,' said Melissa. 'I'm not disposed to argue about it this evening. What do you make of this business about Delia Forbes?' Over the nut burgers, she had put Iris in the picture concerning her encounter with Eddie, the visit to Angy's flat and her subsequent trip to Cheltenham.

Iris thought for a moment, turning her glass to and fro on its painted wooden coaster. 'Very rum,' she said. 'Could be some straightforward explanation, though. Have you told Harris?'

'I've been trying to get him but there's no reply from his home. He's not on duty so he and his wife must both be out. I'll try again later.'

'Seen that artist fellow lately?' The grey eyes were sharp as razor-blades.

'You mean Barney? I saw him in the staffroom this afternoon but he hardly spoke to me.' Melissa had pushed this small incident into the back of her mind; now she remembered it, she realised how much it had hurt.

Iris appeared absorbed in a study of her glass. 'Just as well,' she observed.

'You still think he killed Angy, don't you?' said Melissa resentfully.

'No idea. Just want you to be on the safe side. Know what you're like . . . can't resist poking about when you get a whiff of mystery.' She got to her feet and picked up their empty plates. 'I'll go and get the pud.'

'I've been thinking,' said Melissa while Iris ladled out dollops of home-made fruit yoghurt, 'whoever has been coming to Angy's class and calling herself Delia Forbes must know the real Delia is away.'

'Makes sense.'

'Could it be the same person who goes to the house to pick up the post?'

'No reason why not.'

'So where do we start looking?'

'Neighbours?'

'Unlikely. Old Mrs Rogers has lost a lot of her marbles but she'd surely know if it was someone actually living along there.'

'So it's someone from another part of town.'

'Whoever it is has presumably been coming regularly since last November so he or she must have been seen by other people. It was probably the old woman who told Miss Matthews but I don't suppose she'd have the vaguest notion of the day or time.'

'Assuming whoever it is comes regularly. No guarantee of that,' Iris pointed out.

Melissa sighed. 'It's going to be difficult to get hold of this person. I wonder if the police are doing anything about it . . . I must try and contact Ken Harris.'

'That girl you saw . . . you say she's a social worker?' said Iris, brandishing a tablespoon. 'More yoghurt?'

Melissa held out her plate. 'That's right. What of it?'

'Isn't that Eddie's job?'

Melissa almost choked on a spoonful of yoghurt. 'So it is! Suppose Miss Matthews is based at the same office as Eddie! They discuss their cases and Miss Matthews mentions old Mrs Rogers and how much she misses her neighbour. So Eddie knows the real Delia Forbes has gone away and won't be back for a long time . . . but so what?' The burst of enthusiasm died as swiftly as it had kindled. 'It couldn't possibly have been Eddie who impersonated Delia and anyway there'd have been no point when she lives in the same house as Angy.'

'But another colleague might . . . someone who's in love . . . who's been having an . . . is a close friend of Eddie.'

'You mean, someone who had been having a lesbian affair with Eddie? Hears her talking about Angy and is madly jealous? Iris, you could be on to something!'

Iris winced at this unnecessarily blunt reference to Eddie's sexuality, having already made it clear that she held similar views to Sybil's. However, she pursued this new line with enthusiasm. 'Would have been easy, wouldn't it? Assume Delia Forbes' identity, go to the art class, get to know Angy and wangle an invitation to her flat. Didn't your detective johnnie come across something like that in one of your books?'

'That's right . . . *Mirrors of the Dead.*'

Iris, normally strongly critical when she saw Melissa becoming involved in some mystery, was quite carried away with her theory.

'Of course, she'd have to cook her report sheet or whatever they call it,' she went on, becoming—for her—positively prolix. 'Or she might be a part-timer who's free on Tuesdays anyway.'

'It's certainly worth looking into.' Melissa glanced at her watch. 'I'll see what Ken Harris has got to say. I think I'll be getting home if you don't mind. I want to try him again this evening.' She got up and began clearing the table.

'Leave that. You push off. Keep me posted, won't you?'

'Of course. Thanks so much for the supper.'

There was still no answer from Ken Harris's number. On impulse, Melissa called Barney.

'Melissa! Why are you phoning?' He sounded uneasy.

'Why did you rush off like that this afternoon?'

'I had to get to my class.' He was hedging; she could tell by his tone.

'You aren't usually in such a hurry.' There was silence. 'It's DCI Harris, isn't it? He's warned you off.'

'Sort of. He told me he'd said much the same to you.'

'He hasn't any right to interfere!' said Melissa angrily.

'He suspects me of killing Angy and he's trying to protect you. I can see his point.'

'Well I don't believe you did and he isn't going to be able to prove it.'

'He's having a darned good try. He's taken away some of my clothes for forensic tests.'

'Oh, my God!' A cold tongue of fear licked Melissa's spine. 'What did he take?'

'Several things . . . slacks, a sweat-shirt. The trouble is, I can't for the life of me remember what I was wearing the last time I went to see Angy, or on the day she died. It's all a blur.'

'Well, of course it is. That should prove you're innocent. I mean, if you'd really done it you'd have had a story ready to tell the police once the body was discovered.'

There was another pause before Barney said, 'It's nice of you to call, Melissa, and thanks for believing in me.'

She was on the point of telling him about her investigations but it was all so uncertain and there was no point in raising false hopes. 'I do believe in you Barney,' she whispered. 'See you soon.' There was a lump in her throat as she put down the phone.

She went upstairs and spent some time soaking in a hot bath. Presently, relaxed and generously anointed with body-lotion, she wrapped herself in a fluffy towelling robe and went back downstairs. It was ten o'clock; she brewed a pot of tea and made one more effort to contact Harris. There was still no reply; it would have to wait until the morning. Then she remembered that she had promised to keep Sybil in the picture but decided that could wait as well. Later, she was to ask herself if the decision had made any difference to subsequent events. That was something she would never know for certain.

Sitting on the edge of her bed and sipping her tea, she began jotting down notes of the day's events, separating them into facts and possible explanations. It was rather like working out the details of one of her plots: circumstances capable of more than one interpretation; actions which might or might not be innocent; individuals who might or might not have a genuine motive, the means and opportunity to commit the crime. The difference was that when constructing a plot she was able to invent clues that would subtly direct her readers in the direction of the guilty person while strewing their path with red herrings. In this case, her thought processes were negative, seeking before all else to draw suspicion away from Barney but lacking the vital scene-of-crime evidence which, if Harris's attitude was anything to go by, pointed strongly at his guilt.

And he was innocent of murder; she felt it in her bones. Her talk with Eddie had convinced her that he was telling the truth about his relationship with Angy and that Rodney Shergold was the 'poor sap' who had fallen an eager and tiresome victim to her charms. Barney might experience flashes of impatience and anger, say and do things he would later regret, but she could not believe him capable of the blind, destructive hatred that had driven the knife into Angy's throat.

Of all that she had learned that afternoon, the only possible hope lay in trying to establish the real identity of the woman calling herself Delia Forbes. Yet even as one half of her mind speculated on its significance, the other half reminded her that if she had stumbled on this odd circumstance, then the police would almost certainly have done so in the course of their routine enquiries and, since Barney was still their prime suspect, found a satisfactory explanation. The more she thought about it, the more her confidence ebbed away until she was ready to believe that her efforts had turned up nothing of positive help.

With a disconsolate sigh she stood up, slipped off the towelling robe and threw it over a chair. It was a soft rosy pink; looking at it she thought of Barney's robe of saffron yellow and how he had admired its effect on her. She remembered his touch as he wrapped it around her shoulders and the slumbering animal within her stirred and stretched and unsheathed claws of desire. How had their conversation gone? 'I'd like to paint you.' 'What, in this?' 'Yes . . . no, without it.' And he'd appeared suddenly and endearingly shy, as if embarrassed at the memory of seeing her naked in his bed the night before.

She went to the full-length mirror beside her dressing-table, pulling off the headband she had worn in the bath and releasing the glossy brown hair that tumbled almost to her shoulders. Narcissus-like she studied her reflection, running her fingertips over her flesh, breathing its perfume and recalling Barney's enjoyment of its smoothness. She observed with satisfaction the firmness of her breasts, the flatness of her stomach and the trim roundness of her hips. She peered closely at her face; there were a few lines about the mouth and eyes but at forty-seven that was only to be expected. At least her skin was clear and her neck hadn't started to sag.

'You shall paint me like this if it would please you, Barney dear,' she whispered aloud. 'And love me again . . . please.' Then, feeling foolish, blushing in the empty room like a self-conscious adolescent, she put on her nightdress, got into bed and switched out the light.

She slept soundly and awoke just as the dawn was swelling in a luminous golden tide across the sky. It would be several hours before she could think of calling Harris and she reminded herself that there was a book waiting to be finished. She got up, brewed a pot of coffee, went to her study and started work.

At half-past nine she rang the police station and was told that DCI Harris had just gone out and was not expected back until after lunch. She left a message asking him to contact her urgently, dialled Sybil's number and found it engaged. Frustrated, she changed into her gardening clothes and went out to collect and spread her promised share of

Iris's manure heap—an activity which cleared her mind wonderfully so that when Harris rang at two o'clock she had at her fingertips every point she wanted to put to him.

One by one he shot them down.

'Yes, of course we know about Shergold's affair with the girl but he didn't kill her.'

'Did you know about the spare jacket?'

'Of course. We took it for forensic tests.'

'Did you find anything?'

'Hairs, perfume, make-up. No blood. As a matter of fact, we haven't got around to returning it yet.' Harris gave one of his rare chuckles. 'Do him good to sweat a little. We suspect he found the girl's body on the Wednesday afternoon but we can't get him to admit it.'

'That could be why he went home that day feeling groggy. I met his wife in the village shop and she was very concerned about him.'

'She'd have been more than concerned if she'd known what he'd been up to over the previous few weeks!' said Harris drily. 'Lucky for him, his alibi is as watertight as it's possible to be, unless the college principal, half his staff and all his students are lying. We've checked his story in detail and it fits. What else have you got for me?'

'I went to see Eddie Brady,' began Melissa a little sharply, stung by the note of self-satisfaction in his voice. She was interrupted by another hoarse, gleeful chuckle.

'Quite a character, isn't she? First-class social worker too. I've got a lot of respect for Mizz Edwina.'

'I think you might have warned me.'

'Couldn't do that. Prejudice and so on.'

'I had a friend with me and she was quite upset.'

'Too bad. So what did you get out of Eddie that my sergeant failed to spot?'

'Is it totally impossible for her to have slipped home during the critical time?'

'Totally. What the hell do you take us for, Melissa? Real policemen have brains as well as your know-it-all Nathan.' Self-satisfaction had given way to an impatience that said, as clearly as the words, 'If that's the best you can do, stop wasting my time and let me get on with my work.' Well, perhaps she could give him something to think about.

'Eddie was very jealous of Angy, wasn't she? You should have seen her reaction when I mentioned that Delia Forbes might have been round to see her the day she was killed.'

'Who's Delia Forbes?'

'One of Angy's art students. Don't tell me your men haven't checked her out?'

'I'm a busy man, Melissa. If you've got something to tell me . . . '

Now she had his attention. As concisely as she could, Melissa told him about the missing sketch of Delia Forbes, her subsequent visit to the house in Regency Terrace and the possibility of a plot by one of Eddie's discarded lovers to kill Angy. Even while she was speaking, the theory sounded bizarre and far-fetched, yet there were no more quips or chuckles from the other end of the line, only a series of grunts.

When she had finished, he said quietly, 'That is interesting, Melissa.' She heard papers being shuffled. 'I'm just looking at the report of the officer who called on Delia Forbes. A neighbour told him she'd gone off to see her daughter that morning—that would be the Thursday—and would be back in a couple of days.'

'That must have been old Mrs Rogers. She lives in another world. Time means nothing to her.'

'I'll get Waters on to it right away. Anything else?'

'I was wondering what Angy was wearing when she was found.'

'A plain navy-blue skirt and a white blouse. She'd been wearing it to the office that morning and put on an overall for the art class in the afternoon. We found it, chucked on a chair.'

'She was expecting Rick Lawrence about six o'clock. Lou seemed to think she'd have dolled herself up a bit before he came. That would narrow down the time a bit, wouldn't it?'

'We had thought of that.'

'I'm sorry, Ken . . . I'm just trying to—'

'Don't tell me. The earlier she was killed, the better it looks for Willard because he was in college till gone five, right?'

'Just what evidence have you got against him? It can't be all that strong or you'd have arrested him by now.' There was silence. 'Oh, come on Ken, you've just admitted I've turned up something that might be useful. What about a quid pro quo? You can trust me, can't you?'

'It isn't a question of not trusting you. Our investigations are at a delicate stage . . . '

'Waiting for forensic reports on Barney's clothing?'

'He told you about that? I thought we agreed you wouldn't see him till this was over.'

'We're colleagues . . . we use the same staff room.' No point in admitting to the telephone call; that would mean even less chance of prising anything out of Harris. 'I haven't seen him outside college, honestly Ken.' That at least was true.

'Well . . . ' He was beginning to weaken.

'Just between ourselves . . . ' she begged. The need to know what Barney was up against had become overwhelming.

'There were traces of cotton fibre in the blood on the girl's body that didn't come from her own clothing. Willard owns a cotton sweat-shirt—'

'So do lots of people.'

' . . . which he thought he might have been wearing that afternoon and then changed his mind and said he hadn't,' continued Harris, unperturbed by the interruption.

'Is that all you've got to go on?'

'There's the little matter of his fingerprints all over the flat—'

'They would be. He often went there.'

'As he keeps pointing out to us. However, one or two of those prints are highly significant. On the knife-block, for example.'

'Perhaps he touched it while helping her in the kitchen . . . putting the knives away—'

'His prints weren't on any of the handles. From their position on the block, he'd been steadying it with his left hand while drawing out a knife with his right.'

'So Angy asked him to pass her a knife while she was cooking something.'

'That's what he claims.'

'What about the murder weapon? Aren't there any prints on that?'

'That's our main problem. There was so much blood, and the girl left her own prints where she grabbed at the knife—probably trying to drag it out. Any prints left by the killer would have been completely obliterated. Young Lawrence left his, of course, on the knife and the telephone and the cabinet where the ring was kept, but from the state of the blood it was long enough after death to tally with his story.'

'He could have gone back later and done all the things he claimed to have done . . . '

'He wouldn't have had time. We found the taxi driver who took him and the girl to the station and witnesses who saw them get on the train. Lawrence didn't kill Angy. We've checked his story against the girl's account and it hangs together in every detail.'

'And Barney's doesn't?'

'There are holes in it. He had motive and he's the right build. The angle at which the knife entered seems to indicate that the killer is fairly tall.'

'But no one saw him near the flat that afternoon. His clothes would have been blood-stained. Surely, someone would have spotted him.'

'We found traces of blood in the bathroom. We think the killer went in there to clean up immediately after striking the blow. He probably knew the house was empty and there was little chance of his being disturbed. And no one saw him in the street; that little turning is almost entirely occupied by people who are out at work all day.'

'Are you trying to tell me,' Melissa began, on a low note that she could hear becoming steadily more shrill, 'that after stabbing Angy, Barney locked himself in the bathroom and left her to die while he calmly washed away her blood? He couldn't have done it . . . he'd have been frantic with remorse, stayed with her to comfort her, tried to get help. For God's sake, Ken!' She was almost hysterical. 'What about this psychological offender-profiling you're all supposed to be into nowadays? Think about it! It might save you making complete idiots of yourselves!'

'Try not to get upset.' Harris's voice was unusually gentle. 'I can understand how you feel.'

'Never mind how I feel!' Melissa raved. 'You find Delia Forbes! She'll lead you to the real killer!' With a futile, melodramatic flourish, she banged down the receiver. While she stood staring at it, breathing heavily and conscious that if anyone had made a fool of herself during the past few minutes it was Melissa Craig, the phone began to ring again.

EIGHTEEN

SYBIL BLISS WAS ALMOST INCOHERENT WITH excitement, her voice rising and falling in a series of breathless peaks and troughs. 'Oh, Melissa, there you are! I've been trying to get you for *ages* but your line's been engaged.' A hint of reproach hung round the final words.

'Ages', thought Melissa, meant fifteen minutes at the most. 'I was talking to Chief Inspector Harris,' she said, a little wearily. Her outburst had left her feeling deflated, almost disinterested. She had established the fact that the real Delia Forbes was in Australia and that for the past few weeks someone else had been using her name and address; because of her desperate desire to help Barney she had leapt to conclusions which could be hopelessly wide of the mark. There was probably a perfectly simple explanation, if only she could give her mind to it, but for the moment she seemed incapable of logical thought.

Meanwhile, Sybil was twittering on. 'Well, wait till he hears about this! I simply couldn't *believe* it . . . it didn't seem to make *sense* and I thought I must be mistaken but I'm *sure* I wasn't . . . '

'For goodness' sake, Sybil, what are you on about?' It wasn't really fair to snap like that but Melissa's nerves were still jangling.

'Oh, sorry! You must think me very silly but it's just that I'm so *excited*! I think I've found out . . . '

'Found out what?' said Melissa testily, as Sybil broke off.

'Just a moment . . . I can hear something.'

There was a pause. Melissa pictured Sybil with her head cocked, the way she held it when she was listening to someone, gazing with exaggerated, wide-eyed intensity. 'What is it?' she asked.

'I must have left the garage door open. I think I heard it banging. Hold on, will you?'

There was a clatter as the phone was put down, followed by the sound of footsteps scurrying down the stairs and fading into silence. Half listening, half occupied with looking out of the open window at a flock of rooks riding in circles on the breeze, Melissa was vaguely aware of a succession of faint bumping noises in the distance, followed by returning footsteps. The sounds mingled in her mind with the harsh cries of the birds as she waited for Sybil to pick up the phone again.

Instead, there were rustlings, faint and unintelligible mutterings suggesting that she was looking for something, more footsteps going downstairs, a sharp sound like the slamming of a door and then complete silence. Seconds ticked by and Melissa grew impatient. What on earth was Sybil doing? Surely she hadn't gone out again, forgetting that she had left a friend waiting on the telephone? She strained her ears but could hear nothing. She jiggled the receiver rest, shouted 'Hullo!' several times and eventually, exasperated and irritable, put the phone down. If whatever Sybil had to say was so important, she could call again.

Half an hour later, she had not done so. By this time, Melissa's temper had calmed and her curiosity revived. She went back to the telephone, dialled Sybil's number and waited for the ringing tone. Nothing happened. She tried again. Still nothing. She jiggled the receiver and realised that there was no dialling tone. Something must be wrong with the line. She put down the instrument and went next door.

Not surprisingly on such a mild afternoon, Iris was in the garden. She had dug a trench and was busy shovelling manure into it from an antiquated wheelbarrow, her thin arms in the tightly fitting sleeves of her black sweater swinging to and fro like crankshafts. She straightened up as Melissa approached, pulled off one of her gardening gloves and combed back her hair with her fingers. Her cheeks were rosy from the exercise; with her pointed features and sparkling eyes she looked like an amiable, wholesome witch.

'Getting ready for the runners,' she explained.

'Isn't it a bit early to be planting beans?'

'Not planting yet. Just preparing the ground. Nearly done.' She heaved up the handles of the barrow and the remaining contents slid neatly home. She picked up a fork and stirred the dark mass, grunting with satisfaction. 'What can I do for you?'

'My phone seems to be out of order. Mind if I report it from yours?'

'Help yourself. Be in in a minute.'

Iris stuck her fork in the earth and trundled off down the garden with her barrow while Melissa went indoors, reported her problem to the telephone engineers and wandered back to the kitchen. 'I've given them this number and they're going to test the line and call me back,' she said when Iris came in from the garden.

'Good.' Iris washed her hands and filled the kettle. 'Might as well have a cuppa while you're waiting.'

Melissa perched on the edge of the table and watched her as she bustled about with tea-things. 'It would have to play up just as Sybil was going to tell me something important,' she complained. 'I can't think what kept her so long. I hung on for ages.'

'Probably got talking to a neighbour and forgot all about you. Struck me as a bit of a scatterbrain!' commented Iris, arranging oatmeal cookies on a hand-painted plate.

'Yes, she is rather.' Melissa turned the plate to admire the delicate rose design. 'She does some lovely flower paintings, though. She'd appreciate this.'

'She ought to try her hand at decorating china some time.'

'I'll suggest it next time I speak to her.' Melissa nibbled thoughtfully at a cookie. 'I wish I knew what she wanted to tell me. She was bubbling with excitement. It might have had something to do with the murder because she seemed to think Ken Harris would be interested.'

'Try ringing her now.' Iris jerked her head in the direction of the telephone.

Melissa stood up. 'May I?' She went out of the room but returned almost immediately. 'Her number's engaged.'

'Probably trying to get you. Try again before you leave. Any other news?'

'I told Harris what I discovered yesterday about Delia Forbes.'

'And?'

'He's going to follow it up but I had the impression he was only so interested. As far as he's concerned, Barney is his man and he's simply waiting for the forensic reports to confirm it. I can't tell you any more than that,' Melissa added in response to Iris's lifted eyebrows. 'I did manage to worm a few details out of him but strictly in confidence.'

They fell silent for a few moments as they drank their tea. When the phone rang, they both jumped. 'You get it,' said Iris.

It was the engineer, speaking from the exchange. 'Did you have a call from a Stowbridge number recently?' he asked.

'Yes, that's right.'

'The caller must have left the receiver off. We'll get it cleared for you as soon as possible.'

'Thank you very much.' Melissa returned to the kitchen. 'I don't like the sound of it,' she said. 'It looks as if she never came back to the phone. Whatever can have happened?'

'Found you'd hung up and didn't put her receiver on properly,' suggested Iris. 'Easily done with these modern phones. Did it myself the other day. Didn't realise until it started howling like a demented banshee!'

'Howling?'

'Something they do from the exchange to get your attention. She'll ring again as soon as she tumbles to what she's done.' Iris picked up the teapot and held it over Melissa's cup. 'Want a refill?'

Melissa waved the teapot away, frowning. 'You know, this doesn't make sense. She had something she was simply bursting to tell me. She'd never have waited this long. I don't like the sound of it at all,' she repeated.

'Oh, I'm sure it's all right,' said Iris. 'She'll be in touch presently, you'll see.'

'Supposing she's been taken ill or something? She lives on her own.'

'We agreed she must have been talking to someone . . . '

'I never actually heard voices, except a sort of muttering as if she was rummaging around trying to find something. I wasn't really listening, just waiting for her to pick up the phone.'

'Try again. She may have hung up by now.'

Sybil had not hung up; the line was still engaged and Melissa was becoming more uneasy by the minute. 'I'm going round to her house to find out what's wrong,' she said. 'Thanks for the tea, Iris. I'll see you later.'

'Up to you. Think you're wasting your time.'

Melissa was not given to premonition but the fear that something had happened to Sybil had taken hold and would not be shaken off. 'I've got to set my mind at rest,' she said. 'Iris . . . I don't suppose you'd come with me, would you?'

Iris stared at her. 'You really are worried, aren't you?'

'Yes, I am. The more I think about it . . . '

'Okay, if it'll make you feel better.'

The little street where Sybil lived was deserted except for a British Telecom van parked a short distance from her house. A red and white striped tent had been erected on the pavement and two young men in blue overalls were lounging against a nearby wall, mugs in hand.

'That looks like the answer,' commented Iris as Melissa pulled up. 'Fix one line, foul up two more and then take a tea-break!'

'I hope you're right.'

They got out of the car and walked up Sybil's short drive. Two-thirds of the ground floor of each house in the terrace was taken up by a garage; the door to Sybil's stood open with the car inside but the other three were closed, revealing that the owners had differing and not particularly compatible tastes in colour.

'Look like slabs of rainbow chocolate!' sniffed Iris, pausing to assess the effect. 'Architectural vandalism!'

'We can't all live in listed cottages,' Melissa pointed out as she pressed the bell-push.

There was no movement inside the house. She rang again and rattled the letter-box but still there was no response. She peeped through the slot into the narrow hall with its little polished table bearing a silver letter-tray and a vase of flowers. Everything appeared normal.

'Gone to report her phone out of order!' suggested Iris.

'No. Listen.' From somewhere in the house came a faint, high-pitched hum. 'Isn't that the howler thing you were talking about? Surely she'd have heard that.'

'Must have gone out in a hurry. Maybe a neighbour needed help.'

'I can't believe she'd have gone out and left her garage open. There must be a personal door into the house. I'm going to look.' Melissa led the way, easing herself between the car and an assortment of garden implements ranged along the wall. Across the end of the garage was a workbench with a rack of tools above and a hydraulic jack beneath.

'Don't tell me she does her own car maintenance,' commented Iris.

'I doubt it. I expect that lot belonged to her late husband.' As she spoke, Melissa found the door and turned the handle. It was unlocked. Something behind it prevented it from fully opening and a dark, viscous substance that in the subdued light looked like a patch of oil was spreading from an invisible source and had begun soaking into the carpet. Melissa's heart began to thump as she peered round to see what was causing the obstruction.

She stared down at the floor and the remains of what had been a human being. For a moment she stood transfixed in shock and disbelief; then she screamed, and the

scream drained her lungs until she was all but suffocated.
Like someone drowning, she fought for air, gasping and
retching, covering her eyes in a futile attempt to blot out
the memory of the crushed skull, the shattered features and
the foul, oozing stain.

'What is it?' Iris stepped forward, saw, and turned away
in horror, her eyes like black holes in a face the colour of
bleached bones.

'Something wrong?' One of the telephone engineers,
alarmed by the shrieks, appeared behind them. Dumbly,
they pointed to the open door.

'Jesus!' he gasped, and fainted.

'That's all we need!' said Iris, her nerve restored by this
display of masculine weakness. She knelt beside the young
man as he lay slumped against the wheel of Sybil's car. 'I'll
see to him. You go and tell the other one to call the police.
An ambulance too. Not that they can do much.' She began a
vigorous slapping of hands and face while Melissa, on legs
that would barely carry her, stepped shakily over the inert
form and went for help.

Detective Inspector Clarke had smooth, pink skin, pale
eyes and receding sandy hair. His habit of constantly raising his eyebrows had etched a row of horizontal lines on
his forehead, giving him an air of permanent surprise. He
raised them now at the two shaken women who sat facing
him in the interview-room at Stowbridge police station. His
sergeant, an alert girl whom he addressed as Barbara, served
them all with mugs of strong tea before sitting down with
her notebook on her lap.

'Now, you're sure you feel well enough to make a statement?' he asked for the second or third time. 'If you'd
rather go home to rest and get over the shock . . . '

'No, that's all right, really,' said Melissa.

'Best to get it over with,' agreed Iris. 'So long as you're
okay?' she added with a glance of concern at Melissa.

'Don't worry, I'll be fine.'

'Right then.' Clarke took a swig from his mug. 'I believe
it was you who discovered the body, Mrs Craig?'

'I was the one who saw it first,' said Melissa. She took a sip of the dark, bitter tea but, almost overcome by nausea, she hastily put down the mug and covered her mouth with a handkerchief.

'Just take your time, and tell me exactly what happened.'

Briefly, she related the sequence of events, beginning with the interrupted phone call.

'Do I understand,' said Clarke when she came to the end of her story, 'that you had reason to believe your friend might have been the victim of a violent attack?'

'Oh no, nothing like that. I thought she might have been taken ill or had a fall or something.'

'You say you heard bumps. Perhaps you thought she'd fallen downstairs?'

'Not then, because I heard her come back. It sounded as if she was looking for something. I could hear impatient noises, but I wasn't really paying close attention.'

Clarke's eyebrows jiggled up and down. 'It didn't occur to you,' he suggested, 'that it wasn't the poor lady herself that you heard?'

'Oh, my God!' Melissa felt the room start to spin. Barbara was on her feet in a second, pushing her head forward and speaking brisk words of encouragement. Iris grabbed the hand nearest to her and squeezed it.

'Feeling better? Have a drink of tea?' Barbara held out the mug.

'No, thanks very much.' The sight of the scummy liquid aroused more warning signals from her stomach. She sat up and put a hand to her forehead. 'I'll be all right now. It was just the shock of realising . . . of course, it must have been the killer I heard. How absolutely ghastly!'

'It rather looks,' said Clarke, 'as if this was an opportunist crime. Someone saw the open garage door and sneaked in to see what he could pinch. He probably tried the door to the house, found that unlocked as well and picked up the hammer in case he was disturbed.'

'Sybil was killed with a hammer?' Of course, it would have had to something heavy to cause those dreadful injuries.

'A seven-pounder. He might have brought it with him but more likely it was already there with the other tools in the garage.'

'You mean, he went in quite prepared to kill someone?' One read of such crimes in deprived areas of inner cities, but . . . 'How do you suppose it happened?'

'We can't be absolutely sure of the sequence of events but the victim was hit from behind and fell against the door leading into the garage, so the killer must have been in the house. Maybe he'd already started up the stairs when he heard the lady coming down and dodged round them to hide. From what you've told us, Mrs Craig, she'd heard him come in. He must have come at her as she closed the door.'

'But surely she'd have screamed or cried out? I never heard anything like that.'

'We must assume he took her completely by surprise.'

'But why such a murderous attack? It's brutal . . . senseless!' That someone as gentle and inoffensive as Sybil, with her flower paintings and her harmless little poems, should have been needlessly and savagely battered to death, made Melissa seethe with rage.

'I'm afraid that brutal and senseless attacks are all too common nowadays,' said Clarke, the resignation in his voice making an odd contrast to his air of perpetual astonishment.

'Was anything stolen?'

'We can't find the lady's handbag. We shan't know what else is missing until the relatives get here but it was probably money he was after . . . for drugs, I dare say.'

Melissa closed her eyes and shivered. She felt cold and sick and wished she could crawl away and lie down. What sort of a society have we become, she wondered miserably, that our homes are no more secure from drug-crazed humans than were the dwellings of Stone Age tribes from marauding beasts?

'Is that all you want to ask us?' Everyone turned in surprise to Iris, who had sat bolt upright in her seat throughout the interview, replying in her own brand of verbal shorthand to the questions that came her way. 'She's had enough!' Iris nodded in Melissa's direction and turned fierce eyes on the detective. 'Tomorrow will do if you want to know anything else.' She got to her feet, grasped Melissa by the elbow and hauled her upright.

If Clarke had intended to pursue his enquiries further, he obviously thought better of it under that formidable gaze. He too stood up. 'Yes, that's all for now. Thank you, ladies, you've been most helpful.'

After the artificial light in the interview-room, the late afternoon sun shining directly on the entrance to the police station was like a physical blow to the eyes that tapped a gush of protective tears. Half-blinded, Melissa faltered, stumbled and collided with a burly figure hurrying towards the building. A strong arm prevented her from falling.

'I beg your pardon, Madam . . . Melissa!' The face of DCI Harris swam out of the mist. 'What brings you here? And Miss Ash? Is something wrong?'

Melissa could only nod speechlessly.

'A friend murdered,' she heard Iris explain. 'We found the body.'

'Good heavens!' Harris looked from one to the other in consternation. 'Where? When?'

'This afternoon. In Stowbridge. Your colleague's got our statements. We're going home.' There was a steely ring in Iris's voice that dared Harris—or anyone else— to delay them further but he was more than equal to the challenge.

'Who was the victim?' he asked, looking directly at Melissa.

'One of her students. Can't you see, she's had enough for one day?' snapped Iris.

'You both look as if you could use a stiff drink,' said Harris, softening the natural rasp of his voice with an almost paternal note of concern. 'There's a good waterhole just round the corner. If you don't mind waiting here a second while I . . . '

'Not now. Got to get home.' Iris tugged at Melissa's arm. 'Come on. I'll drive you.'

'I think Ken's right. A drink would do us both good,' said Melissa. There was something solid and comforting about the big detective's presence that was already having a restorative effect.

'Oh, all right.' Reluctantly, Iris relaxed her hold.

'Just wait here a second while I drop this in.' Brandishing a large manila envelope, Harris bounded up the steps and vanished while Iris sat Melissa on a convenient wall and stood over her like a guardian angel, a protective arm on one shoulder.

'You're incredible, Iris,' said Melissa gratefully. 'You must be just as shaken as I am.'

'Not quite. Didn't know her so well as you did. Wonder if they'll get him?'

'The killer, you mean? They've got to get him. If Clarke's theory is correct, he's very dangerous.'

It was several minutes before Harris reappeared. 'Right, that's that,' he said breezily. 'Let's go and have that drink. You okay to walk, Melissa?'

'Of course I am.' How stupid to have been caught tottering about like an invalid. It was hardly the way her readers would expect the creator of Nathan Latimer to react to a crisis, she thought, ashamed of her weakness. Already she was feeling more herself.

Harris installed the two women in a quiet corner of the bar and bought a pint of bitter for himself, a brandy for Melissa and orange juice for Iris. He went back for a plate of sandwiches and Melissa was surprised to find that she was hungry. She ate the food, sipped her brandy and was even able to smile at the sight of Iris peering between the slices of bread to ensure that the contents were acceptable to a vegetarian.

'I've heard of people being accident prone,' Harris observed after a while, 'but you seem to be murder prone, Melissa.' It was the nearest she had known him come to making a joke.

'I should carry some sort of health warning, shouldn't I?' she said wryly.

'How did all this come about, then?'

The tone was casual but it did not deceive Iris. She glared at Harris like a tigress defending a cub. 'I told you, she's made her statement,' she snapped. 'Not up to any more questions.'

Melissa patted her arm. 'It's all right, Iris. I'm quite okay now.'

'You said your friend sounded very excited about what she had to tell you,' Harris continued between mouthfuls of bitter. Obviously he had taken the opportunity whilst in the station of running through her statement. 'Have you any idea at all what it was?'

'None whatever. She was saying things like "unbelievable" and "doesn't make sense", but she never came to the point at all.'

'Try to remember her exact words.'

Clarke had said the same thing and she had tried desperately to comply but it had been like trying to lay hold of darting butterflies. Now, relaxed by the brandy, she felt her reflexes improving.

'She was complaining at not being able to get through because my number was engaged and I said I'd been talking to you. Then she said, "Wait till he"—she meant you—"hears about this!" '

'Have you any idea where she'd been before she phoned?'

'She was going into Cheltenham, to the library and then to call on Delia Forbes.' Melissa felt a tingle of excitement. 'I wonder if she spoke to the person who's been doing the caretaking? Maybe she learned something that could help us find the person who's been using Delia's name.'

'Maybe.' Harris set down his empty beer mug, took out a handkerchief and wiped foam from his mouth. 'Or maybe she just learned from a more rational neighbour that the real Delia has been abroad for six months. Or had you already told her that?'

'No, I hadn't. That was probably it.' As had happened so many times lately, what looked like a flash of illumination had turned into a damp squib. 'Whatever it was, she was so excited that she forgot to lock her door. Poor Sybil!'

'Dangerous thing to do nowadays,' observed Harris. 'I hope you two are careful about security, living in that isolated spot.'

'Give us credit for some sense!' barked Iris, who had been showing signs of impatience. She stood up. 'Going to the ladies'. Then home.'

She vanished through the bar and Harris turned to Melissa. 'I'm glad she's out of the way for a moment. I've got some news that may cheer you up.'

'Really?'

'It's not much help to me, though.' A rueful grin crumpled the craggy features. 'Nothing belonging to your friend Willard matches up with the fibres we found on the dead girl.'

'Oh, thank God for that!'

'Thought you'd be pleased. Not surprised, are you?'

'Not really, but circumstantial evidence can play lousy tricks, can't it? Oh, Barney'll be so relieved—can I tell him?'

'Certainly not, you leave it to us. No doubt he'll call you as soon as he hears.' Harris leaned forward with clasped hands, his forearms resting on his knees and his head bent. 'It puts us back to square one, of course.'

'You mean, in the hunt for Angy's killer?'

'Right.'

'Inspector Clarke seems to think Sybil was killed by a walk-in thief. Could the same be true of Angy, do you suppose?'

'That's something we'll have to consider.' He sighed and stood up. 'Here comes your friend. I'd better let her take you home or she'll eat me alive and spit out the bones.'

NINETEEN

MELISSA SLEPT UNEASILY, HAUNTED BY VI-
sions of blood, twisted limbs, staring eyes and crushed
bones. She awoke early, took a shower, went to her study
and tried to work. Her output was not impressive but at
least she succeeded for a couple of hours in driving the
memory of Sybil's murder into the back of her mind. It
was a brief respite; when, presently, she took a break
and switched on the radio, she found herself listening to
the voice of Detective Inspector Clarke who was being
interviewed by a reporter. She caught only the last few
words: 'the sooner this dangerous person is apprehended
the better', and switched off in frustration.

An hour or so later her telephone rang. She rushed to
answer, thinking that it might be Barney, but it was a
young journalist from the *Gloucester Gazette* who had
interviewed her a few months previously when her latest
book was published.

'Melissa? Sophie. I hear it was you who found that
woman's body. What led you to think a tragedy might
have occurred?'

Damn Inspector Clarke, thought Melissa. Harris would
have kept her name out of it and she had forgotten, in her
agitation, to ask for it not to be revealed. 'The notion of
tragedy didn't enter my head,' she protested, 'but it did
seem odd for her to break off in the middle of a phone call
like that.'

'And you immediately scented a mystery and set out

to solve it for yourself!' said Sophie in a voice of triumph. 'Everyone's asking themselves,' she went on before Melissa had a chance to put a brake on her roller-coaster imagination, 'whether there could be a connection between this crime and the Angelica Caroli murder. "Vicious Killer at Large in Quiet Market Town"—this'll be on the front page of the tabloids!'

'Angy was stabbed,' Melissa pointed out. 'If this was the start of a series of attacks, surely . . . '

'An opportunist killer would use whatever weapon came to hand,' declared Sophie, undeterred. 'The circumstances are similar: doors unlocked, quiet street, easy for anyone to sneak in unobserved. Of course, the police aren't prepared to commit themselves yet but I'll bet that's what they're thinking. By the way, you referred to the Caroli girl as "Angy"—did you know her?'

'We were colleagues, that's all.' This was tricky ground. The last thing she wanted was for the local press to find out that she had a personal interest in finding Angy's killer. Being well known had certain disadvantages for anyone who set a value on privacy.

'Then perhaps you can tell me . . . ' Sophie had seized eagerly on this possible lead and was determined to follow it, nose to the ground.

'You probably know more than I do,' Melissa interposed. 'You go to the police briefings. I presume you were at this morning's?'

'Yes, of course, that's why I'm phoning you. Can you give me some impressions? What did the place look like? Was there much damage or disturbance?'

'I didn't notice any but I never went inside the house. What else did they say at the briefing? Have the police got any leads yet?'

'Not a lot.' Sophie's voice dipped in disappointment, as if she had been hoping for a graphic account of overturned furniture and blood on the walls. 'Just exactly what did you see?'

'I saw a woman's body lying in the passage behind the personal door from the garage,' said Melissa wearily.

'That must have been pretty frightful for you,' said Sophie, her optimism regenerated.

'It was, rather.' Up flashed an image of the hideous thing on the floor.

'How could you be sure she was dead?' No doubt Sophie was hoping for a lurid description. If she didn't get one, she would invent it and she would embroider whatever she was told.

'Her head and the side of her face had been bashed in,' said Melissa. Already, the memory had set her stomach churning. 'Look, Sophie, it was a pretty harrowing experience. I don't really want to relive it.'

'I *quite* understand!' Synthetic sympathy floated over the line. 'Can you describe your feelings when you saw the body?'

Melissa was running out of patience. 'What do you suppose? I was shocked, I felt sick, I screamed. Now could you please answer my question? What else did the press officer say?'

There was a pause; Melissa overheard mutterings of 'shocked', 'sick', 'screamed', as Sophie scribbled in her notebook. She pictured her, frowning in concentration, her lower lip caught by her small white teeth and her short fair curls a-quiver.

The probing continued. 'I believe you had someone with you?'

'My neighbour.'

Sophie pounced. 'Miss Ash? The one who came across that body in Benbury Woods a year or so ago? My, the two of you certainly have a knack of finding corpses, don't you?'

Iris would be furious. She had a poor opinion of reporters after her experience at their hands during that unpleasant episode. 'Look Sophie, do you have to mention names?'

It was hopeless, of course; there was no way Sophie was going to drop this one. At any rate, Joe would be pleased; he always relished a bit of publicity for his authors.

'You haven't answered my question,' Melissa pursued. 'The least you can do . . .'

'Oh yes, the press briefing. Well, there were two British Telecom engineers working in the street . . .'

'Yes, I know. One of them saw the body and passed out cold.'

'Cor, did he! I'll have to get hold of him!' It was easy to imagine the sparkle in Sophie's eyes as she snapped up this morsel. 'They didn't see anything because they were working in their little tent,' she went on, 'but they did hear someone hurrying past and then a car starting up a little way away. And a short while before that, while one of them was getting some tools or something from the van, a car drove past quite slowly as if the driver was looking for somewhere. He didn't see who was in the car and it went up a side road. The police want the driver and the owner of the running feet to come forward . . . and of course, anyone who saw anything suspicious, please call this number . . . the usual stuff.'

'Not much to go on, is it?' said Melissa.

'You never know. Someone may have spotted something. Anyway, thanks for the interview. Bye!'

'Goodbye.' As she put down the phone, Melissa wondered what garbled version of their conversation would appear in the columns of the *Gazette* that evening.

There was a tap on the window as Iris passed on her way to the front door of Hawthorn Cottage. She stood in the little porch with Binkie in her arms, her chin resting on his head; they both gazed at Melissa with calm, unblinking eyes.

'How're you feeling this morning?' said Iris.

'All right, I suppose. How about you?'

'No problems. Did extra yoga last night. Giving a lesson this morning. Three or four people from Craftworks.' Recently, Iris had taken an interest in a group of young artists who had set up a studio in a converted barn in Lower Benbury. 'Care to join us? Settle your nerves,' she added as Melissa hesitated.

'You know I'm hopeless at it. Last time I let you talk me into having a go, I felt as if I'd had a session in a tumble dryer.'

'Rubbish. Out of condition, that's all. Put on some joggers and bring a blanket. Half an hour.'

'Oh, all right. I'll just have a cup of coffee . . . '

'No coffee. Nothing to eat or drink till after.' Iris swung round and marched away. Binkie stared back over her shoulder and Melissa could have sworn that, behind his impassive expression, there was a smirk on his furry face.

'Feeling better?' asked Iris.

'Much better, thanks!' said Melissa warmly. It was true. Despite her scepticism, the slow, rhythmic yoga movements and the controlled breathing had exercised a calming effect. Iris's protégées had consumed their coffee and nut biscuits and departed, leaving the two of them to put the sitting-room to rights.

'Knew it would help,' said Iris with an air of satisfaction as she heaved a sofa back into place. 'Should do a little every day.'

'Perhaps I will. Could you work out a routine for me?'

'Promise to stick to it? No good just now and then.'

'I'll try.'

'Saw Rodney Shergold in the shop this morning,' Iris observed, pulling a face. 'Jumpy as a cat and as cross as two sticks. Eleanor had the cheek to have a tummy upset so he had to fetch his own newspaper. Poor thing! Can't think how she puts up with him.'

'She thinks the sun shines out of his . . . well, you know what I mean.' Just in time Melissa remembered that although Iris had been known, in moments of crisis, to permit herself the occasional 'bloody', she strongly disapproved of vulgarity. 'She's been worried sick because she thinks he's still a suspect.'

'Of Angy's murder, you mean? Is he?'

'As far as I know, his alibi is okay.' Melissa was on the point of telling Iris about Shergold's affair with Angy and the business of the jacket. It was the kind of story that she would relish but with her blunt ways one could never be sure she wouldn't at some time let the cat out of the bag. Not that one cared too much about the feelings of pompous, over-bearing Rodney Shergold but there was

Eleanor to consider. She was suffering enough as it was.

'Any developments? Or does that murder take a back seat now they've got a new one to think about?'

'It certainly hasn't taken a back seat and there have been developments, but I'd better not tell you what they are until the details are officially released.' Melissa pushed the last chair into place and glanced round the room. 'Have we finished?'

'That's fine, thanks.' Iris picked up the tray of coffee mugs and headed for the kitchen, then stopped short. 'Is that your phone?' They listened for a moment; through the wall separating the two cottages came a faint, rhythmic warble.

'Yes, it is. Excuse me if I dash!' Melissa was on her way in a flash, but not so quickly that she missed the knowing look on Iris's face. Almost certainly, she had guessed that the developments had something to do with Barney.

'I was just going to hang up,' he said in response to her breathless 'Hullo'.

'I was next door.'

'I've had a visit from your policeman friend.'

So Harris had been round personally. She wondered how much he had told Barney about the purpose and the result of the forensic tests. Not much, she suspected, and it wouldn't do to reveal what she knew. 'What did he want?' she asked.

'He came to return my gear. I suppose they couldn't find anything to incriminate me. He had the grace to thank me for my co-operation.'

'That's wonderful! I'm so glad!'

'But not surprised, by the sound of it.'

'Of course I'm not surprised. I always believed you were innocent!'

'So you did. Thank you, Melissa.' If he had guessed that she had prior knowledge, he was not prepared to say so. 'I hear there's been another woman killed not far from where Angy lived. D'you suppose there's a connection?'

'There may be. No one knows yet. It was one of my workshop students, Sybil Bliss. She used to go to Angy's painting class as well. I found her body.'

'How dreadful for you! However did that happen?'

'It's a long story and I don't think I can bear to tell it again just now.'

'I can imagine.' The sympathy in his voice was heartwarming. Of course he understood, having been through the same gruesome ordeal. Worse, in fact. At least she herself was not being treated as a suspect. 'Melissa,' he went on, 'when can I see you?'

It was what she had been hoping and longing for but there was no surge of delight, only a strong but strangely detached sense of relief that the worst of his ordeal was over. Perhaps she was still traumatised by shock. Surely, once she was with him, the magic would return.

'How about this evening?' she said.

'I hoped you'd say that. Will you come here for dinner? I cook quite a reasonable steak.'

'That would be lovely.'

'About seven-thirty?'

'I'll look forward to it.' She managed to convey enthusiasm but the feelings came from the head and not the heart.

She put on a coat and walked into the village for some shopping. On her way through the churchyard she was greeted by excited barks from Snappy, tethered to the boot-scraper by the south door. Immediately, she changed course and made her way among the gravestones, stopping for a moment to fondle and quieten the wriggling, prancing little dog before entering the church.

She was greeted by the familiar smell of ancient timbers overlaid with the indefinable atmosphere that clings to the interior of many old churches. Like the wooden chancel rail on which countless hands awaiting the sacrament had laid a patina, and the memorial stones in the floor of the aisle worn smooth over the centuries, the very fabric of the building seemed to have distilled and preserved some essence of generations of worshippers. There were traces in the air of beeswax, metal polish and fresh flowers, and the brass lectern, the candlesticks and the carved pews gleamed in the mosaic of light pouring through the stained-glass windows.

Eleanor, her back to the door, was standing in front of a flower arrangement on a pedestal at the side of the altar. She glanced round as Melissa entered, alerted by the creak of the heavy wooden door, but immediately returned to her task of removing faded blooms and replacing them with fresh ones. She had spread a newspaper on the chancel steps to receive the discarded items and next to it, arranged neatly side by side, were her handbag, a pair of scissors and a flat basket containing some sprays of foliage and white carnations. Melissa stooped to inhale the clove-like scent of the flowers.

'That's a lovely arrangement,' she said.

'Thank you.' Eleanor had uttered no greeting and her voice sounded flat and tired.

'Are you all right?' asked Melissa.

'Why shouldn't I be?' The response was sharp, almost defensive.

'Rodney told Iris you weren't feeling well.'

'Just a stomach upset. I'm all right now.' Eleanor picked up the fresh flowers and began trimming their stems. She kept her face averted but Melissa could see that she was drawn and pale.

'Well, you don't look all right.' Poor thing, she must be having a rotten time just now. 'Do you have to be doing this? Those flowers could last another day or two, surely?'

'It gives me something else to think about,' said Eleanor with a catch in her voice.

'Something else? You mean, beside Angy ... but you really shouldn't ... '

Melissa's attempt to find some words of comfort was interrupted by the sharp sound of metal on stone as the scissors slipped from Eleanor's hand. Instead of picking them up, she moved behind the pedestal as if taking refuge. Melissa took a step forward and saw that she was clinging to the cast-iron pillar with both hands, her face half hidden among the foliage, her shoulders heaving.

'Eleanor dear, what is it?'

'It's ... it's Rodney! I'm sure they think he killed that girl!'

'Oh no, you mustn't . . . ' Melissa began but Eleanor paid no heed as wave after wave of pent-up fear poured out between her sobs.

'Oh God, what shall I do if they arrest him?' Her voice rose to a thin shriek.

'Eleanor, I'm sure you're making a mistake . . . I don't believe the police suspect Rodney.'

'They do! They do!' In the stillness of the empty church, the words echoed and re-echoed as if every rafter vibrated in sympathy. Eleanor released her grip on the pedestal and put her hands over her eyes, rocking to and fro and moaning, 'I can't bear it, I can't bear it!'

For a moment, Melissa was tempted to put the poor creature's mind at rest by revealing what DCI Harris had told her, but immediately rejected the notion. Such a breach of confidence could rebound in all sorts of directions. So she murmured soothing words and patted Eleanor's shoulder until, little by little, the rocking and moaning subsided like the vibration of a spring coming to rest.

'Did you know,' said Melissa when Eleanor at last became quiet, 'that there's been another murder?' There was no response. 'As a matter of fact, I found the body. It was one of my students.'

'Oh, no!' The words were barely audible. 'Oh Melissa, I'm so sorry!'

'No need to apologise!' As an attempt to introduce a note of levity, the words were a disastrous flop. Eleanor succumbed to another shuddering tide of despair.

'Now stop that!' Melissa gave her a gentle shake. 'The police think she—Sybil—must have disturbed an intruder, and there's some suggestion that the same person killed Angy. Sybil had never even set eyes on Rodney so they couldn't possibly suspect him of her murder, now could they? You'll see, it'll be all right, so stop fretting.'

'You really think so?' Eleanor raised a blotched and swollen face.

'I'm sure so,' said Melissa earnestly, and in perfect faith.

'Well, I only hope you're right. It's been so awful,

lately . . . and Major and Mrs Ford keep hinting . . . ' Still convulsively sniffing, Eleanor dabbed her eyes.

'Madeleine and Dudley Ford are a pair of malicious old gossips. Don't you take any notice of what they say,' said Melissa tartly. 'Now, have you finished here?'

'Nearly . . . just these few carnations.' With nimble fingers, Eleanor put the remaining flowers in place before rolling the newspaper into a neat parcel which she carried into the vestry. Melissa heard the sounds of a dustbin lid being replaced and the running of a tap as Eleanor washed her hands. She came back into the church and picked up her belongings.

'Are you going home now?' Melissa asked. Eleanor did not reply. She stood for several moments in front of the altar before turning away and walking back towards the door. Her head was bent and her shoulders drooped as if her fears had been only partially allayed.

Melissa hurried after her. 'Are you sure you're all right? Shall I walk home with you?'

'That would be kind.' Outside, she bent to unhitch Snappy's lead. The dog whined and squirmed with pleasure, jumping up at the two women in turn. 'Down, Snappy!' said Eleanor in the same dead tone she had used when Melissa first arrived.

As they reached the corner of Woodbine Close, Dudley Ford emerged from his front door and came striding down the garden path with Sinbad snuffling at his heels. He had a jaunty air, his panama at its usual rakish angle and his cane swinging.

'Oh, no!' Eleanor groaned in dismay. 'I can't face him this morning. Excuse me!' She scuttled across the road, dragging a reluctant Snappy who was obviously spoiling for a scrap, just as Ford reached his front gate.

'Ha! Good morning, Melissa!' He lifted his hat an inch or two and directed a toothy smile first at her and then at Eleanor's retreating figure, as if ready to return the wave and the greeting that he evidently expected of her. 'She seems in a bit of a hurry!' he observed, implying with raised brow and compressed lips that such haste must hold some deep and possibly sinister significance. That anyone would deliberately avoid him would never enter his head.

Resigned to being detained for several minutes, Melissa forced herself to be pleasant, making suitable replies to his comments on the weather and agreeing that it was a bit unsettled, that frost was still likely to be a problem but was only to be expected at this time of year. She was certain, however, that it was not the weather that was uppermost in his mind. From the way his eyes kept darting to and fro she guessed that he had something more important to say and that he was waiting until Eleanor was safely out of sight and earshot. As she disappeared round the side of her house, he leaned towards Melissa with a sly, knowing look on his face.

'Poor old Shergold has had another visit from the boys in blue!' he confided. 'Shouldn't like to be in his shoes!'

'Really?' Deliberately, she used a tone of cool detachment. She had no wish to appear impolite but there was something about the man that made her cringe. He was so blatantly, shamelessly inquisitive, so ready to place the most sensational interpretation on the smallest of circumstances and, under the guise of concern, to savour to the full the trials and tragedies of his neighbors.

'Brought something in a plastic bag . . . for identification, I shouldn't wonder. Didn't stay long but I expect they'll be back. Part of their tactics, don't y'know. Psychological pressure and all that.' The florid countenance was within a foot of Melissa's face. 'Y'know what, I still reckon it was him who killed that girl, alibi or no alibi. And I reckon his wife thinks so too. She's been going around lately looking like death warmed up.' As if that settled it beyond doubt, he rocked back on his heels, planted his cane between his feet and assumed an expression of profound wisdom.

Melissa's patience had been tried to the limit. 'I don't think we should make that sort of speculation without any evidence,' she snapped. 'The Shergolds must both be under a great deal of strain and it's up to us all to be as supportive as we can. Excuse me, Dudley, I really

must be going.' Without waiting for the inevitable flourish
of the panama and the affected little bow that she knew
would accompany his farewell, she turned round and hurried away.

TWENTY

WHEN BARNEY OPENED THE DOOR TO MELISSA he greeted her with a smile but his eyes remained grave. He stood aside to admit her; in the tiny entrance hall he helped her off with her coat without touching her.

'Do go in. Mind the step.' He followed her into the sitting-room, still leaving space between them. Music played softly in the background as they stood on either side of the hearth, smiling uncertainly at one another like former lovers reunited after a long absence and wondering whether they still had anything in common.

'It's nice to see a fire,' she said, breaking the silence.

'Yes, it makes the room look cheerful, doesn't it?'

'Yes.' A pause. 'That's Mozart, isn't it?'

'That's right. The clarinet concerto. Do you like it?'

'I love all his music.'

'So do I. Won't you sit down? Can I get you a drink?'

She didn't want to sit down. She wanted him to take her in his arms and make her feel once more the strong, swift surge of desire that she remembered from their one night together. Yet, perversely, she found it a relief that he kept his distance. So often since then she had lain awake in the darkness aching for him . . . but that had been before the discovery of Sybil's body and the awful, emotional turmoil that had followed. The knowledge that he was not going to be charged with Angy's murder had aroused profound relief but not elation; his invitation for this evening had brought pleasure but no excitement.

209

It was probably just as well. His own manner was controlled, almost detached. Perhaps he had no intention of making love to her again but had merely invited her round for a meal and a couple of hours of music and conversation, out of a sense of gratitude for her loyalty and her repeated assurances that she believed in his innocence.

She asked for red wine and when he brought it she raised the glass and tried to think of something original and witty by way of a toast but he forestalled her by saying, 'Cheers,' and she could think of no other response. They settled in armchairs and she saw how the standard lamp threw shadows on his face, accentuating the hollows in his cheeks and the overhang of his brow so that his eyes seemed to sink into their sockets and burn there in the firelight like lamps in darkened caves. Only the music and the hiss of burning wood broke the silence.

'You must feel there's a great weight off your mind,' said Melissa at last.

He looked at her with a sombre expression. 'Yes. It's no fun, being suspected of murder.'

'I'm sure it isn't.'

'You know they checked on Doug Wilson and Rodney Shergold as well?'

'I hadn't heard about Doug but in a case of murder, nobody close to the victim gets overlooked.'

'They couldn't find a motive in Doug's case, but they tested some of his clothing just the same.' Barney gave a short laugh. 'They seemed particularly interested in cotton sweat-shirts. We found out later that we each had an identical one from Marks and Sparks. That would have set them a puzzle, wouldn't it, if the fibres had come from one of them?'

She smiled back in relief. The ice, if not broken, was beginning to soften a little. 'It certainly would.'

'I wonder where they go from here?' His face became serious again; he leaned forward and stared at the fire, slowly sipping his wine. 'You said there might be a connection with this latest killing.' He turned to her with a searching expression, as if he suspected her of withholding something.

'They think Sybil was the victim of a walk-in thief—
maybe a junkie, and it's possible the same person killed
Angy.'

'When I think of all the time they've wasted, trying to
prove me guilty while the real killer goes free . . . '

His voice disintegrated. He stood up and began moving
restlessly around the room, fiddling with books and ornaments and adjusting the glasses and cutlery on the table laid
ready for their meal. He had taken great pains to make it
attractive; green candles in crystal holders stood waiting to
be lit and in the centre was a bowl of white miniature roses,
their heads like pale ghosts against the polished wood. He
seemed to be considering it, as if wondering if something
had been overlooked, but when he turned round, the pain
in his eyes was almost too much for Melissa to bear. In
an instant, she was beside him, standing close but still not
venturing to touch him.

'Whoever did it will be caught in the end,' she said
gently.

'Yes, of course.' He stared down at her, his mouth working. 'It's just so awful, not knowing. I lie awake at nights,
seeing her lying there . . . '

'You must try not to brood.'

He gave a despairing little shrug and closed his eyes.
Melissa decided that it was time to be sensible and practical.
Too much sympathy would only encourage self-pity. 'What
about that dinner you promised me?' she reminded him. 'Is
there anything I can do in the kitchen?'

It had been the right thing to say. He squared his shoulders and forced a smile. 'What a rotten host I am! It's
all ready except for the steak. How do you like yours
cooked?'

Melissa stared at the two slabs of raw meat that he took
from the refrigerator and felt her appetite vanish. 'I'm sorry,
Barney,' she faltered. 'I don't think I can face that.'

Instantly, he understood and put the steaks away. 'How
about a quiche? There's one in the freezer . . . I can thaw it
out in the microwave . . . and I've done a salad and jacket
potatoes.'

'That'll be fine.'

By mutual consent, the conversation switched from mystery and death to more mundane topics: the latest political scandal; the protests of wildlife conservationists against a proposed motorway extension. By the time they sat down to eat, much of the tension between them had eased.

'My vegetarian neighbour would thoroughly approve of this meal,' commented Melissa.

'You mean Iris Ash?'

'That's right.' Melissa gave a mischievous grimace as she suddenly remembered the disapproving gleam in her friend's eye on learning where she was spending the evening and, possibly, the night.

'What's the joke?' Barney, too, was smiling as he reached out to refill her glass.

'I was picturing her face when I said I was seeing you this evening.'

The smile faded. 'She's still worried about your safety?'

'Of course not. It's just that she has this *idée fixe* that my agent is the man for me. Truly!' she added as the shadow on his face continued to darken and his head to droop.

'She won't be the only one who still has their doubts,' he muttered, pushing his plate away. 'We're all under a cloud until they find the real killer . . . me, Doug, Rodney Shergold.'

'I haven't seen Doug since the day you . . . since Thursday of last week.' Just in time, she remembered to avoid the direct reference. 'How has he been taking it?'

'I think it shook him pretty badly, but you know Doug. Likes to kid everyone he's the big macho tough guy. Not like poor old Rodney! He's been going round looking like the wrath of God. Haven't you seen him?'

'Only once. I gather he's pretty much on edge. His wife is going round the bend, thinking he's under suspicion, but I'm sure she's barking up the wrong tree. Not that she's the only one. Their busybody neighbour is convinced that he did it.'

'But he's got an alibi.'

'It'd take more than a few facts to convince Dudley Ford that he's mistaken! I haven't a lot of time for Rodney but I really do feel sorry for Eleanor,' Melissa went on thoughtfully, remembering the afternoon's encounter. 'I found her in church earlier on today, howling into her flower arrangement. The strain is really getting her down.'

'Poor thing.' Barney sounded as if he meant it. 'What sort of a woman is she? I picture some self-effacing little creature who won't say boo to a goose.'

Melissa laughed. 'You're not far off! She certainly wouldn't say boo to Rodney but get her out from under his shadow and she's got plenty of . . . character.' She had been going to say 'potential' but felt it might sound patronising. 'It's sad really. She's quite talented but she subordinates all her interests to his. It's almost unhealthy.'

Barney nodded vaguely. It was clear that his mind was once more centred on the hunt for Angy's killer. 'What are the police going to do now, do you think?'

'Just carry on with their usual kind of enquiries: forensic tests, house-to-house visits, appeals for witnesses. They'll be trying to establish whether the two crimes are related or not.'

'Finding your friend's body must have been a terrible shock for you,' he said. For a moment, he had put his own pain to one side to share in hers. She felt her eyes prickle.

'It was awful,' she whispered.

'How did you come to be there?'

Briefly, she recounted her and Sybil's efforts to track down Delia Forbes. 'I keep asking myself what it could have been that she was so keen to tell me on the phone. I can't help thinking it had something to do with Angy's murder, but we'll never know now. Some wretched little junkie saw to that!'

Barney was looking at her with a strange expression, half puzzled, half tender.

'Were you really doing all this on my behalf?'

'Sybil didn't believe you'd killed Angy either. She . . . we both thought we'd like to do something to help.'

'I find that very touching,' he said.

'It seemed a long shot, but we felt we had to try.' She hesitated for a moment before saying, 'We went to see Eddie Brady on Thursday.'

'The man Angy was always talking about? Wasn't he her landlord?'

'Not exactly. "Eddie" is short for Edwina.'

Barney frowned. 'I don't understand.'

'Eddie Brady is a woman. She was in love with Angy . . . very sincerely, very deeply. I don't think there was any commitment on Angy's part but I've no doubt Eddie hoped—and believed—there would be, given time.'

'That explains why Angy thought my suspicions about her being pregnant were so wildly funny,' said Barney, slowly and with some bitterness. 'Why in the world couldn't she have been more honest with me?'

Melissa was surprised that he had taken the news so calmly. She had thought long and hard before deciding that it was best for him to hear it from her rather than risk it reaching him through the more sensational tabloids, but she had braced herself for an outburst of shock, anger, even disgust.

'My guess is that she hadn't come to terms with the situation herself,' she said. 'The more I think about it, the more it seems she was very confused about her feelings. She seems to have been a girl who drifted into relationships because she didn't like upsetting people. Her so-called engagement to Rick was a disaster, and Eddie said . . . ' She broke off, thinking that further revelations about Angy's sex-life would be a mistake, but Barney pounced.

'What did Eddie say?'

'That Angy had started an affair with Rodney Shergold, as a kind of quid pro quo for letting her take the art class. Eddie wanted Angy to end it but said that she was too soft-hearted.'

'Just a girl who couldn't say "No",' said Barney with a quiet irony that held a hint of resignation. Once again, the feared explosion of rage had not materialised. He sat looking at his hands as they rested on the table, palms down, the fingers softly drumming. She thought how long and lean they were, a true artist's hands, and remembered how they had felt when he touched her.

It was several moments before he spoke. 'She never told me about Shergold but it was common gossip how he felt about her,' he admitted at last. 'I didn't like to think of it but Doug Wilson was always making sly innuendoes. You're right about her being tender-hearted, of course. She couldn't bear to see anyone upset. When I think of what I did . . . I'd give anything in the world to undo that quarrel with her!'

'Don't be too hard on yourself. You told me how she taunted you . . . ' Melissa was about to point out that Angy's tender heart had not prevented her from flaunting Rick's ring as if it were her own, nor had she intervened to protect Barney from hurt, but she merely said, 'It was enough to make anyone angry.'

'That's no excuse for hitting a woman.'

'A slap in the face doesn't exactly amount to grievous bodily harm, does it? You must try and forget about it.'

'I suppose so.' He took the hand that, without thinking, she had reached out to him. 'Bless you, Melissa. I can't tell you what it's meant to me, knowing that you cared, even a little . . . '

'I care quite a lot,' she said softly. The warmth of his fingers on hers was like electricity.

'Have you had enough to eat?' he asked. 'Shall we have coffee?' He had it already prepared and he went and fetched the tray. 'What about some more music? A piano concerto?'

'Lovely.'

He put more logs on the fire and she sat on the floor with her back resting against a settle. 'You don't mind, do you? Iris always sits on the floor and I've got into the habit.' It wasn't entirely true but it could very well have been and he showed no surprise.

'You don't look very comfortable. Have a cushion.' He took one from an armchair and put it behind her back. Then he sat on the floor beside her, half turned towards her, leaning on one elbow. They drank their coffee and he

took both cups and leaned across her to put them on the
settle. His arm came down on her shoulder and tightened
round her, pulling her close. She smelled the clean tang of
his breath, felt the softness of his beard and the purposeful
movements of lips and tongue and hands. The air was filled
with sublime music and the sound of burning wood was like
the soft crackle of melting ice.

TWENTY-ONE

ON SUNDAY, AS ARRANGED, MELISSA JOINED Iris and her American cousin for supper. David Burleigh was a retired professor of literature at a New England university, quietly spoken and witty. In normal circumstances, Melissa would have found him stimulating company but that evening she found her thoughts constantly wandering. The shock and mystery of two tragic and violent deaths jostled for attention with a sense of uncertainty over her future relationship with Barney. At ten o'clock, overcome by weariness, she excused herself and went home.

Next morning, she went into the village to collect bread and newspapers. Eleanor was just coming out of Mrs Foster's shop.

'How are you this morning?' enquired Melissa, holding out a hand for Snappy to lick and noticing with relief that some of the strain had lifted from her friend's face.

'Fine, thank you.' Eleanor glanced from side to side and then said in a low voice, 'It's all right . . . what I told you about.' She broke off as if afraid of being overheard and moved away with a nod and a wave. 'I must get back and see to the washing. I think it's going to be fine, don't you?'

'Well, she seems more like herself,' said Mrs Foster as the door closed. 'Been looking like death lately, she has.'

'Yes, she does look better,' replied Melissa, thinking that the return of Rodney's jacket must have convinced Eleanor that he had at last been eliminated from police enquiries.

'Mind you, it's no wonder she's been out of sorts after that dreadful business at the tech . . . and Major Ford tittle-tattling all over the village.' If it was Mrs Foster's intention to express disapproval of the Major's predilection for gossip, the animation in her tone and the wild fluttering of her colourless eyelashes seemed rather to show an unhealthy interest in what he had to say and an eagerness to discuss it.

Melissa had no intention of obliging her. 'I take anything the Major says with a large pinch of salt,' she said crisply. 'If I could just have a wholemeal loaf and the papers . . . and I need a tin of tomatoes and half a dozen eggs.'

'Yes, of course.' Mrs Foster bobbed about collecting the items and putting them on the counter. 'Any news about who did in that poor lady that you found, Mrs Craig?' she asked as she took the money. Melissa shook her head. 'Poor soul, what a way to go. I expect it's made you feel a bit jumpy too, like?' The eyelashes fluttered harder than ever, doubtless in anticipation of some highly-coloured account of the state of Melissa's nerves.

'It did shake me up, but I'm over it now.'

'Yes, well I suppose in your line of business you get used to bodies and blood and things,' said Mrs Foster, as if writing crime fiction was in some way akin to working in an abattoir.

Melissa stowed her purchases in her shopping bag and picked up her change. 'I really must hurry along, I've got a busy day in front of me.'

Late that afternoon she had a telephone call from Joe Martin, just back from a trip to New York.

'Hi, Mel!' he said breezily. 'I see you've been having more fun and games!'

'What's that supposed to mean?'

'I've been catching up on the week's news, and who do I find hitting the headlines yet again?'

'That was hardly my idea of fun and games.'

'No, of course not. It must have been creepy for you, going into that empty house and finding something nasty behind the door . . . hey, that'd make a title, wouldn't it? *Something Nasty* . . . '

Melissa was not amused. 'You make it sound like part of a publicity exercise,' she interrupted. 'It was a very unnerving experience.'

'I'm sure it was . . . poor old Mel. Still, talking of publicity, I hear demand for your paperbacks has shot up in the past week.'

'I'm sure Sybil would be comforted to know that her death had helped such a worthwhile cause,' said Melissa through her teeth. 'Some of us have hearts where you keep your pocket calculator.'

'Sorry, should have known better.' His voice became furry with contrition. 'Well, here's a bit of good news: there's a very flattering piece about *Blow the Man Down* in this week's *Publishing News*.'

'That's nice,' said Melissa bleakly.

'You sound as if you need cheering up. I'm tied up for a couple of days but I could come down on Thursday if you like.'

Something in his tone warned her that his motives were not entirely concerned with her peace of mind and she replied, a little too quickly, 'I don't want any visitors just now, thank you. I've had too many interruptions already and I'm behind schedule with *Suspected of Being Innocent* as it is.'

'*Suspected of* . . . hang on! Is that your idea of a title?'

'Don't you like it? It's sort of double bluff. You'll understand when you've read it.'

'You mean, the prime suspect turns out to be the killer? Bloody useless title. Gives it away before you can open the book.'

She had thought it rather clever and original and felt childishly disgruntled at his reaction. 'Well, you suggest a better one,' she said pettishly.

'I already have,' he pointed out, sounding smug.

'Yes . . . well, it might do.' Privately, she thought it quite promising but she wasn't going to admit it.

'Think about it. Well, if you're sure you don't want me around . . . ' He was letting her know that he was taking her refusal personally.

'I didn't say that.'

'But it's what you meant, isn't it? Okay, I get the message. I'll be in touch.'

Melissa put down the phone and glanced at the clock. It was almost five. She might as well pack up work for the day and start thinking about food.

She ate her supper at the kitchen table, a book at her elbow. When she had finished she wandered into the sitting-room and picked up a newspaper. She felt bored and restless; she didn't really feel like reading, there was nothing worth watching on television and Iris was down at the Craftworks studio giving free advice to her protégées. It looked like a barren evening. Then the phone rang again.

'Is that you, Melissa?' The girl's voice sounded hesitant.

'Why, Lou! How nice to hear from you! How are things?'

'Not very good.'

'Oh dear, I'm sorry. What's wrong?'

'It's Rick. We've split up.' The voice was flat and carefully controlled but it had a tell-tale wobble. 'Melissa, are you terribly busy?'

'I'm trying to be,' said Melissa wryly. 'When I'm not getting caught up in murder hunts.'

'Yes, I read about that in the papers. She was one of Angy's students, wasn't she?'

'She was one of my students as well.'

'And you found the body. Poor you, it must have been ghastly.'

Despite her own problems, the girl was quick to show a real concern. Melissa found herself drawing comparisons with Joe. He too had expressed sympathy but it was a pretty thin veneer over his commercial and sexual preoccupations.

'I hate to bother you with my problems,' Lou went on, 'but you've been so kind and I do need someone to talk to . . .'

'It's no bother. Would you like to come down tomorrow, if you can get the time off?' I need my head seeing to,

Melissa thought to herself. I've just been fending off Joe because I need the time to work . . . but of course, that wasn't the only reason.

Lou jumped at the invitation. 'Could I? That would be brilliant! I rang the office this morning to say I was sick so they won't be surprised if I don't show!' She sounded almost cheerful. 'Shall I get the same train as last time?'

'Why not? I'll pick you up at the station.'

She had barely sat down when the phone rang for a third time. DCI Harris was on the line.

'I wonder if I could call round for a few minutes,' he said.

'You mean now?'

'If it isn't too inconvenient.'

'Of course.'

As usual, his bulk seemed to dwarf his surroundings. Melissa steered him towards the most substantial chair in the room and he lowered himself on to it, tugging at the trouser legs that strained across his massive thighs. He pulled a folder from his briefcase.

'The forensic boys have been pulling all the stops out,' he said. 'We're ninety-nine per cent certain now that we're looking for one person in connection with both killings.' From habit, his eyes, the only small feature in his round, lumpy face, did not leave hers for an instant. 'I know you've already been questioned by Inspector Clarke but there are still one or two points where you might be able to help us.'

'I'll do whatever I can.'

'First of all, would you mind showing me the shoes you had on when you found Mrs Bliss?'

Melissa thought for a moment, then went and fetched a pair of flat-heeled black casuals. 'I was wearing these.'

He took one, turned it over and inspected the sole before handing it back. 'Thanks. You're sure those were the ones?'

'Quite sure. Could I ask . . . '

'What about gloves?'

'Gloves?'

'Were you wearing any?'

'No.'

'You're sure?'

'Absolutely. Ken, what . . . ?'

'Do you happen to know if your friend is at home?'

'You mean Iris? She was out earlier on . . . she may be back. Do you want to talk to her?'

'When I've finished talking to you.'

'I'm sure she'll be more than willing to answer your questions, but I do think you might tell me what you've found,' pleaded Melissa. 'You know it won't go any further.'

'Don't worry, I was going to tell you.' The fleshy cheeks, pushed upwards by one of his rare smiles, almost obliterated the twinkle in his eyes. 'There was quite a bit of dust on the floor in Mrs Bliss's garage and we found one lovely impression of a shoe.'

He handed over a couple of prints. The photographer had used all his skill to bring up the detail of the fine diamond pattern of the sole. 'This was made by the murderer?' murmured Melissa, feeling suddenly chilled.

'We can't be certain but it's odds on,' said Harris. 'It certainly wasn't yours, and we've already eliminated the two British Telecom boys and Mrs Bliss's own shoes. There's Miss Ash to check, of course, but after that . . . '

'Where exactly was the print found?'

'Near the main door of the garage, close to the wall. We think he probably stood there looking out to see if the coast was clear before making off.'

Melissa closed her eyes and pictured a furtive figure, probably wearing denims or a leather jacket with Sybil's handbag stuffed inside it, huddled tense and trembling against the wall, waiting for his chance to slip away unobserved. He must have had blood on his clothing, yet no one had been there to see he had vanished like a wraith into thin air, leaving behind him an innocent woman with her brains spilling out on the floor.

'Are you feeling all right?' asked Harris.

She opened her eyes. 'Yes, I'm fine. I was just thinking . . . it's so strange that no one saw anything.'

'Yes, we haven't had a lot of luck with witnesses. What worries us is that there's every chance he'll strike again. We've issued a warning to the public to be on the look-out and keep their doors and windows secure.'

'Was there money stolen from Angy's flat? I don't remember hearing about it?'

'Her handbag was missing but as there were several people with possible motives for killing her, it seemed like an attempt to make robbery appear the motive. Now, it looks as if it really was someone after the money for a fix.'

'You're sure it's drug-related then?'

'It's the line we're following at the moment, but it's like the proverbial needle in a haystack.' For the first time since she had known him, he showed signs of despondency. The corners of his mouth drooped and his ruddy face seemed to sink into his squat neck like a cartoonist's drawing of the sun going down.

'You asked about gloves,' Melissa reminded him. 'Weren't there any prints on the hammer?'

'No, but there were some fibres which match the ones found on Angelica Caroli's body. Those were so spread around and mixed up with her blood where she'd been thrashing around with her hands and clawing at the knife, it was difficult to establish exactly where they were to start with. Now, we're pretty sure our man wears brown cotton gloves.'

Melissa swallowed hard at the gruesome description. 'Well, Iris doesn't often wear gloves, except for gardening and church,' she said. 'She certainly wasn't wearing any last Friday.' She studied the prints of the shoe again. 'This is a very ordinary pattern, isn't it?'

'There's a bit of wear that might help with identification and a small round patch that could be something stuck to the sole. It's a fairly small shoe so we aren't looking for a heavily-built chap. Probably quite a weasely little bugger.'

There was the sound of a car outside.

'That'll be Iris,' said Melissa. She half got up. 'Shall I pop out and tell her you want to see her?'

'No thanks, I'll drop by when I leave here.' He put the prints away in the folder. 'I'm sorry to have broken up your evening.'

'I wasn't doing anything. By the way, have you found out any more about Delia Forbes?'

'A little. I sent an officer round and he managed to find a more intelligent neighbour who said that Mrs Forbes left a key with a lady who comes round every now and then to check the house and pick up the post. She couldn't remember the name. We're taking steps to contact her.' Harris stood up. 'We've checked among Eddie Brady's colleagues as well and there's no talk of any lesbian triangles so I wouldn't pin too much faith on that theory of yours, especially now that we're pretty sure Angy Caroli was the victim of a walk-in thief.'

'But you must admit it's odd,' persisted Melissa, 'taking someone else's name just to join an art class?'

Harris shrugged. 'People do all sorts of daft things. It's important to find her, though. If she really did call round at Angy's flat, she might have seen someone hanging around . . . it could be the breakthrough we're looking for.' He heaved himself upright as he spoke, making for the door. 'Now, I'll just call in and see Miss Ash and then I'll be getting home.'

As she let him out, she said, 'Remember Rick Lawrence's faithful girlfriend?'

'I remember. Nice kid . . . much too good for that greasy little wop!'

'They've split up. She rang me this evening to tell me.'

Harris grunted. 'Good thing too. Tell her from me to be a bit more choosy next time!' His small eyes searched Melissa's like a dentist's probe. 'Seen anything of Willard?'

'I had dinner with him on Saturday.' She was conscious of the blood rushing into her cheeks and furious with herself for such a schoolgirlish reaction. She tilted her chin in an effort to appear belligerent. 'I assumed we'd been given clearance!'

He shrugged. 'Nothing to do with me now.'

He's still feeling miffed . . . he really thought he'd got his man, she thought to herself. He was a first-class policeman and his hunches were usually right but he'd completely misjudged Barney. She couldn't hold back a smug little smile. 'You can't win 'em all,' she said consolingly.

Lou had dark smudges under her eyes and her face was pale but she showed none of the nervous tension of her previous visit. During the drive from the station she hardly spoke, sitting with bowed head and a wan, wistful expression, but her body was relaxed and her hands lay loose in her lap in a pose of resignation and defeat.

When they reached Hawthorn Cottage she got out of the car and stood for a minute or two looking at the view across the valley. A flock of rooks rose screeching from a clump of tall trees and scattered in all directions like flakes of charred paper whirling away on the wind. Lou dug her hands into the pockets of her red woollen jacket and shivered.

'It's a lot cooler here than in London,' she commented, 'but you've got a smashing view. Rick would love it,' she added, her mouth drooping.

'Come indoors and we'll have some coffee,' said Melissa. 'Then you can tell me all about it.'

It was a simple story: Rick's family, staunch Catholics and fiercely proud of their cultural heritage, had refused to give their blessing to his engagement to someone they regarded as an outsider. Rick had made it plain that he had no intention of defying them.

'They want him to marry a nice Italian girl who'll cook his pasta and give him lots of bambinos,' said Lou, her lip curling in contempt. 'They absolutely doted on Angy . . . thought she was the ideal mate for their precious son! Didn't know her, did they?' The old resentment had resurfaced. 'They were absolutely devastated when she ran out on him and when he and I got together again they wouldn't have anything to do with him. We thought it was just because of the ring and that everything would be all right once he'd got that back . . . but it wasn't.' Lou shut her eyes and screwed up her small pointed features in an heroic effort to hold back the tears but two bright drops squeezed out and hung on her lashes.

'I'm sorry it didn't work out,' said Melissa sincerely, 'but if you'll forgive me for saying so, I never thought that Rick was quite the right one for you . . . and neither did Iris.' She decided not to pass on DCI Harris's comment.

Lou's eyes widened. 'Why not?' She showed no resentment, only surprise.

'Too self-centred and too much of the Italian temperament,' said Melissa. 'All that posturing over the portrait— I'll never forget the way he went barging past you that day—and then running away after finding Angy's body, leaving you to face the music when the police caught up with you. Not exactly the steady, reliable type, is he?'

Lou's deep sigh and soulful expression suggested that steadiness and reliability had not been high on her list of priorities when she threw in her lot with Rick. 'But I love him so much!' she protested. 'And he's so good-looking!'

'Yes, well, so was Guy, but I'm not sure he'd have been the ideal husband,' said Melissa.

Lou sniffed and blew her nose. 'Who's Guy?' she asked through her handkerchief.

'My son's father. He was killed in a road accident before Simon was born.'

'Oh, poor you, how awful! Didn't you say your son lives in America?'

'Yes, in Texas. Here's his picture.' Melissa fetched a framed photograph of a bronzed and beaming Simon, resplendent in Stetson and cowboy boots and mounted on a chestnut horse.

Lou's eyes nearly popped out of her head. 'He's gorgeous! Is he married?'

'Not as far as I know. I think he'd tell me; we're pretty good friends.'

Lou's eyes followed the photograph as Melissa returned it to its place on the shelf. Plainly her heart, though bruised, was far from irretrievably broken.

'Why don't you come and talk to me while I prepare some lunch,' said Melissa. 'I don't know much about the world of fashion so tell me about your job.'

After they had eaten their chicken and stir-fried vegetables, with a glass of white wine and some cheese and fruit to follow, Melissa suggested a walk. They reached the village just as Snappy was having a noisy argument with Sinbad outside the shop. Dudley Ford was waving a menacing stick and Eleanor, looking pink and flustered, snatched up her dog and backed away.

'Quiet, Snappy, silly boy!' she chided him, smiling uncertainly at Ford. 'They don't seem to like one another very much, do they, *khikhikhi*!'

Ford was not in the best of tempers. 'Aggressive little beast!' he growled. 'Didn't expect to meet you!' he added with a glare in Eleanor's direction. 'Usually off out somewhere on a Tuesday, aren't you?' Then, appearing to notice Melissa and Lou for the first time, he remembered his manners and reached for his hat. 'Afternoon, ladies!' His eyes skated backwards and forwards between them, inviting an introduction and identification.

Deliberately ignoring the blatant curiosity in the old man's eyes, Melissa walked past with a curt, 'Good afternoon, Dudley' and called a greeting to Eleanor, who had retreated a short distance before putting Snappy down. She was wearing a bemused expression and seemed lost for words.

Not so Lou. 'What a dreadful old man!' she said in a high, penetrating voice as the door into the shop was flung open to the accompaniment of a furious tinkling of the bell. 'Are you supposed to ask his permission before changing your routine?'

'Major Ford is the ultimate in nosey parkers!' explained Melissa. 'He and his wife between them keep an eye on the comings and goings of everyone in the village. Next time I meet him he'll be pumping me like mad to find out who you are. Let me introduce you. Lou Stacey—Eleanor Shergold. Lou was a friend of Angy's.'

'Oh, really?' said Eleanor.

'We were at college together,' said Lou. 'I was absolutely shattered when I heard what had happened.'

'Such a terrible thing!' Eleanor's green eyes were sombre. 'She was such a good secretary, my husband used to say. He's quite lost without her and you know, they still haven't found him anyone else. It's really very difficult for him.' Eleanor quickened her pace as Snappy plunged forward in a bid to pursue a cat crossing the road ahead. Behind her back, Melissa and Lou exchanged glances.

They parted from Eleanor at the corner of Woodbine Close. In the distance, Melissa spied Dudley Ford striding up the village street towards them. If they retraced their steps they'd walk straight into him.

'Shall we go back across the fields?' she suggested. 'It might be a bit muddy in places, though,' she added with a doubtful glance at Lou's dainty little boots.

'No problem,' the girl assured her.

The sun was warm and every tree, hedge and flower responded with an eager thrust of new growth. A lark filled the air with song, hovering above a field of young corn as if suspended on a thread from heaven. Lou tilted her face towards the sky and closed her eyes.

'Isn't that just beautiful?' she murmured.

Soon they met Harriet Yorke. In her green jacket and tailored slacks, her skin glowing from exercise, she looked as sleek and glossy as the red setter bounding ahead of her.

'We've come this way to dodge Dreadful Dudley,' said Melissa after introducing Lou. 'He was beastly to poor Eleanor outside the shop, just because Snappy barked at Sinbad. He had the cheek to tell her off for not sticking to her regular times! Can you believe it?'

'I can believe anything of that man,' said Harriet. 'His wife's just as bad. My brother-in-law had some business in Gloucester the other week and he called in to see me during the afternoon. From the way that old crow looked down her beak, you'd have thought she suspected us of having an affair. "Ay hope yaw husband knows about yaw visitah!" ' Harriet gave a wicked impression of Madeleine Ford's plummy voice. ' "Yew kneow how people tawk!" I just smiled and said I was sure she'd find an opportunity to mention it to him and she went all pink and sniffy.'

'They sound a real pain in the bum,' said Lou chirpily.

Harriet's smile flashed like a row of pearls and she gave Lou an approving nudge on the arm. 'Oh, they are! Like ferrets up a drainpipe, the pair of them!' Her eyes scanned the field. 'Damn, where's that dog gone? *Ruuufus!*'

'Isn't she gorgeous!' whispered Lou as Harriet went striding off along the edge of the field, calling and whistling, her red-gold hair catching the light as it lifted in the breeze.

'It's reliably rumoured that Dudley Ford fancies her!' said Melissa with a grin. 'That's why his wife never loses an opportunity for a dig!'

Lou gave a little squeak of delight. 'And I always thought country life must be dull!'

'Far from it!' Melissa assured her, thinking how good it was to hear her laughter.

Back in Hawthorn Cottage, Lou said, 'Could you give me the recipe for that chicken dish? It was scrumptious!'

'Of course.' Melissa took her recipe book from a drawer and found a sheet of paper and a pencil. She glanced up at the clock. 'We'd better be leaving when you've jotted that down,' she said, realising as she spoke that she would be sorry to see the girl go. 'You'll keep in touch, won't you, and come and see me again?'

Lou's face lit up. 'I'd love to!' she said. Her eye fell on the calendar that hung on the wall. 'Are you doing anything over Bank Holiday?' she added with a touch of wistfulness in her voice.

'I'm not sure. A friend of mine is spending it with relatives in Yorkshire and he's asked me to join him.' Barney had issued the invitation on Sunday but she hadn't yet made up her mind whether to accept.

Lou, scribbling away at the recipe, glanced up and looked at Melissa with open curiosity. 'Is it a serious relationship?' she asked, her tone entirely matter-of-fact.

It was a question Melissa had been asking herself for the past couple of days but she had not expected to hear it from Lou. For a second, she was nonplussed. When I was in my twenties, she thought, it wouldn't have entered my head to say a thing like that to someone twice my age. Young people have absolutely no inhibitions nowadays. Yet in a way the girl's frankness pleased her. At least, she didn't consider her too old to have a man.

'It's fairly serious but I don't think it's permanent,' she heard herself saying, and it seemed as if she was removing a doubt from her own mind.

Having finished her writing, Lou got up, took the teacups over to the sink to rinse them and then went up to the bathroom. When she returned, she was wearing her red woollen jacket in readiness to leave. Its loose bulk hung on her slight figure, giving her the air of a small girl dressed up in her mother's clothes. Melissa felt a rush of maternal tenderness towards her. Perhaps the poor kid had been thinking ahead to the holiday that, had things gone the way she had hoped, she would have been spending with Rick and his family. Instead, she'd be stuck on her own in a house of mourning.

'We could make it the weekend after,' she suggested.

Lou's face lit up. 'Oh thanks! I'll really look forward to it.'

When she got back from seeing Lou on to her train, Melissa went into the kitchen. The recipe book still lay open on the table and as she picked it up a piece of paper fell out. Idly glancing at it, she saw that it was the recipe for scones that Eleanor had insisted on giving her. She had put it away without bothering to read it but now, for some reason, she glanced through it. The handwriting was not easy to read; the letters were small and cramped and the words ran into one another, giving the effect of knotted string, interrupted at intervals by spiky up or down strokes. It seemed to Melissa to reflect the writer's repressed, submissive disposition, with the occasional streak of assertiveness that had won her the right to keep a dog.

She studied the paper for several minutes before replacing it. It seemed to be trying to tell her something but for the moment its message eluded her.

Twenty-Two

THE FOLLOWING MORNING, SHORTLY AFTER THE postman had called, Iris appeared at Melissa's front door, brandishing a large envelope. She was obviously bursting with news; her eyes shone and her hair, newly-washed and unruly, threatened to erupt from the restraints of the tortoise-shell slides.

'It's come!' she announced in triumph.

'What has?'

'Philippe's prospectus.' Iris followed Melissa into her sitting-room, thrust the envelope into her hand and subsided on to the floor, legs crossed under the folds of her green pinafore dress. 'Go on . . . read it.'

'Who is Philippe and what is he prospecting?' enquired Melissa as she pulled a glossy brochure from the envelope.

'Philippe Bonard,' said Iris with a simper.

'Ah!' said Melissa. 'I asked you about him when you came back from France and you were jolly cagey. Are you having a torrid affair when you go off to the Midi every winter?'

Iris's smile became positively coy but she made no comment. Melissa, noticing the colour creeping into her friend's cheeks, suppressed a smile and began scanning the literature. After a few moments she looked up to meet a pair of eager eyes.

'What do you think?'

'It looks fascinating . . . but you never told me you were interested in study courses in France. Why all the secrecy?'

'Didn't know if it'd come off,' said Iris. 'Question of capital. Philippe wasn't sure he could raise enough to buy a larger place.' She cleared her throat and played with the hem of her skirt. 'Remember I told you he's been running an adult study centre for some time? Terrific demand . . . language and literature courses mostly . . . wanted to branch out into crafts and music and things but needed more space. Then he found this super house.' The hem became more engrossing than ever. 'He asked me—if it came off—if I'd run an art course in July.'

'And you're going to? Yes, I see you are.' Melissa ran her eye down a list of tutors. Among the names, that of Iris Ash, the internationally known fabric designer and water-colourist, caught her eye.

Iris gave a sigh of pure rapture. 'The house is sublime! Wonderful mountain views!'

'Sounds fascinating,' Melissa repeated. She put the papers together and a sheet fell out. She glanced at it before replacing it. It was a registration form for prospective students at the Centre Cévenol d'Etudes, propriétaire Philippe Bonard. Something jogged her memory.

'Leave it with you if you like,' said Iris, rising to her feet and adjusting several metres of green cloth. 'Have a browse.' She glanced out of the window. 'Nice day. Going to do some gardening later on?'

'Mmm?'

Iris waved a hand in front of Melissa's nose. 'Wakey wakey!'

'Sorry, I was thinking.' It was a mild word to use for the activity going on in her head. Her brain was clicking like a machine, wheels turning and cogs interlocking one after the other at a feverish rate.

'Planning to join one of the courses?' said Iris hopefully. 'Come and brush up your French. Philippe's a superb teacher.' She gave a dreamy sigh. 'Must go. See you later.'

Melissa, wondering among her other thoughts what sort of lessons Philippe had been giving Iris, smiled absently. 'Bye,' she murmured.

Iris peered into her face. 'You're miles away. What's on your mind?'

Melissa tucked the registration form into the envelope with the prospectus. 'I'm not sure, but I think I may have hit on the answer to a riddle. I'll explain later,' she added in response to Iris's raised eyebrows. 'I have to go out.'

The minute Iris had gone, Melissa put on a jacket and outdoor shoes and left the cottage. Deliberately taking the longer route to avoid the village centre and a possible encounter with one of the Fords, she reached Cotswold View just as Eleanor was returning with Snappy on his lead and a shopping basket in her hand.

'You're an early bird!' said Eleanor. Her smile seemed a little too bright.

'Have you got a minute?' asked Melissa. 'There's something I have to talk to you about.'

Eleanor hesitated for a moment before replying. 'Yes, all right. I hope you won't mind coming in at the back door. Rodney doesn't like Snappy coming in through the front because of dirtying the hall carpet.'

In the small glassed-in lobby behind the house, Eleanor put down her basket, inspected the dog's feet and wiped them with a towel.

'You can't be too careful, can you?' she said fussily as she unlocked the back door. 'You never know what they walk in.' Indoors, she changed her shoes, hung her jacket and Snappy's lead on a hook and put her gloves and her purse on the Welsh dresser. Then she washed her hands, dried them carefully and massaged cream into them.

'I like to take care of my hands,' she explained over her shoulder. 'Rodney is always telling me what lovely hands his mother used to have.' She began unpacking her shopping, reciting the items as she did so and checking them against a list. 'Tea . . . eggs . . . biscuits . . . ' Not once since they entered the house had she met Melissa's eye. She scuttled about the kitchen putting things away and then took cups and saucers from a cupboard. 'Would you like a coffee?' she said hesitantly.

'Thanks.' Melissa pulled a chair from under the table and sat down while Eleanor filled the kettle, plugged it in and then stood at the sink, staring out of the window. 'It's a nice day, isn't it?' she said without turning round, and her voice had the toneless quality of one whose thoughts are far away.

'Yes,' agreed Melissa. She waited for a moment. Had she herself been in a similar situation, she would have been curious to learn the reason for the visit. Perhaps Eleanor had already guessed and would prefer not to hear. The kettle began to sing and she measured instant coffee into the cups and opened a packet of biscuits, all without a word. Melissa waited until the coffee was on the table and Eleanor, with seeming reluctance, sat down beside her. Her face was pale and there were indigo smudges under her eyes.

'You don't look well,' said Melissa in sudden concern.

'I'm quite all right, really.' Eleanor stirred her coffee with quick, jerky movements. 'What did you want to talk about?' After having avoided eye contact since they came in, she now fixed on Melissa an intense, unwavering stare.

Melissa fingered her spoon. It all seemed so foolish, so trivial compared with the recent horror, yet she knew that what she was going to say would leave a desperately inhibited woman feeling raw and exposed. Throughout this wretched business, it seemed, it had fallen to her lot to break unpleasant news. This was going to be distressing but there was no way of avoiding it. Two women had been brutally murdered and every corner where a shred of a clue might lie had to be explored.

'I know,' she began, 'that you said you couldn't go to any classes at the college because you thought Rodney wouldn't like it.' Eleanor froze in the act of lifting her cup and Melissa's hunch that she knew what was coming became a certainty, even before she went on. 'That's why you decided to call yourself Delia Forbes, isn't it? Is she a friend of yours?'

Eleanor ran the tip of her tongue over her lips. 'How did you find out?' she whispered.

'I recognised your writing on the registration form.'

'Are you going to tell Rodney?'

'I'm afraid,' said Melissa, speaking slowly and quietly as if she were approaching a nervous animal, 'that it won't be just Rodney who has to know. The police particularly want to speak to you. You may be able to help them in their enquiries.'

At the mention of the police, Eleanor gave a start, spilling some of her coffee over her skirt. Ignoring the stain, she put down her cup, her hand groping for the saucer as she kept her eyes fixed on Melissa. Her colour rose and then faded, leaving her as pale as death.

Melissa put out a comforting hand. 'Oh, come on, it's not as bad as all that! They only want to know if you went to Angy's flat that afternoon and if so, whether you saw anyone hanging about. I'll come with you, if you like, and explain why you did it.'

'Did what?' The voice was barely a whisper and the hand that Melissa held in hers was ice-cold.

'Went to the classes in disguise, of course, so that Rodney wouldn't know. I'll tell him I put you up to it, if you like. It was my idea, after all.'

Eleanor continued to stare with the blankness of a figure carved in stone. As if he knew that something was wrong, Snappy jumped up and put his paws on her lap. She showed no sign of being aware of him; he whined and nudged her hand with his nose but still she did not respond. After a moment he gave an uneasy whimper and retreated to his basket.

Melissa was becoming impatient. 'Look, Eleanor, forget all that nonsense about keeping it a secret from Rodney. That's not important any more, don't you understand? The police want to know if you went to Angy's flat that afternoon and if you saw anything.' Still, Eleanor neither moved nor spoke. In her exasperation, Melissa almost screamed, *'Did* you go there? *Did you?'*

Tears began trickling down the colourless cheeks. The sight filled Melissa with compassion but she felt at the same time a faint prickle of apprehension.

'There's no need to cry,' she said, trying to speak gently. 'Just tell me what happened and we'll go to the police together and . . . '

'No!' The word burst from Eleanor's lips like a spurt of flame.

Melissa could hardly believe her ears. 'What do you mean, no? You have to go! You can't get out of it!'

Eleanor buried her face in her hands. Her breathing became harsh and uneven and her shoulders heaved.

'I'm not . . . going . . . to the police!' she gasped.

'Why ever not?'

Even as she spoke, the answer came into Melissa's head with a dreadful, blinding clarity. Twice before she had found Eleanor in obvious distress, obsessed with fears for her husband's safety. Now, it seemed, those fears were only too well founded.

'Oh my God!' she whispered. 'Oh, Eleanor . . . you were there . . . and you saw . . . ' For a moment, stunned by the enormity of her friend's predicament, she too found difficulty in speaking. 'It was Rodney, wasn't it? That alibi was a fake . . . Rodney killed Angy!'

For a moment, Eleanor seemed to hold her breath. Then she lifted her head; her tears had stopped flowing and her eyes were two points of green fire.

'How dare you accuse my husband!' Her voice was almost a snarl, thick with rage, barely recognisable. She got up and stood over Melissa, glaring down at her. 'Apologise at once!'

'I . . . I'm sorry,' stammered Melissa, feeling more bewildered by the minute. 'I must have misunderstood . . . but you must have seen something . . . or someone.'

As she spoke, a new fear came into her head. Was it Barney whom Eleanor had seen? She couldn't remember telling her anything that might have betrayed her feelings for him but it was possible. Was his story after all a pack of lies? Had he been back to Angy's flat that Tuesday afternoon after all and been seen by Eleanor, and had she all along been keeping silent out of friendship? The thought was like a blow to the stomach and she winced with the pain of it. But no, her reason told her, that didn't make sense either. Eleanor would never have kept quiet when her precious Rodney was under suspicion.

'Tell me, please!' she implored. 'What did you see?'

Eleanor backed across the kitchen until she was standing against the edge of the work-top that ran between the sink and the cooker. Silhouetted against the window, she drew herself erect and flung out both arms, as if she were on a stage and about to give a public performance. The fingers of her right hand brushed against a wooden knife-block like the one in Angy's kitchen. She appeared to be pointing at it and, for a split second, gave the illusion of being about to execute some grotesque conjuring trick.

'I didn't see anyone,' she said at last, and now her voice was high-pitched, breathless, almost infantile. Her right hand closed round one of the knives and she pulled it, very slowly, from the block and ran a finger along the blade. Suddenly, she gave one of her husky, nervous giggles. 'I know who did it, though, *khikhikhi!* I know the name of the murderer!'

Anyone would think she was talking about a party game, thought Melissa. Even now, she could not bring herself to believe the horrifying truth. The strain has got to her, she thought wildly, she's having a nervous breakdown. Any minute now and she'll go right over the edge. Rodney should be sent for . . . if I could just get to the phone . . . but first, I've got to calm her down and get that knife away from her.

'I'll tell you what,' she said in a soothing voice. 'Why don't you come home for lunch with me and tell me all about it? I can't stay . . . I'm expecting an important phone call. And do stop playing with that knife . . . you'll cut yourself.' Desperately ad-libbing, she half rose.

'Don't move!' said Eleanor. She had a foolish grin on her face and she made a little stabbing gesture in Melissa's direction. 'You still don't understand, do you, *khikhikhi!*'

Melissa's stomach tightened and something cold went crawling up her spine. Eleanor . . . Eleanor had killed Angy . . . she was face to face with a murderess who was armed with a knife. Somehow, she must distract her attention. Her eyes swept the kitchen for inspiration and fell on the pair of gloves lying on the dresser. Cotton gloves. Brown cotton gloves . . .

Eleanor was still holding the short, wickedly pointed blade directed towards Melissa. Her eyes were unfocused and her lips were moving. Melissa's heart was hammering like disco drums. Keep calm, she told herself, try to look and speak normally. Say the wrong thing, make the wrong move and she'll go berserk and come at me with that knife. She had been sitting bolt upright on the wooden chair; now she forced herself to lean back in a more relaxed position. Snappy, still restless, came and sat beside her and she held out a hand to him. He licked it eagerly as if anxious for reassurance.

After a while, Eleanor slowly lowered the knife. 'I didn't mean to kill her,' she said in a voice that was almost normal. 'It was because of the things she said about Rodney, you see.'

'Tell me,' said Melissa.

'She offered to lend me a book—an art book—and suggested I call round to collect it. She told me where she lived . . . it was a scruffy little bed-sit at the top of a horrid old house.' Eleanor screwed up her face in ladylike disgust. 'In the class that afternoon she'd been teaching us to draw heads and she showed us some of her work . . . sketches of people in the college. There was one of me and one of Rodney.' The voice faltered for a moment and then continued in a flat monotone, as if she were repeating a lesson.

'When I got there, she'd spread out all the sketches as if she'd been admiring them. She was very conceited, you know, about her own work. We talked about the drawings and she picked up the one of Mr Willard and said, "Poor Papa Barney, I'm afraid he's very cross with me and he's going to be even crosser when he knows all about Eddie." Did you know,' the look of disgust returned, 'that Eddie was a . . . a woman? Angy was . . . one of those!'

'Yes, I knew about Eddie,' said Melissa. 'What else did Angy say?'

'She gave a funny little smile, like a cat. She was rather like a cat, didn't you think so?'

'In some ways. Do please go on.'

'I pointed to the drawing of Rodney—it was really rather good, I thought—and I said, "That's a good likeness of Doctor Shergold," or something like that and . . .' Eleanor's breathing quickened again and her grip on the knife tightened, 'do you know what she said?' She swallowed hard, chewed her bottom lip and swallowed again, as if she were trying to bring herself to utter an obscenity that in normal circumstances would not so much as enter her head.

'Well, what did she say?' prompted Melissa.

'She said, "Oh, that pompous little fart"! I could hardly believe my ears!' She was seething with well-bred outrage.

The tension had become almost unbearable, yet the words had come as such an anti-climax, and sounded so incongruous when spoken by Eleanor, that Melissa felt an insane desire to laugh.

'It's not funny!' snapped Eleanor.

Melissa put her face to rights. 'No, of course it isn't. I'm sorry.'

There was another pause. A contemplative look had come over Eleanor's face. When she spoke again, her voice held a note of weary resignation.

'Right from the day she started working for him, I realised that Rodney was . . . well, rather taken with Angy. I know him so well, you see . . . he couldn't keep anything from me. There was something about his face when he spoke of her . . . and then one day . . . it was the day you first had tea with me . . . they'd been out together somewhere . . . on business of course, it was quite legitimate but I knew something had happened between them. His jacket smelt of perfume and there were long, reddish hairs on it.'

Melissa gave a little sniff to show her contempt for such behaviour.

'I didn't blame him in the least,' insisted Eleanor, with a quick frown of reproach. 'He's such a clever, talented man and I'm so ordinary and plain. I've always felt terribly honoured to be his wife but I've often asked myself what he saw in me.'

I could tell you, thought Melissa grimly. Daddy was Principal at Brigston and was seen as an academic ladder, only Daddy very inconsiderately went and died before Rodney got past the bottom rung. He must have realised he was never going to get far without that influence and had been taking his disappointment out on his wife ever since. Yet such was her devotion to him that her loyalty and admiration had remained unshaken.

Aloud, she said, 'You shouldn't sell yourself short all the time, Eleanor. You're very talented . . . Angy herself said so.' Mention of the name brought her mind back to reality. 'Did you tackle Rodney about his affair with her?'

Eleanor winced and appeared shocked. 'Of course not! I told you, I didn't blame him . . . only,' her face took on a wistful expression, 'I couldn't stop wondering what she looked like . . . what sort of a person she was. The more I thought about it, the more I felt I had to know. I had the idea of pretending to be Delia and signing on at the art class for a term. I went to a shop selling theatre costumes and bought a wig and some plain glass spectacles. It was rather fun . . . I felt very daring!' For a moment, the pale, round face lit up with a childlike amusement as she relived the memory.

'You were telling me what happened the day you went to Angy's flat,' Melissa reminded her.

'Oh, yes, so I was.'

The minutes ticked by. When, at last, Eleanor spoke again, her voice had a metallic edge and the sentences came one after the other with the precision of clockwork, with only the occasional hesitation.

'She put down the sketches and went into the kitchen. She was going to make a cup of tea. I followed her. She had her back to me, getting out the tea-things. She was talking about herself and her . . . affairs. She said she'd had several men as lovers and decided she preferred women. And then . . . and then . . . ' The momentum faltered; Eleanor seemed to be steeling herself; the final words tumbled out

in a rush as if borne on a choking wave of hatred and anger.
'She said, "When that little squirt Shergold comes round for
his weekly bit of nooky, it'll be the last time. He'll have to
go back to screwing his wife." That's what she said!'

'And that was why you killed her?'

Eleanor drew a deep, shuddering breath. 'It wasn't only
that,' she whispered. 'It was what she said after. She gave a
silly giggle and said, "I hope for his sake the poor cow never
takes a lover and finds out what a pathetic little prick her
husband's got." ' In a swift change of mood, Eleanor drew
herself up to her full height·and with both hands round the
knife handle made vicious downward stabbing movements
in the air. Her nostrils flared and her eyes flashed. 'How
dared she say that about my Rodney?' she hissed. 'How
dared she?'

At last, Melissa understood. It was rage at the insults to
her husband, not his infidelity, that had driven the wife to
murder the mistress.

Eleanor was still gripping the knife and a row of whitish
spots like little pearl buttons ran across the back of each
hand . . . the hands that she had always kept smooth and
immaculate in order to please the man who for twenty-five
years had dominated, undervalued, denigrated and finally
betrayed her.

Slowly, the pearly spots faded as Eleanor slackened
her hold. Her head drooped, her shoulders sagged. Now,
thought Melissa, now perhaps I can persuade her to hand
it over. But before she could speak, Eleanor said wearily:
'What will happen to me? Are you going to call the
police?'

'Don't you think it would be better if I called Rodney
first?' suggested Melissa. 'And perhaps you should talk to
your doctor . . . '

'Oh no!' Eleanor's eyes widened in sudden terror. 'Don't
call Rodney! I don't want him here!'

She made a sudden bound, catching Melissa completely
off-guard. A moment before, she had been leaning back
against the edge of the sink, drooping and defeated. Now,
she was out of the kitchen and halfway down the hall.

'Eleanor, where are you going?' Melissa yelled, dashing after her. By the time she reached the foot of the stairs, Eleanor was on the landing. Still clutching the knife in one hand, she rushed into her bedroom, staggering in her haste and lurching against the frame before practically falling through the door and slamming it. Melissa tore up the stairs, seized the handle and pushed but Eleanor had thrown her weight on the other side. For a moment or two they struggled while the door shifted and vibrated a couple of inches this way and that; then the resistance increased as if something had been wedged against it.

Melissa pounded on it with her fists. 'What the hell do you think you're playing at?' she shouted. 'Come out of there!'

'Go away!' said Eleanor, her voice muffled.

'Open this door!'

'No!'

'What are you doing?'

'Never mind.'

Melissa stopped hammering and tried to think rationally. 'You're overwrought,' she pleaded, trying to sound calm. 'Let me get you a drink.' Anything to keep her talking, stop her doing something stupid. She pictured Eleanor sitting on the edge of her bed, the knife in her hand and despair in her heart, and shuddered at what she might be contemplating.

'I don't want anything,' sobbed Eleanor. 'Leave me alone.'

The telephone rang suddenly and Melissa nearly jumped out of her skin. 'I'll go and answer that,' she said.

'No!'

'It might be Rodney.'

'Leave it!'

The bell rang and rang. Stealthily, terrified of provoking the distraught woman into doing herself an injury, Melissa inched her way down the stairs and into the hall. As she reached for the receiver, the ringing stopped. She glanced back upstairs; from behind the bedroom door came the sound of muffled crying. Thankful for a modern push-button telephone that was virtually silent, she tapped out

Rodney Shergold's office number. 'Sorry, Eleanor,' she muttered as she waited for the ringing tone. 'There's no way you can hide this from him.'

His telephone voice was high-pitched, staccato, almost hectoring. Anxious not to alarm Eleanor, Melissa gave her name in a low voice. 'Please come home at once,' she said. 'It's an emergency.'

'What's that? Speak up, I can't hear you!' he snapped.

Drat the man, how could anyone who claimed to be so clever be so slow on the uptake? She cupped her hand round the receiver. 'It's an emergency . . . get home!' she repeated.

Still he was not satisfied. 'What sort of emergency? Can't Nell deal with it? I've got work to do!'

'Nell *is* the emergency,' said Melissa in a fierce whisper. 'Don't ask questions, just get home as quickly as you can.' She put down the receiver, ran back upstairs and tapped on the bedroom door. 'Eleanor, are you all right?'

There was a muffled sob. 'Who was on the phone?'

'It stopped just as I got to it,' said Melissa, praying that her call to the college had gone unnoticed. 'Now, why don't you come downstairs and have that drink?'

'I don't want a drink. Melissa, will you do something for me?'

'Of course. What is it?'

'Look after Snappy. Rodney doesn't like him, you see.'

It took a second or two for the implication to sink in. Then, in a panic, Melissa grabbed the handle of the door and began shaking it and screaming, 'Eleanor, you *must* let me in!' She flung herself against the unyielding wood but only succeeded in bruising her shoulder. Frantically, she raced back downstairs, snatched up the telephone and put in an emergency call to Detective Chief Inspector Harris.

'Please let me in,' pleaded Melissa but there was no response from the other side of the door. She gave it another shove; it seemed to yield a little. By yanking it to and fro she at last managed to prise it open far enough to get an arm through the opening and dislodge the chair wedged under the handle. Throughout her struggles, there had been neither sound nor movement from Eleanor. Her heart thumping in dread of what she might see, Melissa stumbled into the room. It was empty.

One window stood open a bare couple of inches and the others were closed; plainly, Eleanor had not taken that way out. For a moment, Melissa was at a loss; then she spied another door in the corner. Of course! She must be hiding in the en suite bathroom. She went across and tapped softly at the door.

'Eleanor? Are you in there?'

'Yes.'

The voice was quiet but at least she was still alive and conscious. Melissa tried the handle but the door was locked.

'Eleanor, listen to me. Don't do anything foolish. Just let's talk for a little while. Now, why don't you come downstairs . . .'

'There isn't time.'

'What do you mean, there isn't time? What have you done?'

'It's no use, Melissa. I can't bear any more.'

It seemed, from the direction of the sound, that Eleanor was lying on the floor. Melissa bent down to catch the words.

'I can't live with the nightmares,' Eleanor faltered, her voice unsteady as a leaf blown in the wind. 'Every time I close my eyes I see her face . . . she was crouching at the cupboard with her back to me and she turned round and straightened up just as the knife was coming down and it went into her throat. I'll never forget the look on her face.'

Melissa felt her knees buckle and her head began to swim from stooping. She slid to a sitting position on the floor, noticing as she did so the smear of mud from her shoes that soiled the thick, delicate carpet. As if that mattered at a moment like this . . . yet she found herself thinking that Rodney Shergold would have a fit when he saw it.

Outside, a tractor rumbled past and an aircraft droned overhead. Nearby, a dog barked and a woman's voice soothed it. A car door slammed; Harriet Yorke was preparing to go out. Melissa scrambled to her feet, rushed to the window and called out, but she was too late. The sound of the engine drowned her voice and in a moment the car had driven away.

Feeling drained and utterly helpless, Melissa returned to her seat on the floor, certain now that nothing she could say would persuade Eleanor to come out, if indeed she was still capable of getting to her feet and unlocking the door. When the police came they would break it down. They must be here soon; it seemed an age to Melissa since she had called them, yet when she glanced at her watch she saw that it was barely five minutes. Surely, nothing that she had done to herself could have made her unconscious in such a short time.

She was about to call through the door when Eleanor said, 'Melissa, are you still there?'

'Yes, I'm here. What is it?'

'I just wanted to say . . . I'm sorry about Mrs Bliss.'

It was a second or two before Melissa grasped what she meant. In the shock and confusion of Eleanor's confession, the fact that Angy and Sybil had been struck down by the same hand had simply not registered. Now, the realisation was like a blow to the solar plexus.

'Sybil? Of course, you killed Sybil as well! But why? What had she done to you?'

Eleanor's voice, though weak, suddenly became as chatty and matter-of-fact as if she were speaking about the weather. 'I nearly bumped into her coming out of Delia's house, *khikhikhi!* Wasn't it silly of me? I was pretty sure she'd recognised me and I was worried about that so I followed her home. I had to stop her telling anyone.' There was a short silence before Eleanor murmured reflectively, 'Angy did deserve to die, don't you agree, after what she said about Rodney? But it was a shame about Mrs Bliss.'

For all the depth of emotion in her voice, she might have been apologising for allowing Snappy to jump up with muddy paws. Even if they get her out in time to save her, thought Melissa despairingly while Eleanor alternated between rationality and childish prattle, they must surely find her unfit to plead.

From outside came sounds of car doors banging and footsteps hurrying up the front path. A key turned in the lock and Shergold's voice was raised in petulant anger, demanding to be told what was going on and being curtly answered by DCI Harris's rasping bark. Melissa scrambled to her feet and lurched on to the landing.

'Up here!' she called. 'For God's sake, hurry!'

She went back into the bedroom and her heart seemed to stop at the sight of the bright scarlet stain seeping from under the bathroom door and spreading over the peach-coloured carpet. As the owner of the house rushed into the room followed by a seemingly endless procession of police and ambulance personnel, she shrank against a wall, shaking uncontrollably as she stared down at her right hand, sticky with Eleanor's blood.

Somehow, she found the main bathroom and got her head over the handbasin in time to avoid throwing up on the pale blue carpet. Her teeth were chattering as she rinsed away the mess, washed her face and hands and dried them on one of a row of towels that had been carefully arranged on a rail in graduated sizes and varying shades of blue. Disturbing them seemed like an intrusion, as if the towels were there as part of the decor and not intended for practical use. Still shivering, she sat down on the blue candlewick toilet-seat cover and put her head in her hands.

She could hear muffled thumps and a jumble of men's voices; they must be trying to force open the en suite bathroom door. She wondered how long it would take them, how much blood Eleanor would lose before they got to her, whether they'd get her to the hospital in time to pump more into her so that she'd be fit to go through the due process of the law. She longed to slip out of the house and go home but knew it was her duty to stay and talk to Harris. Anyway, there'd be a man posted at the door to ask politely if she'd be kind enough to wait. She wandered downstairs and into the kitchen. There by the back door were the shoes that Eleanor had been wearing that morning. She picked up the right one and stared down at the brass-headed drawing pin embedded in the sole.

It seemed an eternity before she heard the tread of feet coming down the stairs, slowly, as if carrying a burden. There was more slamming of doors and the ambulance siren began to wail as it drove away. Hearing her name spoken, she went into the hall. Harris was there and behind him stood Rodney Shergold, his slight figure dwarfed by the detective's bulk. He looked dazed and his eyes were slits in a face the colour of Cotswold stone.

'Are you all right, Melissa?' said Harris.

'I'm fine. What about Eleanor? Is she . . . ?'

'Still alive but lost a lot of blood. Sergeant Waters is going with Doctor Shergold to the hospital. I'll drive you home and we'll talk there.' She swayed and he caught her arm, calling over his shoulder, 'Have you got any brandy? Mrs Craig's out on her feet.'

Shergold passed a hand over his eyes. 'I'm not sure where she keeps it,' he muttered. He glanced helplessly round him and then up the stairs. 'What on earth possessed the stupid creature? Causing all this trouble! You should see the mess . . . the carpet's ruined!'

'Don't worry about a drink, I'll be okay,' said Melissa to Harris. The idea of accepting anything from Rodney Shergold filled her with revulsion.

She felt something brush her legs and heard a soft whine. Snappy had crept out of his basket and was pressing himself against her as if reminding her of her promise to his mistress. She could feel his body quivering as she bent down to fondle him.

'Poor little chap,' she murmured. 'I'll take care of you.'

Shergold's face darkened. 'Get that disgusting animal out of here!' he said, scowling.

She picked up the dog and went into the kitchen to collect his lead. 'Shall we go?' she said to Harris, and without so much as a glance at the master of the house, she led the way to the door.

TWENTY-THREE

'WHAT FIRST PUT YOU ON TO ELEANOR SHER-
gold?' asked Harris when Melissa had stumbled through
her story.

They were sitting in the kitchen at Hawthorn Cottage.
Melissa had led the way there, muttering something about
coffee, but it was Harris who, after pushing her with surprising gentleness into a chair, had filled the kettle, found
the brandy and poured some into a glass for her. Now, he sat
at the other side of the table, calm and relaxed and looking
more like an invited guest than a detective investigating a
murder.

'It was a recipe for scones,' explained Melissa. 'She gave
it to me months ago but I never glanced at it until yesterday.
It rang a vague bell but it wasn't until this morning that the
penny dropped.' She explained how the application form in
Philippe Bonard's prospectus had acted as a trigger. 'Even
then, it never occurred to me that she had killed Angy; I
just thought she'd pretended to be Delia Forbes to get to
the art classes without Rodney knowing about it. In a way,
of course, it was just that. I don't think the idea of murder
entered her head until she heard Angy making those cracks
about him.'

She closed her eyes in a futile attempt to obliterate the
scene in the kitchen at Cotswold View: Eleanor, arms
upraised, hands clamped on the knife, eyes blazing with
hatred and vengeance as she relived the moment when her
rival rose and turned, like a sacrificial victim, to receive the
fatal thrust.

'She must have gone absolutely berserk,' she muttered.

'That might be true in the case of Angy but from what you tell me, when she killed Mrs Bliss she knew exactly what she was doing.' Harris's meaning was obvious; there would be no question of a court finding Eleanor unfit to plead.

Melissa played absently with her glass. 'You know,' she said, 'all the time she was talking to me, up there in the bedroom, she was like a child caught out after doing something naughty. First she was trying to justify it, then saying how sorry she was, then laughing . . . '

'Laughing?'

'While she was telling me how she went into Angy's room, when she'd finished washing away the blood after killing her, she sounded almost gleeful, as if she was describing a playground game.'

'She went in there? What for?'

'To retrieve the sketch of herself that Angy had drawn. She sounded quite proud of herself for having thought of it, and for remembering to keep her gloves on all the time. She described how she'd picked her way to avoid stepping in the blood, just like she steps round puddles when she's walking the dog.'

Melissa inhaled long and hard to quell a spasm of nausea at the memory of Eleanor's foolish, self-satisfied giggle. Her eyes went to the corner where Snappy had settled down on an old blanket, entirely at home. What a mercy, she thought to herself, that there were no children . . . but perhaps, if there had been . . . who could tell?

'She certainly covered her tracks pretty well.' Harris shifted on his chair and it creaked in protest. 'Led us a merry dance.'

'I should have realised earlier that she'd been coming to the college,' said Melissa thoughtfully. 'She once spoke of Barney as if she knew him, and only yesterday Dudley Ford said something about her being out on Tuesday afternoons. Sooner or later, it would have come out that she was using Delia Forbes' name.'

'Next week, to be precise,' said Harris. 'She's expected back on Wednesday.'

'And all the time you thought Barney Willard was the murderer,' she reproached him.

'Ah yes, Willard.' A strange expression flitted across the big detective's features. 'I hope you . . . ' He broke off; it was the first time she could remember any hint of hesitancy in his manner.

'What do you hope?'

He rose from his chair and turned away, ignoring the question. 'I'd best be going,' he said. At that moment, the phone rang. 'Would you like me to take that?'

'Go ahead. It might be for you anyway.'

He lumbered out of the room, returning after a few moments. 'That was Waters, calling from the hospital.'

'Yes?'

'Mrs Shergold died a few minutes ago without regaining consciousness.'

It was a pitiful way for a woman's life to end, but Melissa felt only relief at the news. Survival would have left Eleanor without hope or comfort; death was by far the lesser affliction.